No Abiding City

Carolyn Sanderson

In memory of Harry

CONTENTS

Chapter One

The last of them had died now, the very last of those who shared his blood. It was the watching at night that had been the hardest. During the day there was so much to do: water to pump, fires to tend, food to find. When they were hot, he sponged them, wrapped them tenderly in blankets when they shivered; tried, mostly without success, to coax liquid through parched lips. It was at night when he sat alone with his thoughts that the dread overcame him until, exhausted, he sprawled in helpless sleep. After the last grave was dug, there was nothing else to do. He waited for the sickness to find him, but it didn't.

For a while he stayed, out of habit, going about the daily chores, dazed, but without others to care for there seemed little point. Around him, the few neighbours still left were packing up.

'You should go,' said Sadie from the end of the lane, come to say goodbye. 'There's nothing here for you now.'

Leave or stay: what was the difference? He no longer had a purpose. So he left. It gave him something to do, some sort of shape to his days. He took with him a few belongings, and what was left of his grandmother's healthmakings, and set off, taking a road he did not know to a future he could not imagine.

The red kites, gliding effortlessly above the landscape, watched as the young man trudged along the road. Swooping, they came close enough to see the tumble of dark curls on his head and the bundle on his back, but he was of no interest to them, not yet. Later, maybe …

It was a shock, the way they crowded round him. He hadn't been expecting people, hadn't expected anything, really, except somewhere to shelter from the afternoon glare. They were all talking at once, mouths opening and closing, so many voices; he couldn't make sense of any of it.

It was the elderly lady, as she limped across the open space at the centre of the clearing, who made the difference. She walked with difficulty, and he wondered absently if he had anything in his pack that might help. There was something about her that reminded him of his grandmother.

When she spoke, her voice was as warm as her smile.

'You look tired. Been walking long?'

He nodded. 'Feels like forever.' His voice felt strange in his mouth.

'Then stay with us a while.'

'Is that all right?' He was not used to all this. 'How do I...? Is there someone I should ask? Do you have a leader?'

The grey-haired man seated at the centre of the clearing was in the act of slicing open something that had once been a living thing; he had long ago outgrown the squeamishness of those who watched, their faces half- averted. Now he paused, aware that something was going on, over near the treeline: another new arrival. Ah well, let them come; let them all come. The earth was for everyone.

The small group seated around him shuffled up to make room as the dark-haired newcomer approached, his steps slow as if questioning his right to be there. He sank gratefully down onto the soft grass, easing off his bundle and stretching his aching shoulders. He wasn't sure what to do next.

The other spoke first. 'Welcome, stranger.'

Hesitantly, the younger man asked, 'Would it be all right if I stay for a while?'

'Oh, you don't have to ask me. I just live here.' There was gentle amusement in his voice.

'Oh? The others seem to think you are their leader.'

The other man thought for a moment. 'Perhaps that's because I was here first.' He paused. 'But, you know, the natural world doesn't belong to us; we belong to it. Anyway, young man, what's your name?'

'Jonas.'

'I'm Will.'

Some of the others joined in then, offering names he instantly forgot, and information he struggled to retain.

'Old Will has lived here his whole life, haven't you, Will?'

'…knows everything there is to know about living out here…'

'Catches food, cooks it…'

'Lights a fire to cook on…'

'Makes things, all sorts…'

'He can mend anything…'

'Knows everything about survival…'

Jonas looked at the old man and wondered how old he really was. Not as old as he looked, at a guess. Living out here must have aged his appearance, but somehow it suited him; it made him seem at one with his surroundings. Now he was holding up his hands in mock horror as the others praised him.

'Enough, enough…' He was laughing as he turned to Jonas, but his words were serious. 'Don't listen to their nonsense, Jonas. Remember: you should never believe what people tell you until you have tested it out for yourself.'

Jonas' mind flew briefly to the strange rumours he'd been hearing, but it was late; that topic could wait for another day. He found himself a space at the edge of the clearing, unrolled his blanket, and stretched out. As the sun sank low, the murmurs of conversation died away; fires were dowsed, and sleep overtook him.

It was the song of the birds that woke him next morning, stealing into his sleep and mingling with his dreams. Even before he was fully awake his heart lifted at the sound. They were coming back; each day it seemed that there were more of them. For a while he lay there without opening his eyes, exulting in the sudden pure joy of being alive. It was a new feeling. In all honesty, feeling anything at all was new. At the shrill mewing of the red kites his eyes flew open, and he looked up, his gaze held by their graceful flight as they hung almost motionless in the unseen currents of air.

Around him, the bustle of early morning activity was increasing. He eased himself up, stretching stiff muscles and yawning. The days of walking had been arduous, and his arrival at the clearing overwhelming. He threw a final glance skyward and then, recognising a need to respond to a more earthbound call of nature, he made his way to a grove not far from the river, where he found the place designated for the men. Afterwards, throwing off his crumpled tunic and scarf, he plunged thankfully into the water, washing away the dust and weariness of travel. It all still seemed unreal. How long had it been since he had found himself amongst so many people?

Back up at the camp, Will seemed impressed that Jonas knew how to start a fire, and that he carried his own flints and kindling.

'Not under the trees, mind,' the old man warned him.

Jonas smiled wryly.

'It's a pity no-one listened to that advice before the forests burned!'

In the early days, he hung back, remaining on the periphery of things while the life of the encampment went on around him; after everything that had happened, self-sufficiency was already second nature. Was he lonely? If he was, there was no sense dwelling on it. He was used to loneliness. It had been lonely before, when his parents had followed the little ones into the grave. Nothing could be lonelier than that.

Today, he was watching from his usual position on the edge of things; everyone here in the Woodlands seemed to have a purpose. Over in the central space, near the main fire, the older folk were keeping an eye on the children as they played. The elderly lady, the one with the limp, was amongst them, smiling even as she chided the naughty ones. The children called her Granny Tabitha. Shyly, Jonas moved over to speak to her, but before he had gone more than a few paces a heavily built man appeared from the tree line and planted himself squarely in front of the old lady. Even from where he stood, Jonas could see the man's limbs were taut with agitation.

'You know, Ma, I've had enough of this,' the newcomer said, ignoring the others present. 'There's talk of heading out to find the place. No more of this hanging around.'

Jonas noted the anxious look that crossed Tabitha's face. He wondered if there was anything he could do to ease the tension, but another man was already on his feet. He was calm, but Jonas saw that he wore a slight frown.

'Wait a minute, Sam, slow down. All we've heard so far is rumours, right? Do we even know for certain that the place is real? We don't know of anyone who's seen it, do we? And even if it is a real place, or was, is it possible that it's still standing? Come on, think about it: after all the damage and destruction, after the fires and the floods and the loss of life? Really? Do you honestly think it's still going to be there?'

Sam waved his words aside.

'So what's the alternative?' He was shouting now, white knuckles showing in clenched fists. 'Stay here and do nothing when there's a chance of something better? Is that really all you want out of your lives?'

His raised voice was attracting attention, and some of the others began to drift across to listen. A young woman, joining the group, spoke up.

'It's just another story, Sam, don't you realise? Like all the other stories we've been fed. A world lit up by screens, when you could see other people and other places no matter how far away. I mean, who really believes in that any more?'

'So you don't even want to go and see if it's true? You don't want to find a place where the machines still function? Where food is there just for the taking, stacked up on shelves, with robots to do all the work?'

'It *was* all true once,' said Tabitha quietly. 'In my grandparents' day there were screens and machines, and there was a benevolent government that cared for people's needs.'

6

'Yeah,' snarled Sam. 'And took half their earnings in exchange for the favour.'

Tabitha looked at him sadly. 'But it's all gone, Sam, the good *and* the bad. It's not coming back. We have to face a different future.'

Jonas became aware that Old Will had joined the little group. Taking note of the younger man's worried expression, he invited him to walk with him.

'You know,' he said, laying a kindly hand on Jonas' shoulder, as they moved away from the others, 'People need their dreams, and sometimes they're the wrong ones. It doesn't really matter whether the place exists or not: life will go on, somehow. What does matter is the here and now, and how we prepare ourselves for the future.'

'Will, I don't even understand what this place is that they're talking about.'

'Neither do they, truth be told. You must have heard some of the rumours, though?'

'I've heard people talking about The City, or some such place…'

'That's about the size of it. Different people have seized on different visions of somewhere they think they can return to - a past that never really existed.'

Perhaps it was because he seemed so completely alone that Old Will began to take Jonas under his wing; sometimes they went fishing together in the clear water of the river upstream, and other days Old Will showed him how to set the rabbit traps. Jonas needed no lessons in how to make do and mend – what else had he been doing for most of his life? Now he enjoyed the new skills Old Will was able to teach him: the felling of the coppiced wood, the seasoning of the timber; the carving

7

of useful items like spoons; the making of carefully jointed wooden stools.

'You know, you have a talent for working with wood, Jonas,' Old Will said one day as Jonas handed over another of his carvings for inspection. 'You should keep at it.'

He found he liked the feel of the wood in his hands, the fresh smell that arose from the cut edges. As he worked, he imagined the sapling struggling into life against all expectation, growing stronger by the year. He marvelled at the skill of those who had learned to cut only enough to enable regrowth, taking what was needed and nothing more. He thought of the living things hidden in the bark, nestling among the leaves, tunnelling among the spreading roots.

Newcomers were arriving daily. Jonas wondered where they were all coming from. He asked Old Will about it.

'Oh, news gets around.'

'So, how did you come here?'

'I was born here.'

'Really?' Even as he said it, Jonas realised that it made perfect sense. Old Will was so completely at home here that it was hard to imagine him anywhere else.

'Yes, really. Back when things started to get serious, my great-grandparents saw the writing on the wall, so they left it all behind…'

'They left behind civilisation?'

'If you could call it that. What *they* called it was muddle and mess: the choking cities, the fear, the corruption. Out here they found a way to live closer to nature, free as the wind…'

The older man paused, his face creasing into a wry smile. 'Not that the wind was exactly free by then, of course, once other fuels had become unacceptable, or unavailable... or the cause of bitter conflict...' He sighed. 'No, the wind was greatly in demand.'

Jonas nodded, waiting for him to go on. He wondered what he was thinking in the silence. Finally, he prompted him:

'So you've been here all your life?'

'Pretty much. I travelled about a bit when I was younger, but I always ended up back here - didn't much like what I saw out there. Yes, this is how I've always lived, just like my parents and grandparents before me - off grid. And now everyone's off-grid!' He laughed. 'Never used to have any trouble with the neighbours, either, because there weren't any...'

'So, what happened?'

'Well, at first it was just a trickle. The people who showed up here were pretty bewildered, as you can imagine, but mostly glad to be here in the woods where it was cooler and more sheltered from the wildstorms. I had to show them how to do the most basic things, of course: how to gather the dried sticks, you know? How to stack them, how to strike the flints; how to cook vegetables; how to prepare meat.'

He hesitated, glancing at Jonas as though checking him out.

'There were always a few who vomited when it came to skinning and butchering the rabbits.' There was another pause. 'To be fair, it wasn't a pretty sight, and the early traps I made were, well, somewhat inhumane. But you know what, Jonas? As people grew more and more hungry, they found that they could be inhumane too. They ate what there was because there wasn't much of it.'

He became silent again, and Jonas tried to imagine what this sort of survival must have felt like for those people, fresh from the devastated towns.

The red kites looked on impassively. They were not starving. Carrion was plentiful in those days; it was other things that weren't. If they had cared to look down, they might have seen the two men heading purposefully east; they might have noted the scattered bands straggling over many miles, small knots of people sometimes stopping to hear what the two men had to say, while others moved apparently aimlessly, dazed and confused.

Chapter Two

Gradually, Jonas began to join some of the others in the evenings as they prepared and cooked their food, listening without comment to the friendly chatter. Then he would return to where he had set out his few possessions, right at the edge of the circle. It seemed generally understood that, once you had claimed a space, it was yours for as long as you stayed in the Woodlands.

A little family had also set up camp near the edge; perhaps they had chosen that spot because of the new baby that was clearly on the way. He recognised them from the confrontation that had taken place between Sam and Tabitha, when the man had reasoned calmly with Tabitha's angry son. Each time he returned to his pitch, they gave a friendly smile and a wave, and Jonas gave a nod in return. He would have liked to exchange a few words with them, but didn't know the words to use. Then he had an idea, and began work on a new project.

Each day, over in the central space where people were at work making and mending, he began to shape a little wooden cradle of his own design, smoothing it with a whetstone, oiling it with the fat of a wild duck. He found himself smiling as he worked, but the smile faded when he looked honestly at the finished cradle: it seemed hard and inhospitable for a tiny infant. When asked, Will gestured to a pile of plucked feathers; in the encampment, nothing was discarded before a use had been found for it. Combined with local mosses, they made a soft mattress. Now he was ready to present his gift.

Their eyes were on him as he approached, and he hesitated; it had been so long since he'd really spoken to strangers that he felt uncertain. They had another child, a girl who watched with wide eyes as he approached. She was holding a crudely carved doll. Then the man nodded and the young woman smiled at him, and he held the cradle out to them.

'I hope you don't mind? I, er, I couldn't help noticing…'

The young woman blushed and looked down at her bump.

'Not too long now, we reckon,' said the man. He was a little older than her, although it was difficult to tell for certain. He ran his fingers abstractedly through his matted hair. 'The fact is…' he looked embarrassed. 'That's a beautiful cradle, but we don't have a thing to exchange for it.'

'Oh, no, I'm not selling it.'

The woman looked up at him then, her eyes bright. Jonas placed it gently on the ground beside her.

'Will it do? For your new baby?'

They accepted the gift gladly, insisting that he sit down with them for a while. The little girl placed her doll gently in the cradle and began to rock it.

'I'm Robin,' said the man, holding out a hand awkwardly. After a slight hesitation, Jonas took it; the old taboos no longer held, surely?

The woman's name was Alison, and her glance kept returning to the cradle. Jonas turned his attention to the child.

'And what's your name?'

'Oh, she doesn't speak yet,' said the father, gathering her into his arms. 'Her name's Skylark.'

The child looked about four years of age.

When he felt the urge to stretch his legs, Jonas spent time walking, observing the land about him. There was a dark mound, some distance away, bright patches glinting here and there in the sunlight. Old Will appeared from somewhere, making him jump.

'You'll see plenty of those middenheaps around here.'

Jonas turned to face him. Old Will was still staring in the direction of the mound, seemingly lost in thought.

'There they are: all the things people thought they needed and then found they didn't.' He gave a mirthless laugh and then his mood changed as he shrugged his shoulders. 'You'll find all sorts there, Jonas, but some of it will be worthless plastic: try not to disturb that, because if it gets loose…'

Jonas nodded his understanding.

'But you'll probably find plenty of household things that can be mended, too: you know, pots, pans, things like that, and knives, scissors: they can be sharpened. Even some textiles can be cleaned if you do it properly.'

Jonas was pleased to take this on; no-one else seemed to be scavenging, and he liked the sense of having something to offer to the community. For hours at a time, he lost himself, rummaging amongst the forsaken possessions of former generations, amazed at what had been discarded.

He began to bring back all sorts of treasures, beating out the dents in the cooking pots and scouring them with ash from the fire to bring them up shiny as new. Old Will showed him which kind of stone was best for grinding the blades of knives and shears, and explained how the sun's rays, so dangerous in the wrong place, were perfect for disinfecting the fabrics he brought back and washed in the river.

The first time he went down there it aroused amused curiosity in the women.

'What have you got there?'

The tone was friendly enough, and so he held out the fabrics he had brought, still all jumbled together in his arms.

'Hmm,' one of them said, 'These have seen better days!' She ran a tentative finger over them. 'What are they?'

Jonas explained that he had reclaimed them from the middenheap. The others gathered round, their washing abandoned for the moment.

'Well, yes,' said someone else, 'They're good quality. If you can get them clean they could be useful.'

'That's what I'm hoping. The threads could be unpicked and used to make something else, maybe… or they could serve for bedding.' He submerged the bundle, watching as it billowed and spread in the water, the colours brightening already.

'Don't you have any soap?' asked the first woman.

He shook his head ruefully. How could he have failed to think of that? The woman walked a little way along the bank and returned with a jar of liquid. He watched, fascinated as she shook it until it foamed up.

'Here,' she said, thrusting it into his hand. 'I want the jar back, mind.'

Later, they showed him how to grind up the horse chestnuts himself and how to steep them in water, and he promised to make enough to repay what he had used. He was fairly sure he could find some unbroken glass jars at the middenheap for them, too. He was becoming part of the community.

The rumours Jonas had heard on his way to Old Will's encampment began to resurface; they swelled to become news, big news, spreading like the floodwater that in places drowned out everything else and left a coating of black slime to rot the crops and choke the animals.

Robin described it as spreading like wildfire, adding, 'There was a phrase people used to use: they said that things *went viral*.' At the lifting of Jonas' eyebrows, he added, 'Of course, that's considered bad taste now. But wildfire – that's different, isn't it? Everyone knows what that is: the choking air, the sickening fear as it approaches, the sudden change of direction...'

'I've heard all sorts of rumours. Do you think anyone believes in them?'

Robin shook his head. 'Some do, but I'm sure most people take them with a pinch of salt. They think it's just another story, like when the word goes round that someone has found a deserted warehouse full of food, you know, still edible, perfectly preserved through the disaster years.' His laughter was hollow. 'Now if you'll believe that...!'

'I hope you're right, Robin, although...'

As time went on he had found himself observing the young families with their children, parents wanting only the best for them, as parents have always done, skimping on their own food to feed them, telling them there was nothing to fear, that all would be well, while their faces told a different story.

'Mm?' Robin was waiting for him to finish.

'Well, it's just that, I don't know, some of the grandparents seem to have caught the same fever as Sam, you know, filling the children's heads with tales of how the world was before, feeding them with discontent...'

Robin had to agree that it was a worry.

Granny Tabitha was different, though. As Jonas sat one morning, whittling wooden spoons, he saw her struggle to her feet to stop a small child getting too close to the fire. Clearly, her legs troubled her more than she would admit, and, once the child had been safely delivered to its parents, he went over to her with one of his wooden stools.

'Here, Tabitha. It's not quite so far down if you sit on one of these.'

She gave him her bright smile as she sat, and began to ask how he was settling in.

'I'm doing fine, but you seem to be having a bit of trouble moving about. Are you in pain?'

'Oh well, you know... I'm getting old, Jonas.'

'Is it pain, or stiffness?'

She shrugged. 'A bit of both, really.'

'My grandmother was a healer,' he said. 'I have some of her herbs and salves in my pack. Would you let me see if I can help you?'

Before Tabitha could reply, Sam appeared, wearing his perpetual scowl. He ignored Jonas and launched back into the argument that seemed always simmering below the surface.

'It's all very well for you, Ma,' he was saying now, 'You've lived your life; but what about us and our children, eh? What sort of future is there for them here, living like this?'

Tabitha seemed undaunted by the bitterness in his tone.

'It depends what sort of future you think is best, Sam. Out here, in the Woodlands, there's no more fighting. We're close to nature.' She glanced round at the resurgent trees, the green plant life showing here and there beneath them. 'You can see: she is beginning to repair herself already.'

The old lady had struggled to her feet now, and stood looking earnestly up into his troubled face. 'Your

16

children have never known anything different: this is their normal.'

She gestured towards young Swallow, weaving a grass basket with the help of an older child.

'Look how contented she is.'

The child looked up at that moment, smiling, gap-toothed. Her grandmother had no way of knowing it, but Swallow was the image of the child Tabitha had once been; yet a vast gulf separated their childhoods.

Irritated, Sam stumped away.

Chapter Three

The red kites soared serenely, high above the world, uncaring of the change and tumult far below. The two men they had been watching as they headed east were nearer now; before long they would reach Will's encampment. A wild sense of purpose drove them on and, most of the time at least, blotted out the ache in their limbs and the hunger in their bellies.

The big man made a sudden lunge to the right, almost knocking his companion off his feet.

'Well, come on then, aren't you hungry?'

'Yeah,' said the other. 'Starving.'

The path was overgrown, and the big man kicked savagely at the tangle of brambles, outraged to find them daring to block his way. His smaller companion was some distance behind.

Approaching the battered front door, he turned briefly to look over his shoulder.

'Well come on, Joe! What are you waiting for?'

No sound came from inside. The door gave way easily. Most doors did when the big man was involved. As Joe caught up, he found himself gagging; the big man seemed unaffected by the smell. The sight of the woman on the bed had no effect on him either. He headed straight for what had once been the kitchen.

'No, wait, Brendan…I think she's still breathing.' Joe's voice was timid. He knelt beside the bed, his nose and mouth covered with his rag of a scarf.

Big Brendan was too busy ransacking cupboards to pay him any attention. None of them contained food.

'Bastards!' he said. 'Bastards!'

He came to the last cupboard: it was locked. Raising his fists, he began hammering furiously on it, until the hinges gave way. It swung outwards.

'Hey, Joe!' His tone had changed. 'Come and see – we're in luck!'

Reluctantly, Joe joined him in the kitchen. The smell was no less strong, but in this room it was not the smell of disease but of rotting wood, of water-soaked flooring, and possibly of sewage. Big Brendan was holding out a clutch of tins, their labels long since faded.

'Look at this lot!' His voice was loud in the enclosed space. 'We'll eat well tonight, Farmer's boy! Quick: find a bag! We'll take as much as we can carry.'

Joe began searching the drawers. The warped wood came apart the moment it was released from the runners; the contents fell with a clatter to the ground. Joe followed them down, scrabbling ineffectually amongst spoons and strainers and the accumulated domestic clutter of long ago. Big Brenden, pausing in the act of emptying the cupboard, turned and hauled him roughly to his feet.

'You're not going to find a bag in amongst that lot, idiot!'

'No, Boss, I'm looking for a tin opener.'

'What?' Big Brendan threw his head back in a coarse laugh. 'You don't think we're going to eat in amongst this stink, do you?'

'No...' Joe's voice was tremulous. 'But the lady, in the other room...'

'She's past it. No point wasting food on the dying.' A thought struck him. 'You didn't touch her, did you?'

Joe shook his head. No-one, not even he, would take such a foolish risk.

No-one knew where the news came from originally. Some said it was definitely true because they had heard it from somebody who had heard it from someone else, who had spoken to an actual person, someone who had escaped from there. Escaped? Was it a prison then? Others had it on good authority that it had existed for years, long before things turned bad. So what was it for? Who lived there? One view was that it was where the old government had gone when they saw the writing on the wall; furthermore, they were still there, formulating plans for a future in which the land would be green and fertile again, the sea levels would fall, the bees would come swarming back…

'Yeah,' said Big Brendan, spitting in the dirt. 'And pigs will fly!'

'Yeah,' echoed Joe Farmer. His main function in Big Brendan's life was to act as his echo. It lent a sense of veracity to Big Brendan's assertions.

There was a lot of wildfire news in those days: someone would pick up a rumour about a stash of tinned goods, or a generator still working intermittently, or even a field full of cabbages, or turnips, the sort of thing people wouldn't have been seen dead eating back when things were different.

Much had fallen into disrepair over the disaster years. Power supplies were limited and unreliable; things wore out, or broke and could not be fixed. The first thing that went was the internet: what use screens and keyboards, platforms and apps, when the need was for basic foodstuffs to feed hungry people? The brilliant young minds of the cyber generation proved to be not so brilliant when it came to tilling the soil and weeding crops.

But even without the old cyber-skills, people are still people: they found ways to communicate without the help of the worldwide web. After all, human beings had been doing just that for thousands of years. So person spoke to person; they passed it on to someone else, who passed it on, and in this wildfire way, the news spread.

The red kites, had they cared to, might have watched as the two men continued eastwards, weighed down by the bags they carried. They might have noticed how Joe stared wistfully at the neglected fields, the ruined farmhouses, the sad remains of the once fertile land. Big Brendan didn't call him Farmer's Boy for nothing.

In the camp, time passed, and the days and the weeks rolled into one. Some of the people made attempts to set up shops of a sort: a rickety stall at the front of someone's shelter displaying a sack or two of gritty flour, a few shrivelled roots, a handwoven blanket. The currency was whatever the shop owner needed: fresh fruit, a pair of shoes, a roughly formed cheese.

A kind of society began to form, but like societies always and everywhere it wasn't long before disharmony broke out. There were arguments about the value of goods in the shops, petty jealousies about who had the best site for their shelter; one woman accused another of stealing her shoes; another spilt her neighbour's soup.

That was exactly the moment when Big Brendan and his sidekick Joe Farmer stumbled into the clearing.

It was late, and people had begun to settle down. Smoke drifted through the camp, carrying with it the age-old smells of cooking; a small child wailed briefly, and elsewhere a mother could be heard singing a lullaby. As a gentle breeze ruffled the treetops, bringing welcome relief after the heat of the day, Jonas stretched out on the soft grass and found to his surprise that he was contented. This wasn't such a bad way to live; he could be happy here, living out his days making things, eating what nature provided.

His eyes were just starting to close when a sudden commotion brought him sharply back to full wakefulness. It seemed that there were new arrivals in the camp. He got to his feet and found that a small crowd had gathered around the newcomers. Soon the whole camp was wakeful again.

The wildfire news had reached the Woodlands in the shape of the big man and his companion. They brought the news that the place Sam talked about incessantly was real after all: that after all the destruction, all the ruin, all the decay, the semi-mythical seat of power had survived. It was true, they said: the site of The City had been located! This was news that could not be stopped; it flew from mouth to mouth through the camp, spreading like the old sickness. There was little sleep that night.

Next morning they all got up slowly, the news still sinking in. The newly arrived pair, a big man with a lot to say for himself, and his quieter companion, were already at the centre of an excited group of people when Jonas joined them.

The questions came thick and fast.

'Are you sure?'

'How do you know?'

The big man laughed scornfully. 'Don't you people know anything? Everyone's talking about it. The news is everywhere.'

'Yeah,' said the other man. 'The news is everywhere. You should just listen to what Big Brendan is saying.'

'Yeah, thanks, Joe mate,' said the other, rolling his eyes. Even Big Brendan sometimes tired of his sycophantic shadow.

The questions continued: where was it? How far? Some asked if Big Brendan could take them there. Granny Tabitha spoke from where she sat, her back against the trunk of a large oak tree that had seen better days. She spoke firmly, her voice surprisingly strong for an old woman.

'There have been rumours of this kind before,' she reminded them. Heads nodded. Hope was exhilarating, but they all knew it often led to disappointment.

'I'm not talking about rumours. This time is different.' Big Brendan's voice was harsh in contrast to Tabitha's. He paused deliberately to create expectation in the crowd. All eyes were on him now; the crowd held its breath.

'I'm telling you: it's there. It's still standing. And...' He allowed himself another dramatic pause, 'Someone has made it out of there. One of *them*. What more proof do you want?'

Once the excited babble had died down, Tabitha asked, 'Have you spoken to this person? Have you seen The City for yourself?'

Big Brendan was clearly untroubled by embarrassment or self-doubt. 'I didn't need to see it. I've spoken to those who have.'

'Yeah,' said Joe Farmer.

There was a buzz of excited conversation, which subsided as the crowd parted to allow someone else through. The old man stood calmly facing Big Brendan for a moment, before turning to make eye contact with those watching. There was a respectful hush. Against the weathered skin of his face his eyes were as bright as those of a much younger man.

'So you think this place will be full of marvels for you to just help yourselves to?'

Big Brendan stared; this wasn't the way it was supposed to go. He didn't take kindly to being challenged.

Will spoke again. 'Even if it is, are you sure those are the sorts of things you really want?'

Big Brendan started blustering again.

'Of course it's what we want! Do you think people want to carry on living like this?' He gestured disdainfully at the makeshift shelters, the cooking fires, the meagre possessions lying about in heaps. 'And if they try to stop us, we'll take them anyway.'

There was only a muted cheer at this. There had been so much fighting; could they really stomach any more?

The man standing next to Jonas spoke up.

'Wait a minute, though. Do we actually know what goes on in there? I mean, is it possible that it was built to protect the structures of government? You know, when they saw what was coming, so they could organise and regroup, get the country running again? After all, they made an Accord with the people, didn't they, the SAR?'

Granny Tabitha joined in once more from her seated position. 'Then they will help us. That's what governments are for, isn't it? To protect the people?'

The rest of her words were drowned out by several other voices.

'You'll be waiting a long time then!'

'What did that lot ever do for us?'

'Only a fool would believe that.'

Big Brendan spat on the ground; Joe Farmer gave a sneering laugh.

'No, listen to her...' began Robin. 'Tabitha has a point.'

A few joined in with murmurs of agreement, but then the doubters began again.

'The only thing they were protecting was themselves!'

'That's the way of this world – everyone for themselves.'

An agitated woman called out from near the back of the crowd, 'Yeah – we all need to look out for ourselves now. No-one else will, that's for sure!'

'No! You are wrong.' Tabitha was standing now, although it had cost her an effort. Her legs were clearly troubling her a great deal that day and she was breathing heavily, but now her voice rang out powerfully. Jonas sighed; he had tried to ease her pain with the herbs and ointments in his bundle, but to no effect.

The clamour stopped.

'You are wrong,' she said again, turning to face the woman. 'You are so wrong. It's not a question of everyone for themselves. If we are to survive we need to look after each other now.'

After that there was a burst of talking and shouting as the crowd fragmented into disparate groups. Big Brendan bellowed to make himself heard again.

'You fools! Do you really think they're sitting around working out how to help the poor? When did governments ever do that?'

'Yeah,' said his echo. 'When did governments ever do that?'

Big Brendan started up again. 'We all know how much government accords are worth! And the Shanti Accord Regime are the worst of the lot!' He made a circle with his thumb and forefinger.

'This is what the famous Accord is worth. Zero! Zilch! Less than nothing! Oh, it's all right for them, isn't it? They've got everything they need: plenty of food, water coming out of taps, electricity... Why should they care about us?'

There was a hubbub at this. He raised a hand.

'Oh yes. Didn't you know? There are ways of generating electricity in that place. They probably still have the... what d'ya call it... Interweb!'

'Yeah,' his companion added. 'And screens and all that stuff.'

There were howls and whoops at this.

Someone else said, 'All right: so if we don't think help is coming from The City any time soon, what are we going to do about organising ourselves here and now? We need to work together if we're going to have proper shelters and...'

The speaker was interrupted by shouts, the big man's voice carrying above them all.

'I'll tell you what we're going to do: we're going to join up with the People's Army and we're going to storm that place. It's time for the people to rise up and claim what we're owed!'

The shouting resumed, and this time the big man let it go on uninterrupted. Jonas turned away in disgust. With some meaningless rhetoric, the big man had managed to whip the crowd into a state of near hysteria. He knew already that he disliked him, and he didn't often take an instant dislike to others. Did the People's Army even exist?

Returning to his pitch he found that Robin and Alison were already back, resting. Little Skylark was sleeping soundly on the ground between them; she had her doll clutched tightly in her skinny arms. He was glad they were not swayed by the wild talk; that level of angry disagreement wasn't something they needed right now.

The next morning, Jonas came across the big man as they were both heading down to the river. He nodded a greeting, and the big man gave a curt nod in response. Neither spoke for a while as they splashed water on their hands and faces. It was Jonas who broke the silence.

'So,' he asked, warily, 'How did you get to hear the news about The City?' The man looked ready to explode if not handled carefully. 'You said you've spoken to someone who has proof?'

For a moment the big man acted as if he hadn't heard, but then he turned, red in the face, squaring up to him aggressively.

'What do you mean?'

Jonas took a step back. 'I was just wondering, you know? Do you trust the person you've spoken to? From what I understand, no-one's been near it since before the disasters. A lot of people don't believe it's even real.'

'Course it's real. Everybody knows what's going on there. And, like I said, *if you were listening,* one of them has come out from there. Living proof, see?'

Jonas remained where he was, shaking the water from his hands, and waited for further elucidation.

In the silence, the big man began to bluster. 'Besides, loads of people have seen it. Stands to reason, doesn't it? The rumour wouldn't be going round, would it, if no-one had been there?'

'So, what sort of place is it? What does it look like?'

'Well...' Big Brendan bent down to fiddle with the fastenings of his boots. Still looking at his feet, he answered, 'Well, obviously, it's a fortress, equipped for defence. Gives them an all-round view of anyone approaching.'

'Including the People's Army,' Jonas murmured.

27

'Well, yes, but, well, they won't be expecting people on foot, will they? They'll be on the lookout for machines and things. The People's Army will be able to slip under their systems, get right up close…'

'So, how big do you reckon it is?'

By now the big man's complexion had gone from red to purple. He sucked in air through clenched teeth. 'Do you know…' he hissed, 'I'm sick to death of being put down and patronised by people like you. Always think you know better…just because I'm…' He appeared to have run out of words.

Jonas waited calmly. Eventually, with an effort, the big man spoke again.

'Well, clearly, it's going to be huge. Obviously! I mean the whole SAR Regime, and their families, and their hangers-on… after all these years, there must be hundreds of them. At least.'

'I'm surprised,' said Jonas, 'That's all. I mean, we thought that everything of any size had been pretty much flattened.'

'Well, clearly The City wasn't!'

Big Brendan turned on his heel and strode past Jonas, jarring him with his shoulder and almost knocking him off balance.

Jonas gave him a few seconds' start before heading up to the camp. 'So…' He smiled grimly to himself. 'He doesn't actually know anything for certain.'

Chapter Four

Once back at his pitch, Jonas began to prepare breakfast. He had taken to making himself a kind of porridge from the oats he and some of the others had gathered and stored. The land beyond the trees must once have been part of a farm, with well-delineated fields and boundaries, but rather like the people, the oats had gone wild, and now grew everywhere. Old Will had shown him how to gather these and other grains to rub between two huge stones set up for the purpose. Mixed with water and a little wild honey and left in the warmth, the grain mysteriously absorbed yeast from the air, and after the dough was left to swell for a few hours it could be baked in a fire-scorched mound of clay to make something he called bread. It was fairly gritty, but edible, and filled you up satisfactorily. The problem was how to store the grains, because the local rodents were rather partial to them too. Jonas was just wondering whether he could fashion something rodent-proof from the metal containers he'd noticed at the middenheap the previous day, when his thoughts were shattered by a shrill cry of pain.

For a moment he was back in that place where he'd been as a terrified little boy when his brother Jack was born. His father had calmed him and explained that all women made that noise when a baby was coming, that it was all right because Granny was with her. Granny had been a real doctor when younger and knew how to help get the baby out. His father had been right: the yelling stopped, all was well, and when he was let in to see his mother, she was smiling at the tiny, wrinkled thing. Lifting her face, she had a beautiful smile for him too, and in that moment he knew for certain what love was. As the years passed and the others arrived, there was always enough love to go around, and when his youngest sister was born he had been there when Granny told his mother to pant, hard, while she unwound the cord from around the baby's neck. She had made him watch.

'You may need to do this yourself one day,' was all she would say.

Later, when she took him with her, visiting neighbours in need, he did indeed assist her, under her instruction. There were times too when the baby got stuck, and on one occasion Granny had shown him how to sterilise a knife in the fire and make a small nick to give the baby room. She had also shown him how to stitch up the wound afterwards, and he had even tried it himself, with trembling fingers.

The memory faded as another agonising scream filled his head. Alison's time must have come! In a few strides he was beside his neighbours. Something seemed to be wrong. There was no-one else about. The others must be back over on the other side, listening to the big man, who had started up again with his nonsense.

Robin was holding his little girl against his chest, tears streaming down his face.

'I don't know what to do,' he sobbed. 'It wasn't like this last time.'

'Would it be OK if I take a look?'

He addressed Alison, but she was beyond hearing. Robin nodded his assent.

When it was all over, Alison held the baby to her breast, beaming broadly as her neighbours came by to offer their congratulations.

'It was Jonas,' she told them. 'The baby was stuck, and he got him out. I thought I was going to die back there, but Jonas was so gentle, and it was all over very quickly.'

It may have felt quick to Alison, and he was glad for her sake that it had, but to him it had seemed like years, and he was still trembling from the shock of the responsibility he had just undertaken.

Robin looked around, hoping to find something to give him, but could find nothing. 'I don't know how I'll ever thank you. I have nothing to repay you with.'

'I'm just relieved all is well,' Jonas told him. 'But actually, I could use your help carrying some things back from the middenheap, if you wouldn't mind.'

Robin got to his feet as though ready to set off there and then.

'Oh, no, not now! In a few days or so. You need to stay here with your lovely family for a while. And,' he glanced over to where Alison's eyelids were drooping, 'I think Alison is in need of some rest.'

Robin knelt beside her on the grass and took the tiny baby gently from her arms.

'It's all right,' he whispered. 'We have a beautiful cradle to put him in.'

He had been more nervous than he'd realised in the heat of the emergency. It was good to leave all that behind and step into the river, wading out to the centre where it was deeper. Jonas allowed the cooling waters to wash over him for some considerable time, but when he returned to the clearing, he saw to his dismay that the crowd was once more gathered around the big man. It seemed someone had asked how they were to get to The City.

'It's east of here,' the big man said. 'We just walk towards the morning sun. Easy!'

'But is it far?' someone else wanted to know.

'Not so far when you consider what we have to gain from going there.'

Jonas groaned to himself. Why were people so easily impressed by such evasive talk? Big Brendan met every question with a non-answer and followed it up by asking questions of his own.

'So are you going to hang around here in the woods doing nothing for the rest of your days, or are you coming with me to storm that place and give those lying, cheating politicians what they deserve?'

Joe Farmer gave a cheer, which was picked up by a number of people in the crowd.

'Are we going to get some of what they've got for ourselves?'

More cheering.

'Are we going to send those scumbags packing? Prison's too good for them I reckon. Are we going to take our country back again?'

The cheering this time was mixed with a low rumble of dissent. The crowd had begun to disperse, and Jonas caught a few words here and there.

'What's the point? They're bound to have weapons, better than anything we've got.'

'Yeah, but what else do we do?'

Someone else said, 'There's something about that man I really don't like,' and his companion replied,

'He's as bad as the SAR if you ask me.'

Jonas went over to where Tabitha was sitting once more, propped up against the oak tree. She patted the space beside her, and he joined her under the cool, green canopy.

'What do *you* think?' he asked her.

She looked at him with her bright eyes, smiling. 'Different people say different things, don't they? You've

32

heard Big Brendan's version. But others say it's more like a garden, with a roof of clear glass to let the light in.

'That's definitely not what Big Brendan says.'

'No. Well, he wants it to be part of the old war machine, doesn't he? Keeps going on about guns and machines and things.' Tabitha was fiddling with a charm that hung about her neck, a crudely fashioned wire shape. She tucked it carefully inside her dress, and said wistfully, 'I know what I'd like to believe: that it's a place where things grow; where there is light and peace and certainly no weapons.'

Jonas smiled and thanked her. Granny Tabitha's version was much to be preferred to Big Brendan's. How wonderful if she were right! But how could they know for sure?

He was still deep in thought when he returned to his pitch next to Robin and Alison and their little family. All four of them were sleeping soundly, and he smiled with satisfaction. Life would go on, with or without The City, whether or not it possessed a glass-domed garden.

The following morning the whole encampment was awake early amidst a great deal of noise and bustle. It seemed the big man and his companion had really set the wildcat among the birds. Already people were gathering up what belongings they had; some were looking around for wood to use as clubs. Jonas was asked about the possibility of finding weapons at the middenheap, or whether there was any way of sharpening their knives. He shook his head and kept quiet about the grinding stone, wishing he had the courage to say directly that he had no intention of helping them prepare for violence, and that they were fools to follow the even bigger fool who had come into the camp and disrupted all their lives.

No Abiding City

Opinions were deeply divided: on the one hand there were those who thought the only way forward was to return to the past as soon as possible, with its screens and robots and cities of glass and steel, and that it would take force to achieve their vision. Others preferred to look to a new future, different from the past. Some even said that their little society here in the Woodlands was how life was meant to be and why change that? Where before there had been petty squabbles and minor disagreements, now Big Brendan had managed to create factions, and this time it was serious.

Jonas spoke to Robin about it, out of Alison's hearing for fear of upsetting her with talk of violence. She remained oblivious, awed by the new life she held in her arms.

'I don't believe he even knows where it is, or even if it really is still standing.'

Robin agreed. 'No, he says it is, but if he's asked a direct question he has nothing solid to say. I think he's just telling people what they want to hear. Have you heard what Granny Tabitha says about it?'

Jonas nodded. 'The domed garden? Quite a nice idea. But who knows? Not Big Brendan. He seems to have persuaded quite a few to go with him, though... '

'You're not thinking of going, are you?'

Jonas hesitated just long enough for Robin to raise an eyebrow.

'No, not going with him, not to find The City, definitely not. I don't actually want to go anywhere at all... but if someone went with him, to keep an eye on him or something...I feel as though we should be trying to stop him, get him to see the harm he's doing...'

'Do you think that's possible?'

Jonas shrugged. 'If enough people joined together...'

'I'm sorry, but I really don't think…'

'Oh, no: this isn't the right time for you, not now, not with…' He looked over to where Alison was calmly nursing the baby. 'No. You have your family to look after.'

'And yours is…?'

'Gone. All gone.' He looked down, briefly. 'It's OK, I'm used to it. But…' Jonas smiled, sheepishly. 'But the habit of trying to look after people hasn't gone. Even when I'm not very good at it.'

'It must have been hard for you.'

Jonas turned away. How could he even speak of it? He had been so long without friends, without anyone to confide in, not since his grandmother…' He sighed.

'Oh well. That's all in the past. We need to look to the future now, don't we?'

Before Robin could offer further sympathy, Jonas asked brightly, 'Anyway, what about yours? Your parents? Any other family?'

Now it was Robin's turn to sigh. 'We don't know where they are. Everyone got scattered a while back, you know, when…'

Jonas nodded. 'Of course. Have you tried finding out?'

'We've asked people. I'd like to help Alison find her mum, especially now, with the baby… And I'd really like to find my brother…'

They lapsed into silence. Finding family suddenly felt a whole lot more important than finding a militarised City – or even a peaceful glass-roofed garden - which might or might not be there at all.

The bustle continued around them for the rest of the day. By early afternoon a group of around thirty people had gathered at the big stag-headed oak tree on the edge of the clearing. They must have agreed that as the meeting place. The big man was swaggering around, boasting about what he would do to the SAR leader and any of his cronies if he ever caught them. He'd picked up a long hazel switch from somewhere and was whipping it hard against the trunk; the more nervous members of the group jumped each time he did so.

Unable to bear it any longer, Jonas set off to the middenheap, walking at twice his normal speed for the first kilometre and only slowing down when he was almost there. He had already located a number of steel drums over at the far side, thinking they would make useful storage containers. The question now was how to get them back to the campsite. He contemplated rolling them, one at a time, but the thought of rolling them all the way with his back bent, especially on the uphill stretches, quickly ruled that out. He needed some means of transporting several at once. It set him to thinking though, and he searched around instead until he found a set of wooden boards that he could just about manage on his shoulders.

Back at the camp it was noticeably quieter. The warmongers had left, and a kind of stunned silence seemed to have settled over the rest of the little community. The afternoon sun was beating down relentlessly, and Jonas resisted the temptation to snooze. Instead he sought out Will, who was tinkering with some old copper pots.

'See, here,' Will said. 'With the dents knocked out they'll be...' He came to a stop. 'OK, Jonas, I can see you're bursting with something. Why don't you sit down here and tell me?'

To his relief, Will encouraged his idea of making a cart, and agreed to work on it with him. The planks he had brought back with him suggested the general shape and size, if he could find more of them. The wheels of course would present a problem.

'It's a specialist job,' Will said, shaking his head. 'The wood has to be heated and shaped and ideally bound with metal rims to stop it wearing down too quickly. I don't know of anyone round here with the skills for that. Although...'

'Yes?'

'I don't suppose you've found any wheels on the middenheap?'

Disappointed, Jonas shook his head.

'OK, well don't be despondent. It's a little further, but I know of a place where there are sure to be some.'

The derelict bicycle factory was indeed a source of wheels, surprisingly stout ones, with good thick tyres not yet showing any signs of perishing. Within a week Jonas' unconventional cart was complete, and with Robin's help he had been able to use it to transport the steel containers and a number of other useful things from the middenheap.

'So,' said Old Will one morning as they were finishing their breakfast. 'Have you decided what you are going to do?'

'Do? About what?'

'About the rest of your life.'

Jonas shook his head.

'Perhaps you should go and see what's happening out there.'

'Go in search of The City?'

Will laughed, nodding and shaking his head at the same time. 'Maybe.'

'I don't want to join some great movement for revenge,,,'

'No, but supposing you could do some good? Persuade people there's another way to live without returning to the past?'

It was as if he could see inside Jonas' head.

Jonas continued to make things, but in time the days grew monotonous. The weather stayed quiet, and there had been no newcomers for some time. Robin and Alison had finally left weeks ago in the vague hope of finding news of Alison's family. The parting had been painful on both sides, and even though they had begged him to go with them, Jonas had been convinced that there was something else he needed to do, if only he knew what it was.

Now, the empty space alongside his pitch made him feel restless as well as sad, and he recalled the conversation with Old Will. Was there really something he could do, something worthwhile? After a night in which he slept badly he found that he'd reached a decision.

Old Will was unsurprised when he told him. He helped him select the tools he would find useful on his journeying, pointing out that he would be able to teach others some of the skills he'd learnt in the Woodlands as he travelled, as well as using his gift for healing. At the last minute he thrust into Jonas' hands a small wooden chest, neatly partitioned inside.

'For your herbs and ointments.' He must have seen Jonas rummaging awkwardly in his pack each time he had need of any of his grandmother's remedies.

'You're sure you'll be all right?' Jonas asked Old Will as he loaded up the cart. He had added a raised frame, with strong fabric stretched across to give shelter at night and keep his simple belongings dry in wet weather.

'Aye,' said Will, looking amused. 'I've always been all right. It's the others that aren't.' He had never been much of a talker, all the time Jonas had been there; out of practice, perhaps, after living alone for so long.

Jonas turned away to hide his grief at parting, and perhaps Old Will did, too.

'Off you go now, lad. You have work to do.

Chapter Five

Jonas met no-one for several days. One morning, as he pushed his cart along an ancient, rutted roadway, he saw someone up ahead. The figure was wrapped in a cloak, head down, shoulders bent, seemingly oblivious to his approach. As they drew level, he saw from the outline that it was a woman. Women did not usually travel alone these days.

'Good morning!'

No response.

He tried again. 'Good morning! Where are you headed?'

She turned then and he saw her eyes, large in her pale face. As she made to run, she staggered and slowed to a halt, where she remained, watching him.

It was a new thing, to have someone afraid of him, and the feeling was uncomfortable.

'Please, don't be frightened. Are you hungry? I have food.' He could read the hesitation in every line of her body. He understood: people who offered food could be dangerous.

'Wait,' he said, holding his hands up, palm outwards, before going round to the back of the cart and lifting the cover. He had some bread in there, hardening but still edible; Old Will had encouraged him to make extra provisions as he prepared for his journey. Jonas broke off a piece and held it out to her at arm's length. He smiled encouragement, but her expression did not change. Finally, he placed it on the fallen branch of a tree and returned to his cart.

'My name is Jonas,' he said, once more lifting the cover. This time he pulled out a small package of smoked meat - another of the skills Old Will had taught him for preserving food. He hoped she had strong teeth: it tended to be tough. This he placed beside the bread.

Her expression remained wary.

With a final nod he took up the handles and heaved the cart forward, giving the frightened girl a wide berth. There was a barely perceptible nod from her in return as he moved on.

If the omnipresent red kites had cared to look down, they would have seen that there were very few people on the road; in truth there were very few people anywhere; so many had died, if not from the sickness, then from fire or flood or starvation. But all that was nothing to them; they continued their flight.

Having lost those closest to him made things easier for Jonas in some ways, for now there was no-one else relying on him; yet the habit of looking out for others was strong, and after his encounter with the young woman, he found himself reflecting on what more he could have done. It was one thing to give her bread and meat, but if he could have taught her to grind the grains and make bread, or trap the wild animals for food, surely that would have been better?

He was following an old track through the devastated remains of what had once been a forest. The charred skeletons of ancient trees reared up on every side, ghostly spectators of a world gone mad. Jonas had plenty of time to think. If The City did exist, whatever it looked like, it was surely nothing more than a relic of the past, like these trees, a past that held much unhappiness and suffering. Why seek out something like that when it was possible to begin building a new world? But then, what would that world look like? He hoped that people might no longer be afraid of one another, like the young woman, too terrified even to accept food from his hand. That didn't seem right. People would need to support and help one another, in practical ways as well as through friendship and trust. He gave a deep sigh. Where did he fit in to all this?

A sudden movement ahead brought him abruptly out of his reverie as he hauled on the cart, his feet making ruts in the soft ground as he dug his heels in, desperate to slow it down, to prevent a collision, to stop something terrible from happening.. It was a child, a little girl.... And he knew her. He shouted as loudly as he could, but she continued without so much as turning her head. No, oh no, no, No, No, Noooo...!

The cart swerved to the right as Jonas pulled on it with all his strength, but its momentum carried it forward until the moment of impact, and Jonas found himself on the ground half beneath it. There was no sound from the child, only the horrifying thud as they collided. Then there was silence.

'Skylark? Sky?'

The mother's wail of fear and anguish rang through the dead trees, penetrating the darkness of Jonas' thoughts. Slowly, he hauled himself out from the cart. Alison hadn't even seen him as she emerged from the trees, didn't see him until he had been standing at her side for minutes that felt like hours.

She looked up at him then and he saw the track her tears had made through the dirt on her face. His own tears were yet to be shed. The child made a tiny fluttering movement of her hand, and they both bent closer. Jonas fought down his own feelings of shame and guilt. His grandmother used to say, 'Where there's life there's hope,' and he remembered how she had told him that it was

42

possible to give life back by breathing your own breath into that of the other. He had never seen it done, though; it was normal to avoid other people's breath for fear of contagion.

'May I?' His voice was shaky. He wasn't even sure what he was trying to do.

Alison nodded, relinquishing her place beside the little girl. Jonas laid her out on the soft earth, gently feeling for broken bones. She didn't react. He opened her mouth, pinching her nostrils closed, and took a deep breath. He placed his mouth over hers, willing his breath to enter her, to revive her. He did this repeatedly, looking anxiously each time to see if her tiny chest had begun to rise and fall. There was nothing.

Alison had moved round to the other side. Suddenly she let out a cry. Jonas stopped and followed her gaze. Beneath Sky's head was a dark stain, growing and spreading even as they looked. He tried to shield Alison's view, but she had seen enough, and as she raised her eyes to his they both knew.

It was at that moment that Robin came crashing out of the forest, his body hung about with bags, the baby in his arms. He took in the meaning of what he saw instantly and moved to comfort Alison. Jonas stepped back from the little family group.

It was Alison who broke the long silence. 'She ran out in front of the cart,' she told her husband. 'Jonas did everything he could to warn her. He tried to stop the cart, but it was too late.' Her sobs were muffled by Robin's shoulder.

Jonas staggered further away into the tree stumps. After a few paces he found himself face down on the forest floor, sobbing into the dead twigs as he had never sobbed when his grandmother died. All the pain and loss of those years, watching his own loved ones dying, one by one, came flooding out. He cried for Sky and for the world.

Later that evening, when Alison and Robin had finally persuaded him to go with them to their camp, he sat silently as Alison went over the events of their daughter's death yet again.

'Jonas tried everything,' she said. 'He even tried to give her his own breath. But it was too late. There was nothing anyone could have done.'

Jonas neither heard nor saw them, hunched in a heap of his own misery. Gently, they fed him, wrapped him in a blanket, and, unknown to him, watched over him as he slept. When he woke, his eyelids still swollen, the first thing he saw was Alison, sitting with her back against a tree trunk, cooing to the baby as she fed him. Some detached part of Jonas' mind noted that the child had grown.

He refused breakfast with a shake of the head. No words would come. He remained, lying there, staring inwards to the darkness that was all he could see. It was laughable: he had wanted to make the world a better place, but instead he had destroyed someone else's world. How could they be sitting there, so calm, doing the ordinary things, when their child lay, wrapped in her little blanket, the blood and gore still seeping through. He had caused that.

The sun rose, reached its zenith, and began to fall again. Dimly, he heard their whisperings, saw their looks of concern as they glanced in his direction. He had still not uttered a word.

A thought began to take shape in his mind; there was one last service he could perform for them.

'Jonas!'

There was surprise and relief in Robin's voice as he reacted to the sight of Jonas standing, stretching his cramped limbs and heading towards the cart. He still had no words. The cart was where it had come to rest, skewed across the track. He walked slowly around it, almost fainting when he saw the mess on the front corner. Drawing breath, slowly and with a great effort of will, he lifted the cover and searched for the spade.

It was not the first grave he had dug: far from it. In the faces of Alison and Robin he saw again the stunned grief of his own parents as they watched him place a small bundle in the hole and cover it up. They had made their final goodbyes, as Sky's parents were doing now; they had done it over and over, until it was their turn, and Jonas was the only mourner left at the graveside.

After he had shovelled the earth back, carefully and gently and with tears obscuring his sight, they stood there, the three of them, Alison and Robin holding tightly on to their baby son, the child who was all they had left, who would never know his sister.

In the long silence Jonas remembered other things: how his parents had spoken words of love and comfort as they buried their children; how they had never stopped believing that the world was basically good, that human beings were basically decent, and that there was always hope.

Robin was speaking; his words slowly penetrated the fog of Jonas' thoughts.

'She brought us joy while she lived, and we will miss her always. We are thankful that she lived, sorry that she died, but there will always be something of her that lives on in us.'

His voice broke, and Alison continued for him.

'Loving our little girl, who was born different, was a gift we were given. We continue to have hope in a better future, and even as we mourn Sky, we rejoice in the birth of our son, and in the friendship of Jonas. Without him, we would not have this other child to cherish...'

Jonas could bear it no longer. He turned and ran, blundering through the blighted forest, unmindful of cuts and bruises and tears to his clothing as he caught himself on the jagged branches of what had once been trees.

He had no idea what time it was when he came to his senses. The night was dark around him, and he heard the sound of an owl, far off. He could have borne it if they had shouted, accused him, beaten him, thrown stones at him. It was what he deserved. But to be so kind, despite their own grief; that was too much.

Rain began to fall. It wasn't like the rain back in the Woodlands, where the trees had leaves and the raindrops made a pleasing music as they fell. The rain here was water, falling straight and determined. Here was his punishment, straight from heaven itself. He laughed, a strange, unearthly sound out there alone in the darkness. By morning there would be nothing but a mound of wet earth, and Jonas buried beneath it.

The rain must have stopped as suddenly as it had started, because when Jonas came to again it was morning. A weak sunlight filtered through the dark branches, falling on his face like his mother's kiss. He realised he had been dreaming of her. It was true what Alison had said as they buried the child: the dead do live on in us if we let them. It must have been something of his mother, or his indomitable grandmother, that now urged him to stand up, keep moving to stave off the shivers, and return, however much he dreaded it, to his life.

They were there, by the cart, as he staggered the last few steps. Alison stepped forward and embraced him.

'You'll get mud on you,' he said, weakly.

'It'll wash.'

'So will you, Man,' said Robin, turning towards him. 'What'll it be first, breakfast or a bath?'

While they were eating, they talked of ordinary things: the weather, the state of the roads, what Robin and Alison had seen on their travels since they left the Woodlands. Finally, when he could stand it no more, he tried to tell them how desperately sorry he was.

Robin spoke before he had finished.

'We understand that, but look, it was an accident. Alison saw what happened. You tried to warn Sky, you tried to stop the cart...'

'You see...' Alison took over. 'She was different. You must have noticed? She never learned to speak because she couldn't hear.'

She looked down for a moment. Jonas realised this was difficult for her.

'I used to think it was my fault, something I'd done when I was expecting her...'

Robin reached across to place a hand on her arm. He shook his head.

'Alison was ill when she was first pregnant. We always wondered if that had something to do with it. But...'

He fixed Jonas with his gaze. 'You were not to blame for the accident.'

Just then the baby, asleep in the crib Jonas had made, gave a loud burp, and they all laughed.

'Does he have a name yet?'

The parents exchanged a glance, and Robin continued, 'We're still deciding. Now off with you, Man, and get cleaned up.' He pointed to a depression in the forest floor some metres away. 'There's a small pond over there.'

Three days later, and Jonas was still with Robin and Alison, still following the same track. His friends had failed to find any trace of Alison's parents, but that was unsurprising; so many people had been lost. Jonas was still struggling to balance the joy he might have felt at being reunited with them, against the agonising reality of what had brought them back together. The baby was gurgling happily in Alison's arms; the cradle and some of the contents of Robin's bags had been transferred to Jonas' cart. As they walked, it became clear from the trodden earth that increasing numbers of people had passed the same way, and then suddenly diverted to one side. The undergrowth had begun to spring up beneath the trees here, and the green freshness was a cheering sight. Before long they heard the sounds of voices mingled with the familiar clanging of iron pots and pans. Soon they caught the scent of woodsmoke, and for the first time since the tragedy Jonas recognised that he was ravenously hungry.

The settlement that lay before them as they emerged from the treeline was ramshackle, but not unpleasant. The people were friendly and offered them a space to set up camp. When Jonas looked around for his own space, Robin said, 'Don't be daft. You're with us now.'

When they were settled and the baby fed, some of the men came over to them. A stocky, red-haired man welcomed them.

'I'm Fletcher,' he said, shaking hands without hesitation. His companions stepped forward to do the same.

'Tommy. How do.'

'Ginger. Good to meet you.'

Fletcher spoke again. 'Where have you come from, friends?'

Robin spoke for all of them, introducing Alison and Jonas.

'We've been on the road a while; met up back at Old Will's place, in the Woodlands. Have you heard of it? A camp rather like this one. Really nice, friendly people.'

He smiled, and Fletcher smiled back.

'Well you've come at a good time. You're not the only newcomers. We've been getting lots of visitors, with all sorts of news – some of it almost incredible!'

Jonas felt his heart sink. Not The City again!

'Anyway, you'll be hungry, and we've a stew in the pot that will stretch to three more.'

Ginger, who, judging by his flaming hair, was probably Fletcher's son, added, 'Tomorrow I'll show you where you can find your own food.'

'Is there any wild game here?' Jonas asked. He was thinking of the traps somewhere under all the baggage in his cart.

'Aye, plenty, if you can catch it!'

A sudden sound of bleating caused Jonas to turn his head sharply.

Ginger laughed. 'Oh, no' he said, firmly, 'Those goats aren't for eating. We keep them for milk. My mother makes cheese: it's good, too.' His gaze swept the woods behind Jonas. 'There are wild goats to be hunted, though, as well as the usual deer, if you're quick enough; and then you can trap the rabbits – no shortage of those.'

When they had eaten, with gratitude, the stew of plain vegetables brought to them by Fletcher's wife, Alison asked Jonas to hold the baby for a few moments while she attended to a call of nature. He stood there with the precious bundle, entranced by the child's wide-awake stare as he took in the sights around him. A sudden banging of pots startled the child. Well, this one wasn't deaf, at any rate.

Alison appeared at his side, and regretfully he handed the baby back.

'I'll go and set the traps now. Should be a good chance of catching something over there.'

Alison stopped him. She looked up at him, her eyes brimming.

'I never forget that we wouldn't have him if it wasn't for you.'

Jonas accepted her words, for what else could he do? But did saving one child's life really cancel out the death of the other?

He set off for the cart, giving them a wave as he went.

Robin called after him, 'By the way, the baby's name is Jonas.'

Over the following days and weeks Jonas' cart attracted a lot of friendly interest, and he was soon persuaded to open it up to show fellow villagers its contents. When they realised that he had tools, and also the skills to use them, Fletcher and Tommy suggested he set up a sort of workshop just outside the main camp, where there would be more space and less likelihood of disturbing other residents with the noise and bustle. Jonas had found his time sharing with Robin and Alison a great joy, even though it was still hard to shake off his sense of guilt. He was sorry to end that time, but he also welcomed the opportunity to give something useful to the community.

'It's not as though you won't be seeing us most days anyway,' Alison consoled him, and Robin added that anyway, at least he wouldn't be woken up by the baby during the nights if he was a bit further away. It was true that little Jonas was wakeful now; he was teething, and it was clearly a very painful business.

Jonas began with the stools. His neighbours had found plenty of fallen branches when making their shelters, and so he began to show them how to shape the smaller pieces for the seat, how to make joints so the legs would fit smoothly. He made spinning tops from the offcuts to amuse the curious children who had gathered round, enthralled, to watch this new activity.

Then someone pointed out the willow trees growing down by the river, and together they harvested the whip-like lengths to dry, and after a few days put them into soak. Once they were supple, the little group sat contentedly, first weaving the base and then inserting the side stakes to shape them upwards. They talked as they worked, as people always do, and the conversation wove in and out and around to the rhythm of their willow-weaving. Jonas heard stories of survival and loss, fear and contentment.

As the willow work became more widespread Jonas was able to leave them to it. There was a middenheap close by. He wandered over there each day and started bringing back small items: children's toys, hessian bags, shoes. There was an informal sort of barter in the village, and Jonas found that these items would ease his way to many of the ordinary things he needed. Alison had begun to teach some of the women how to weave blankets using the unravelled threads of old woven garments, and Robin instituted gathering parties in search of such fabrics.

No Abiding City

The time passed easily, and Jonas began to feel the same sense of belonging, of wanting to stay, that he had experienced back in the Woodlands with Old Will. Talk of The City still bubbled up from time to time, and he listened, perturbed, aware that people were trying to get their heads round the idea of the place and whether or not it could possibly be real. None of the people who spoke about it claimed any first-hand knowledge: it was always someone who had passed through, visitors, strangers who had heard from somebody who had heard from somebody else, and so on.

As time went on, however, interest in The City only increased, and with it the certainty in many people's minds that it was worth finding. He still sometimes heard it described as a kind of city, although no-one seemed to have any clear idea of what that really meant. Jonas wept inwardly. Would they really risk the peace of their settled existence here to go in search of a dream that might turn out to be a mirage? And if Big Brendan succeeded in his plans of joining up with the People's Army, it could turn out to be far worse; a truly alarming nightmare. The more the people talked, the more disquieted Jonas became.

He was collecting timber one morning, with the help of two of the men, Jim and Harry. They were talking about The City.

'You're not serious about trying to find it, are you?' he asked.

Harry looked up from the pile of slim branches he was attempting, with difficulty, to fix into a bundle. '

What? Yes - best idea I've heard of in a long time.' He gave up on his bundle and the sticks fell with a clatter. 'I mean, how else are things going to move forward?'

'So, tell me, what do you really know about that place?'

'Well, if that's where the SAR is, then it's going to have everything we need. Stands to reason: fuel, communications, all the things people had before. Houses, tall buildings... more like a proper city, like there used to be. That has to be a good thing, doesn't it?'

Jim joined the conversation. 'And food! Easy food; none of this trekking about looking for it, or having to catch it.'

Harry laughed, and Jonas joined in. It was known throughout the encampment how much Jim loved his food. Beneath his laughter, though, he was worried. He had noted the increasing shift from Brendan's fortified stronghold to an old-style city. He tried out the other version he'd heard. 'I've heard it might be a kind of garden, with a glass roof?'

The others looked confused.

'Well, yes, it could be, I suppose,' said Harry, slowly. 'A city, with a garden. Covered over by a dome. I guess.'

Their easy acceptance of the shifting definitions worried Jonas: that they were prepared to leave behind all they knew to set off in search of...what? He tried again.

'My grandmother was a healer: she'd been a doctor, back when she was young, when you could still get hold of supplies and medicines.'

'And that's another thing they're bound to have there,' said Harry.

'But you don't know that, do you? Anyway, what I'm trying to say is, my grandmother used to take me out with her when people needed help. I watched her: she never once rushed to prescribe treatment. She always insisted on examining her patients carefully, to establish what exactly the symptoms were before she prescribed any course of action.' He paused for a moment, saddened;

it was that careful examination of sick patients that in the end had cost his grandmother her life.

They were looking at him intently. What did this have to do with The City?

'You see, the point is, it's not a good idea to act on anything before you've had a chance to establish the facts.'

'Oh well, if you want to know the facts, then you should come and hear what our latest visitors have to say.' Jim's eyes shone.

'They'll be at our camp meeting tomorrow, after supper.'

Chapter Six

It was evening, and Jonas was packing away his tools for the night. It had been a good day: a small group had watched as he carved, shaped and jointed wood, and in return they had shown him how they twisted fibres to make yarn. Tomorrow he would attempt to find the middenheap some recently arrived neighbours had mentioned. He was running short on materials and was sure that if he searched he was bound to find treasures left there long ago by those who didn't know the value of what they discarded.

The community had developed a pattern of eating a meal together once a week. This involved a lot of preparation in the hours leading up to it, and there was a definite lightening of the atmosphere as they sat together preparing the vegetables and cutting up the meat, when there was any. While some of the families took on these tasks, others were out gathering firewood, or collecting wild fruits.

Until his arrival here Jonas had found nothing to differentiate the days, and he had long ago lost track of them, but now he was happy to be reminded by the cheerful activity that it was Friday. He took pleasure in the sense of structure the regular communal meal gave to the passage of time, and began to look forward to Friday evening, with its social contact and feeling of relaxation.

With the tools packed away, he walked the short distance to the main camp, just in time to receive his bowlful of stew. It contained wild goat; he had shared in the hunt and capture of the animal the previous day. Now he was sitting near Robin and Alison, but was miles away in his mind, off on some train of thought of his own. What an arbitrary thing it was, to divide the days and weeks up in that way, to give them names... It might be Friday, but did anyone even know what month it was any more? He would have been hard pressed to guess at the season, given that the idea of seasons had long ago largely outlived reality. Sudden bursts of extreme weather still led some people to try to name them, but there was no regularity to them. Was time a purely human construct anyway, born of life on a planet that revolved around a star in what its inhabitants had chosen to call a year? Did time exist at all in deep space, where there was nothing to mark its passing? He sighed. So much knowledge had been lost.

A rising volume of noise at the far side of the settlement brought him out of his musing and back to the here and now. Of course: the new arrivals, due to bestow their mad views about The City on the inhabitants of the peaceful settlement! It was irritating. Why spoil a pleasant Friday evening? He hadn't intended to go and listen to them, but looking around now he saw that most people were drifting over in that direction. Perhaps he'd better go and see what was happening. Leaving his bowl on the stool, he moved cautiously closer to the crowd. Robin said he might join him later.

By the time Jonas got there most of the community had already gathered, and he stood on the edge, watching over the shoulders of the other people. For a fleeting moment he saw them as if from outside: the dishevelled clothing, items found and flung together, many tied up with homemade twine; the men's beards roughly trimmed, the women's hair tied back or plaited. The scarves that hung about their necks or covered their mouths were mostly frayed. Jonas breathed in the stale odour of people whose lives were focused on survival, not appearance, and for a few seconds his memory brought him back to the sharp antiseptic smell that pervaded his grandmother's house; keeping clean, she said, was part of the healing process. Then the memory was gone, and he knew he must smell the same as those around him, have the same dirty streaks across his face, the same sprigs of wild herbs in his teeth, the same stains on his garments. The next moment he had shaken himself free of those thoughts. There were no mirrors out here, and who needed one? Who actually needed to know what they looked like? Life was basic. He felt a sharp pang of sympathy for the people and their need to focus on the dream of a better life; but then his irritation with the newcomers returned. It was unkind to raise the people's hopes. What would happen when they realised that it was a false hope?

The crowd had begun to spread out now, leaving a sort of arena in the centre, where a large, broad-shouldered man was holding forth. Jonas didn't need his neighbour to whisper the name of the big man in order to recognise the speaker. It seemed that Big Brendan was everywhere.

'I tell you, this is the future: a place where there is no more grubbing about in the soil to produce your food. A place where there is no sickness, a place where machines do all the work, where you are safe from fire and flood and wild animals...'

Well, his oratory had certainly improved.

'... so why should they have it all to themselves when it rightfully belongs to all of us? Why should...'

A voice from the crowd rang out. 'Why should we believe you? How do you even know all this?'

'Well, because, because... we've heard. From people who know...'

'Yeah.' This was Joe Farmer filling the brief silence. 'They're starting to come out of there...'

'Have you actually spoken to someone from the City? You, yourself?'

Big Brendan looked daggers at the speaker. He didn't seem all that pleased with Joe either.

'We've spoken to people who've seen them. Isn't that good enough for you?'

Jonas smiled inwardly. Big Brendan's oratory might have improved, but he was still full of bluster when anyone challenged him.

'The fact is, they're growing weak in there; their defences are down. It's ours for the taking, I tell you...'

Some of the people cheered. Jonas ground his teeth in frustration. Couldn't they see he was just making things up on the spot to please the crowd?

People began arguing with their neighbours.

'What's wrong with staying as we are?' The woman next to him muttered. Jonas recognised her as one of the originators of the Friday meal movement.

'Yes, but it's got to be worth a try,' said someone else.

Suddenly, someone shouted, over the general noise, 'We're doing OK out here!'

Big Brendan turned on him menacingly, and the voices faded away; breath was held to see how Big Brendan would deal with the challenge.

'What, you want to stay like this for the rest of your life, poking about for food and water every single day? When you could be warm and safe in The City?'

His tone oozed scorn.

'Warm and safe and with machines to do all the work!' This was Joe Farmer.

'Machines to do all the work, Yes.' Big Brendan repeated. 'No illnesses, no babies dying. Living a long and healthy life. They have machines and electricity and the internet and more food than you can eat in a whole month of Fridays! They have all the things our great-grandparents had, all the things they've taken away from us, all the things that are rightfully ours!'

There was general cheering at this, the dissenting voices drowned out. Suddenly, it seemed, the communal goat stew was no longer so attractive.

'They may have the power now, but it belongs to us…'

There was more cheering.

'That place belongs to us…and it's ours for the taking. They've grown fat and lazy in there.'

'Yeah – fat and lazy.' Joe Farmer added his voice to the general noise.

'Join me, come and meet up with the People's Army. Follow the trail eastwards. The conquest of The City will be the easiest thing ever. They don't deserve to have the place. I tell you, it's our destiny: all we have to do is walk in and take over.'

There was no stopping the crowd now. The cheering continued, and Big Brendan let it. He was basking in his moment of glory.

Then the cheering faded. The crowd were watching what Big Brendan, in his self-absorption, had failed to see. A slight figure, tall and pale, had joined him in the circle and now stood facing him, as though to do battle.

'You don't know what you're talking about!'

The voice was not raised like Big Brendan's, but its quiet, assured calm demanded attention.

'Oh, and you do, do you?' His voice was a snarl.

'Yes, I do. There is nothing in there that will improve the life of anyone out here.'

'Oh, out *here*,' he said. 'Out here's a lost cause.' He looked round at the crowd, oblivious to the confused looks of his hearers. 'The only way to improve life out here is to get in there, out of the wind and the rain and the burning sun. Out here is finished!'

The crowd was silent now, waiting to see what would happen next.

The young woman looked round at the crowd. Jonas hadn't seen her around the settlement before, although there was something about her... She stood upright, her shoulders back. Her simple dress, made of some fabric Jonas couldn't identify, was soft, unspotted, like her pale skin; it lent her a glow; she seemed surrounded by an aura of light.

'These things you want to take by force, the technology, the artificially grown food, the chemicals, the isolation from the natural world, the things our ancestors had: were those all really so good?'

'You don't know what you're talking about, you stupid woman! Why should *that lot...*' - there was such venom in the way he spat out the words that the woman next to Jonas shuddered - 'Why should *they* have all the comforts of the past? With those machine things to do all the work? Keeping the food stores to themselves?'

His gaze raked the crowd.

'Did you know that they can communicate with the other elites, right across the world? They have *screens* and tele-things and...'

The murmur that greeted this was mixed – some of the crowd cheering, some calling 'No!' and 'Rubbish!'

He chose to acknowledge only the supportive voices.

'When things got serious, they scuttled off in there, taking all the stuff that really belonged to us. It's time we went in there after them and took back what's rightfully ours!'

This time the cheering voices were louder.

The young woman waited patiently, unruffled. She spoke as calmly as before.

'Most of what is in there would be of no use out here. The technology wouldn't work outside. The wonderful food you are lusting after is grown in artificial conditions. It's mostly pure chemicals – not a patch on what you eat here, fresh from the earth. In there, there's no daylight, no sunshine, the air is filtered, there is no rain, only water that is constantly recycled – is that really what you want?'

'Daylight doesn't put food in our bellies, does it?'

Jonas couldn't hold back any longer. 'Well, actually, it does. Daylight, and sunshine and rain - that's what makes food grow.'

Someone else in the crowd called out in reply, 'And rain and heat destroy it.'

Brendan swung round to face Jonas, a desperate triumph in his voice. 'You see? I tell you - life out here is finished. We all need to get under cover… that's the future.'

Before Jonas could respond, the young woman replied again.

'No, it's the past!' This time she raised her voice a little. 'And what about the people who don't get inside? How much space do you imagine there is in there?'

'Well you tell us, Miss know-it-all.'

Brendan paused. Jonas could see his mind working.

'How come you know so much about it anyway?' His face twisted in an unpleasant scowl. 'But of course, you don't know anything, do you? You're just making all this up.'

A bit rich, coming from him. Jonas began to edge his way forward.

Big Brendan turned to the crowd again, raising his voice. 'She's making this up – probably planning to go there herself and doesn't want us to follow...'

He took several steps towards her, standing menacingly close. Jonas had pushed through to the front by now and was close enough to hear the words he hissed in her ear.

'Or is there something you know that we don't? Do you know someone, is that it? Someone that's been there? Or...' he came closer still, looking at her strangely. The girl turned her head; Jonas could imagine the stench of his breath. 'Or are you in league with someone on the inside?'

He looked angry enough to strike her. Before he had time to think Jonas had stepped forward and, to his own baffled surprise, grabbed the woman by the wrist.

'Come on Rosie,' he said, with as much authority as he could muster. 'Time we were going.'

Caught off guard, she stumbled, and he was able to drag her with him. The crowd roared with laughter at this unexpected turn of events. They parted to let them through, and Big Brendan was left fuming, unsure what to do next.

Despite the woman's resistance, Jonas refused to let go of her wrist before they had crossed to the far side of the clearing and lost themselves in the trees. When he finally let go she turned on him in fury.

'What do you think you were doing? How *dare* you?'

Her tone was no longer calm. Jonas found that he was trembling.

'I'm sorry if I was a bit rough, but I've come across those people before – Big Brendan and his mates. They're going round stirring up discontent and hatred. They're pretty vicious, truly.'

She wasn't listening.

'You *idiot!*' She wheeled around as if intending to return to the crowd. 'Now they'll be more determined than ever to try and find it.' Then she turned back, the fight suddenly gone out of her.

'I'm sorry, but I was worried they'd turn violent. You seemed alone and, well I thought you needed help…'

'Well I didn't.'

Her pale face had reddened a little and there were tears at the corner of her eyes, belying her protestations.

'Are you alone?' Jonas asked. 'Is there someone I can get for you?'

She shook her head.

'Come with me and I'll find you somewhere safe until things calm down.

He wondered whether she would refuse to get into the cart, but she settled down as well as she could amongst the various implements stored there, and didn't even demur as Jonas covered her with a blanket.

'Are you hungry? I'll get you some food,' he said, without waiting for a reply.

Things had quietened down when Jonas went back over to the central fire to fetch some more stew. The crowd had mostly dispersed, although he could still hear Big Brendan and a few of the others talking over each other in angry voices.

Once persuaded to eat, it was clear that the young woman really was hungry. She was seated on one of the wooden stools, spooning up the stew, and only spoke again when she had finished it.

'Why Rosie?' she asked.

'First name that came into my head. I thought I'd get away with it if it looked as though I knew you.'

63

She gave a slight bow of the head in recognition of his reasoning.

'Actually, I do sort of know you…'

She turned her head away. 'No, I don't think so.'

'Well, we have met before.'

For the first time, she seemed afraid.

'It's all right…it's just that I met you on the road a while ago. You were hungry.'

She looked at him properly now. 'Jonas.'

'You do remember me!'

They were both quiet for a time

'So, are you going to tell me your real name?'

She hesitated. 'Rosie.'

'OK, you don't trust me. I understand.'

'That's not the point. It's safer.'

'OK,' he said again.

She finished the stew and handed him the bowl. He would have to be satisfied with that, at least for now. Moving across to the cart, he raised the frame once more and told her she would be safe in there, under the canvas, until morning. He would be sleeping underneath, as he often did, so she was to call out if anything happened.

Jonas woke the next morning to a fine mist. The ground was damp and he had trouble starting the fire to make the breakfast porridge. He made his way into the main settlement, but a kind of heavy silence lay over it, which explained itself when he saw that a number of the campfires were deserted. The ground where the meeting had taken place the previous evening was trampled, and a trail of footsteps led out to the main track, the one that had brought him here all those weeks ago with Robin and Alison. He crossed over to their shelter, anxious, but found that they were still sleeping. He was relieved. They had too much sense to go off with a hothead like Big Brendan anyway.

Their neighbour looked out and commented gloomily on the weather.

Has Big Brendan gone?' he asked her.

'Him!' she said with disgust. 'Him and half the village…chasing rainbows.'

He waited for more.

'Went at first light, heading east.'

'So do you believe him, that he has proof?'

'What proof can there be?'

The woman's husband appeared behind her.

'Well, your woman seemed pretty convinced.'

'My… oh, you mean Rosie! Well, you know what it's like when they get an idea in their heads…'

The man nodded in agreement and the woman elbowed herhusband in the ribs.

'That's because some of us women have far better ideas in our heads than you, that's for sure.'

The pair disappeared back inside their shelter and Jonas returned to his campsite next to the cart. The water was boiling at last, and he busied himself with the porridge, throwing in a handful of small purple fruits towards the end. They were right, those people, though. Where had Rosie – whoever she really was – got such definite ideas about life in The City? Could she be right? She was certainly the only person Jonas had heard express such detailed opposition to it.

As he approached the cart he was half-prepared for her not to be there, but there were sounds of her stirring and so he cautiously lifted a corner of the canvas. She sat up abruptly, as though ready for flight.

'Whoa, it's all right. Look, I've made breakfast.'

She gave him an almost-smile.

'So this is your mission in life – to feed me every time you see me!'

He laughed. 'Looks that way!'

She climbed out of the cart and seated herself on the stool he offered, accepting the bowl that he handed to her.

'So, is that really better than – what was it you said? Food grown artificially that is mostly chemicals?'

She ignored the question.

'And how do you know what the food is like in there anyway?'

She ignored that question too.

They ate in silence for a while, and then Rosie indicated that she needed to respond to a call of nature. Jonas was reluctant to let her go by herself, but the alternative was clearly unthinkable.

Finally, he said, 'Can you hold on for a minute or two? I'll go and get my friend Alison. She'll show you where the women go, and she can take you down to the river to wash too. Is that OK?'

Rosie nodded, her smile gently amused at his embarrassment.

When he got to Robin and Alison's shelter he was relieved to see that they were already up and breakfasted.

'Oh, we've been up for hours,' Alison replied in response to his apologies for disturbing them. 'Little Jonas had us up before dawn. His teeth are really bothering him, poor mite.'

Jonas had a sudden memory of his mother walking back and forth in the night with one of his young siblings, desperately trying to rock the child back to sleep, until his grandmother appeared with a paste she had made to rub on his gums. He wished he knew the recipe.

'That was an interesting show you put on last night,' Robin said. He didn't need telling that 'Rosie' and Jonas were strangers. 'It was high time to stop all that dangerous talk.'

'But too late to stop half the village falling under his spell,' said Alison, handing the baby over to Robin. 'Now, what was it you wanted me to do?'

Later, when the women had returned from wherever the women went, Rosie and Alison sat down with Jonas. He had unpacked some more of his wooden stools so they didn't need to sit on the damp grass. The conversation turned, inevitably, to Big Brendan and The City.

'I don't think anyone else will trouble you.' Jonas told Rosie. 'Most of these people are really good folk. It's just that they get wound up by the likes of him. There's been a lot of talk about The City recently. Until now I don't think people really believed it existed, but then Big Brendan and his cronies started talking about how they had proof…'

A haunted look passed over Rosie's face, but she shook herself and it was gone. Alison remembered that she hadn't fed little Jonas and made her goodbyes. Jonas and Rosie sat in silence for a while. There was something bothering Jonas, and he wasn't sure how to put it into words, but it was Rosie who broke the silence first.

'Why have they called the baby after you?'

'Because we're friends.' He was not to be put off. 'Why did you talk about The City and what it's like in there with such… ' What was the word he needed? 'With such *knowledge*?'

She replied so quietly that for a moment he wondered if he had really heard her.

'Because I *know*.'

She looked at him, and he read truth in her eyes. There was silence between them again. There was so much Jonas wanted to ask. How did she know, really know, not like Big Brendan and all his blustering and his 'someone who'd spoken to someone who knew someone who...'? At the same time, he was weirdly afraid to ask. There was something about her that disturbed him.

Finally, he said, 'I wish you'd tell me your real name.'

All she said was, 'I'm sorry.' Then, in an abrupt change of tone, she asked what he was planning to do that day. He told her about his intended trip to a middenheap he hadn't yet explored, adding, 'Why don't you come with me?'

To his surprise she said she would, and they set off just as the sun was showing itself and the mist had begun to disperse.

Chapter Seven

They walked in silence for some time. The directions Jonas had been given were rather vague, but after a couple of false starts, they caught sight of what could only be the middenheap. Rosie wrinkled her nose.

'It usually gets worse before it gets better,' Jonas said, with a laugh. 'You'll get used to it. How do they dispose of waste in The City?'

'Is that a trick question?'

'Why would it be?'

She sighed. 'Everyone wants to find it. They want to know the way there. They want to *be* there.'

'Not me. I thought you knew that from last night.'

She conceded that with a nod. 'I know you think that big man's ideas are dangerous.'

They were negotiating their way through an area of broken and scattered stones. Jonas offered her a hand, which she refused impatiently. When they were back on even ground, she added,

'And I know you think I can't look after myself.'

She strode ahead of him. He read her annoyance in the line of her shoulders, and wished he could find a way to get past her defences. Surely the best way to defeat the crazed thinking about taking over The City was to learn more about it, and it seemed Rosie was the one person who could help with that.

She continued to stride ahead of him, her chin tilted upwards, and so she missed the protruding block of stone that tripped her up. She went down heavily, with a little cry of pain. Jonas walked forward to stand beside her.

'So, what now?'

Reluctantly, she asked for his help. 'Could you help me up, please?'

She was rubbing her ankle. Her voice seemed to have got smaller. Jonas bent down to examine the damage.

'My grandmother was a healer. If you'll let me, I can probably tell you if you've done any real harm.'

It was clear that the ankle wasn't broken, but Jonas thought she would have a nasty sprain. He bound it up as best he could with his scarf. A dark bruise was already forming, deep purple against her pale skin. It was clear that she wouldn't make it to the middenheap and back. They would have to return to the camp.

'Could we rest for a while, first?' Her eyes were following the fluttering of two pale blue butterflies, with a kind of hunger Jonas had seen before only in small children. The insects danced tirelessly among the bell-like flowers of a ragged shrub beside her, and for a while he forgot everything else in watching them with her.

Then his practical side reasserted itself. He had some water with him which he gave her, and then sat patiently beside her, thinking about what to do next. She could probably walk, but might need help. He looked around for wood that might serve as a crutch. It was a pity, too, to lose so much time from his expedition, as he really needed to source some new materials; but then there was always tomorrow, he supposed. There was always tomorrow: one day was very much like another.

After a bit, she said, 'I'm sorry.'

'Sorry for tripping up?'

'Sorry for being ungrateful.' There was a pause. 'I'm not used to being helped by strangers. I know you meant well last night.'

Jonas nodded a brief acknowledgement. 'Big Brendan and his lot really worry me. What they're saying is harmful, and most people don't stand up to him. I think he was shocked by your opposition last night, but he really looked as though he was going to strike you.'

'You're right, he is dangerous, or at least his ideas are.' She looked around at the blighted fields and crumbling masonry. To their left a drift of bright poppies led her eyes to the horizon, where a broken tree stood in silhouette. A breeze stirred, sending its few remaining leaves floating lazily down.

'People need to know the truth. It's the only way to stop him.'

'And you know what the truth is?'

She didn't meet his eyes, but said, in a low voice, 'Yes.'

He didn't respond at once, his head full of questions. How did she know? Was her truth any more valid than Big Brendan's? Yet somehow he believed her. She did know.

'There's a small copse over there,' he said, clearing his throat. 'I'll see if there's anything there you can use to help you walk.'

On the journey back, they talked intermittently. Leaning on the improvised crutch was clearly an effort, but despite that, Jonas had the impression that Rosie was enjoying herself. They stopped frequently, and each time she took in great lungfuls of air, letting them out again with a sort of satisfied sigh. He pointed out to her the housemartins, darting about in pursuit of insects, their movements mirroring those of their unseen prey. She laughed aloud at the sight.

'The problem is…' He was thinking aloud now. 'The problem is, people need certainty. One way or another, they need to know the truth. Then they can decide…' Decide what though? What real choices were there?

He was startled when she spoke suddenly, decisively. 'I know where it is.'

He hadn't expected that.

After a moment or two, wondering if she would say more, he asked, 'And is Big Brendan right? About travelling
due east?'

She nodded. 'It's a little more complicated than that when you actually get there, but yes, he's right.'

'So...' Jonas hesitated, wondering where this would lead. 'You've been there. You know where it is.'

As he looked at her, she turned her head aside. There were tears on her cheeks.

'Yes,' she said at last. 'I know exactly where it is, the place they're looking for, and I could lead them there to prove it's the opposite of all the good things they have out here.'

'And that's the problem, isn't it? You can only convince them it's not what they want by giving them what they think they want.'

'And it's the one thing I don't want to do,' she added quietly.

It was after midday by the time they made it back to the camp. Rosie was clearly exhausted, and Jonas took her to Alison and Robin to look after her. He toyed with the idea of spending what remained of the day by heading back to the middenheap, but his enthusiasm had seeped away. Instead, he went out into the woods to search for comfrey to make a poultice; Rosie's ankle would heal faster with some help, as well as plenty of rest.

On his return he made his way over to Alison and Robin's shelter. They were not sitting outside in their usual spot, and he supposed they had gone in, out of the glare of the sun. Rosie must be inside with them. After calling softly and getting no response he headed back to his own encampment to make up the poultice. As he was putting the finishing touches to it, Robin and Alison appeared from the direction of the river. The baby was slung across Alison's back in a shawl. Robin appeared inclined towards conversation.

'Pity you lost the chance to search the middenheap.'

Jonas shrugged. 'There's always tomorrow.'

'Perhaps I'll come with you then. I've had an idea about making a wheel to catch the wind – you know, like the old wind farms? Only on a much smaller scale of course. It could be used to turn things – maybe even the stones we use to grind the grains.'

'Yeah, that'd be great, Robin. Tomorrow it is.' He gestured to the mixture he was still holding. 'Anyway, I've made up this poultice – should help the swelling go down.' He placed it in one of the small willow baskets. 'I'll come over with you to dress her ankle.'

Alison looked surprised. 'Oh, has she gone back over to our shelter?'

'Gone back?'

'She said she was coming over here to get some sleep.'

Jonas looked around, as though she might be hiding in plain sight somewhere in the small clearing.

'Haven't you seen her?'

Robin walked the few steps to the cart. 'Could she be sleeping in here?'

Even as he began to raise the frame, Jonas knew she wasn't there. There was a kind of emptiness about the cart he couldn't explain.

Later, after they'd searched the camp and asked several people, Jonas knew he had to accept that Rosie was

73

gone. There was nothing to suggest she'd been forced; no-one had heard anything, and the crutch he'd made for her was gone too, as was her travelling cloak. The only footsteps away from Jonas' encampment were the uneven ones of someone with a sprained ankle leaning heavily on a crutch.

He felt uneasy. Rosie - whoever she was – had left without telling him, and although his common sense told him that she had gone of her own free will, the scene with Big Brendan was still vivid in his memory. If she continued to speak out as she had, he or someone like him was going to take her claims seriously and attempt to force her to take them to the City, or the domed garden, or whatever the place was. If it was anything.

He ran over and over in his mind the things she had said; she seemed very definite in her knowledge of The City's location. Her repeated assertion that out here was better than in there suggested strongly that she knew something for a fact. But how? And why would she say that the last thing she wanted to do was take others there? Then there was the matter of her name: why on earth keep it secret? How would having it known put her in danger?

Jonas and Robin made it over to the middenheap the following day. They travelled along the same path as the one Jonas had taken with Rosie. The poppies and butterflies were still there, the trees still shedding their leaves, the rough stones and tall grasses. He remembered how Rosie had seemed to delight in them. It made him think of little Jonas, throwing his chubby arms and legs about in rapture at each new sight. He turned and smiled at Robin.

'Little Jonas would love all this.' He gestured at the butterflies, and sighed. 'I do hope he will grow up in a better world than the one we knew.'

'We'll have to try and make it a better one, won't we?'

They continued walking in silence. Jonas' thoughts went back to Rosie. Yes, she had delighted in the simplest of sights, and yet she wasn't childlike; indeed there was something about her that suggested a deep seriousness, a sadness, even.

He wandered about the heap of decaying matter, unsure of what he was really looking for now that he was here. He kicked aside a heap of rotting carpet and found beneath it some sturdy metal boxes. They might be good for food storage.

'I saw some metal drums here the other day, before Big Brendan turned up and disrupted everything. Not too big to carry, if we took one each.'

Robin had his back to him; as Jonas watched, his friend slipped from view on the unstable surface. There was a clanging sound.

'I think I've found them!'

'Are you hurt?'

'No, I just lost my footing. Oh look…!' He pointed to what lay below the metal drums. 'You know, they'd be useful too, and they're light. We could carry them back inside the drums.'

'Ah.' Jonas hesitated. 'Should we, though?'

'What, because they're plastic? Well, if we're going to use them that would be no worse than leaving them here would it?'

'It's just… you know, plastic…?'

'We really need food storage, though, don't we?' He looked at the metal containers Jonas was still holding. 'Those're pretty rusty. Don't you think these would be safer?'

They selected boxes of suitable size and stowed them inside the metal drums. A little further searching located lids for the drums.

'That should keep the rats out.' Jonas grinned with satisfaction, and sat down for a rest. 'So, what do you make of Big Brendan and all his talk of The City?'

'He's certainly all fired up about it.'

'But can he really know anything?'

'I don't know. He's convinced he knows what it is and what goes on in there, but I can't quite believe in his vision somehow…'

They sat for some time, blinking into the sun as it sat low on the horizon ahead of them.

Jonas frowned. 'It doesn't square with what Rosie said about it.'

'About the technology they have being of no use to us out here?'

'Yes, and about the food and so on…'

'She certainly wasn't keen on following him there, was she?'

It almost felt…' Jonas hesitated. 'It almost felt as though they were talking about two completely different things. You know: Big Brendan sees it as a kind of fortress…'

'A what?'

'A place that's built for defence against an enemy.'

Robin nodded. 'And that doesn't seem quite like the dome Granny Tabitha used to talk about.'

'And neither of those quite squares with what Rosie was saying.'

Jonas got to his feet, rubbing his back. It was hard work, clambering about on the shifting, stinking heap. 'I'll need a good dip in the river when we get back, that's for sure.'

Robin laughed. 'Yeah, I don't think we'll be very popular until we've cleaned up a bit.' He scrabbled about for a last look in the spot where they'd found the plastic boxes. 'Oh, what's this? Are these any use, do you think?'

The box Robin held up turned out to contain a collection of plastic combs, of a kind Jonas had only seen before in his grandmother's room.

'I suppose some of the women would welcome these. The thing will be to take care of what we do when we
dispose of them.'

'You could sell them, Jonas. You know: in exchange for things you need.'

He handed the box to Jonas, but now something else had caught his eye. It looked like a metal pole with a small wheel attached.

'Hm. I wonder?'

Jonas waited.

'Yes. You know what? I think we could add sails to this; we need large, flat panels of some sort…'

The following Friday the communal meal was less convivial than usual. With the numbers down, the members of the community were more scattered than before, and somehow the heart seemed to have gone out of things. Even the food was unappetising. Jonas left early and slept badly. All the next day he was restless, and even being asked to look after little Jonas for a while failed to soothe him.

'Sorry, Alison,' he said, as he handed the child back. 'I can't seem to settle him today.'

'Course you can't: you're unsettled yourself.'

Robin arrived back from the river with a pile of wet washing.

'The whole village is unsettled.' He began draping the wet baby garments over the lower branches of a tree. 'So did she talk to you, then? Rosie?'

'She stood by what she said to Big Brendan. She insists that we're better off outside The City.'

'Do you think she knows what she's talking about? More than Big Brendan?'

'Definitely more than him! And, yes, she seems to know something.'

He decided to tell them how she had become tearful when she told him that she had been there.

'What, inside?'

'No, I don't think so. At least ... well, maybe. That might explain how she knows about, you know, chemicals and artificial food and so on.' Why had it not occurred to him before? She had said the last thing she wanted to do was go *back* there.

'I've been thinking,' he said, at last.

Robin left the rest of the wet pile on a stool and came and sat beside him. 'Yes, I think we realised that.' He gave him a friendly grin.

'If, as Rosie said, the only way to prove to Big Brendan and his lot that it's not a good place is to let them see for themselves... then it makes sense to go there, doesn't it?' Jonas looked from face to face. 'Doesn't it?'

'Does it?' Alison looked dubious.

'I just feel that, if there's a movement growing, you know, people joining him, like the people who left here...'

'That you need to do something.' She smiled, sadly. 'You've decided to go, haven't you? You're heading east again.'

They sat quietly for a while, Jonas silently cursing Big Brendan. He had felt such contentment in this place alongside Alison and Robin and his little namesake, and now it had been destroyed. He blamed Rosie, too, for unsettling him, making him wonder what the truth was, challenging him somehow to act, even though he hadn't the faintest idea what action he should take. The only thing he knew was that he had to travel eastwards.

He slept heavily that night, and dreamed of his family. He was a child again, out exploring, but he had taken a wrong turning and got lost. Forcing down his panic, he remained where he was, knowing it would be easier for them to find him if he stayed in one place. He had waited all day, but when no-one came, he set off again, deeper and deeper into the forest. He woke without knowing if he had ever found his way home.

It was still early, but he forced himself to prepare a breakfast of porridge and herbal tea, which he consumed without tasting, and then set about the business of packing up his belongings. They had to be placed in the cart in a certain order, not only to make them fit in, but also because it was difficult to steer if the balance wasn't right. Some things would have to be left behind; but which? He fussed over it for a long time, packing and unpacking until finally he told himself to just get on with it and go. He thought about Rosie, how she had left without saying goodbye. He knew he couldn't do that, although he dreaded the moment of parting from Alison and Robin. He went all around the camp, saying his goodbyes and making the excuse that it was time for him to move on, he had things to sell, skills to teach. They accepted his explanation and waved him on his way. So many had left now; he was just one more.

When he came to Alison and Robin's shelter, he almost faltered, but forced himself to call out, 'Well, I'm off now!'

They came out at once, Alison carrying a bundle.

'Here, this will keep you going on your first day.' She handed over the bundle, and he sniffed it. There was fresh bread and homemade curd cheese in there. Alison and Robin had recently taken to keeping a nanny goat.

Robin held little Jonas up for him to kiss. Jonas took him in his arms and the child stared solemnly back.

'Be brave, little man. Your parents love you so, so much...'

He turned to Robin and Alison.

'I'll never forget you... or what I did to your family. I'll never forget how you forgave me...'

'No, Jonas, none of that.' Alison's hand was warm on his arm as she spoke. 'We've said long ago all that needed to be said about Sky.'

Still Jonas hung his head.

'You are our friend, Jonas.' Alison was looking up at his face, forcing him to see her, to see her expression. 'If it wasn't for you we wouldn't have this precious little one. He would have died before he had a chance to live.'

'And if it wasn't for me...'

'Jonas.' Alison leaned close and spoke softly. 'Of course we mourn our little girl; it would be strange if we didn't. But it was an accident, and we have never blamed you. You tried to warn her, but she didn't hear you; she never heard anything in her life. We saw what happened: it could not have been avoided.'

Jonas travelled a long way that day. He walked, pushing the cart without noticing where he was. When he set off, the sun was low in the sky, and as he continued it rose to meet him until it was overhead. The tears he shed afresh for Robin and Alison's daughter became the tears he had never shed for his long-lost brothers and sisters; he wept for his parents, for his grandmother, and for the world he had never known.

That night he slept under the cart, glad of the food his friends had given him. At dawn he was confused and had to wait for the clouds to clear before he could determine his way forward. He continued for some days, only stopping to make camp long enough to forage for food, light a fire and sleep. It was hard going with the cart; it was heavier than it had been when he'd left Old Will. Since the early days in the Woodlands his life seemed to have been nothing but a series of partings. He was used to being on his own; it had never troubled him before, but something within him had shifted. Well, he would just have to carry on as he had always done, putting one foot in front of the other.

Chapter Eight

One night there was a fierce wildstorm, so wild that he climbed into the cart and huddled down under the cover, crouching amongst the pots and pans. The wind tore at the canvas cover, and he was forced to hold on to it all night to stop it being ripped away. He slept very little.

In the morning he peered out to a sight of broken branches and scattered leaves. The ash from the previous night's fire had been sent swirling around the camp space before settling at the edges, and the wooden bowls he had carelessly left out were nowhere to be seen. Breakfast didn't seem worth the effort, somehow, and he tightened the ropes over the cart and set off without even washing.

For long stretches he saw no-one, and then he would suddenly find a settlement ahead of him, hidden in a little dip, or perched defiantly on a hill. Each was different; in some places people had found a way to construct shelters that resembled houses, with doors and windows; in other places they had taken over the ruins of old buildings, living in amongst the tumbledown walls and broken roofs. Sometimes he spent the night camped near the road alongside other travellers, and once or twice he ventured into an encampment to ask permission to stay the night, but it was never longer than that; always there was something within him that kept him moving forward.

One day he had walked without stopping, deep in thought, only beginning to slow as his legs grew tired. Thoughts continued to circle round and round in his head. Where was he going, really? How could he find a way of revealing a better world? Was there even a way? He found he had walked further than he intended, for the sun was now low in the sky. Time to stop and make camp for the night. He chose a spot next to a stream, and sat for a moment, thinking about the future. He was so absorbed in thought that he failed to hear the two men approaching, although they made no attempt to be quiet.

'What do you want here?' The speaker, the shorter of the two, was unkempt, surly.

Jonas rose stiffly to his feet.

'Good evening, fellow traveller!' He offered a handshake, which was refused. Ah well, people were still naturally wary. 'This is a fine spot for an overnight stay.'

There was no immediate response. Jonas regarded the two men; they were unlikely travellers, carrying no possessions. The second man, the one who had not spoken, walked over to his cart.

'What's this?'

Jonas explained wearily that it contained tools and equipment, a few examples of the things he could make, or perhaps help others to make, when the man cut him short.

'Why?'

'Well, you never know what you'll need when you're travelling, do you?'

Any talk of offering himself as a teacher seemed all wrong now, with the two men eyeing him suspiciously.

'Anyway, what about you two – are you travelling with others? Family, perhaps?'

The first man laughed, and Jonas caught a glimpse of blackened teeth.

'We don't travel, not now.' He waved his arm to something behind him that Jonas could not see. 'Not now we have the village.'

Jonas was surprised. 'You've built a village?'

The other man said, 'Not built exactly…' but gave no further explanation. The vague hostility Jonas had sensed when they first arrived seemed to have eased a little, and on impulse he asked if he might visit their village.

'Aye, OK, come in the morning,' the tall one said, and they set off with no further civility.

The kites had seen it all before, or their long-ago ancestors had. They had seen the earth heaving and cracking; seen the seas pouring in and pouring out. They had retreated to warmer climes when the land froze over, and returned to find the world green again beneath their wings.

They had watched, impassively, as the earthbound creatures crept across the landscape, building their solid nests of wood and thatch; had seen them torn down and rebuilt in ever greater numbers, more solid than ever, in brick and mortar, and then destroyed again. It was all one to them.

The strident sounds of the robin's territorial call woke Jonas, far too early for someone recovering from a long and tiring journey. As he slowly opened his eyes, the sounds of thrush and blackbird joined in, so loud they seemed to be right inside his head, drowning out every thought for a while. He lay there absorbing the sound, feeling at one with the natural world.

Then the previous night's encounter came back to him, and other memories began to surface. He saw in his mind's eye his childhood home. He too had lived in a village, what was left of it; their house - the doctor's house - had been made of crumbling red bricks, weathered by the wildstorms and softened by the flooding. He remembered his mother weeping over the destruction of her garden one year, for their village was low-lying and the sandbags hadn't been enough to keep the water out. It had brought with it a foul stench and left behind a coating of oozing black mud.

They had moved then, up to the higher ground, taking possession of a stone-built home long abandoned after its occupants had died. His mother had worried that they would catch the sickness there, but Granny had assured her - Jonas remembered listening from behind the door - that it could not live outside the human body for long. That house had stood firm against the winter winds, and kept them cool in summer, but it wasn't a comfortable home. Food was becoming ever more scarce, and people were dying in even greater numbers than before. He remembered the tenderness of his mother as she nursed his young siblings, the sagging shoulders of his father as he went out foraging each day and returned exhausted each evening, his bag almost as light as when he'd left.

He got up. Memories of home were painful. His knees and back reminded him of how far he had walked the day before, and new memories of his grandmother welled up; how she had long given up on the medicine she had studied as a young woman, the supply of medical equipment and drugs erratic at best. She had returned to the wisdom of her ancestors and found remedies in the woods and fields that surrounded them. What was it she'd used to ease aching joints? As he searched for the plant, he kept remembering her voice, always matter-of-fact, hiding her own fears so as not to pass them on to the others. Because he was the eldest, she had sometimes taken him with her as she searched for the herbs she needed; in the bare kitchen of the stone house he had been privy to the making of her salves and potions. He had accompanied her on some of her trips to the other families, carrying home the small gifts of food she accepted in exchange for her healing.

As he waited for the pot to boil up the bundle of comfrey leaves, slowly adding some of the white willow bark he always kept in the cart, Jonas sighed. Now that he had let himself remember those times, he was faced with the memory that never truly went away: the look on her face the day she came back from treating Sadie's family; the way she would not let him come close to her. She had taken herself off to her room without a farewell, and he had grieved for her ever since.

Ah well! He sighed as he stirred the pot and began to strain off the liquid, pulping what was left into a paste for use later when it cooled. His grandmother had passed on to him some of her knowledge, and he could offer it along with his making and mending skills. It was no use regretting the past; he would look forward and not back.

Two hours later, fed and with the ache in his limbs eased, Jonas and his cart were heading in the direction indicated by the two men. On his approach he was surprised to see that the village was not the ramshackle collection of crude shelters he'd expected, but a series of square buildings, shabby survivors of the past. He wondered what he would find there.

Whenever he had happened upon collections of dwellings previously, he usually found himself surrounded by a small crowd of curious children and barking dogs. Here it was different; in fact it was eerily quiet. He wondered if the two men had failed to tell him the whole story. He walked cautiously down the main street, avoiding the potholes in the tarmac. The roads that remained from the past were so much worse than the new roads that were slowly emerging from the land: roads made by the passage of feet and animals, that could be repaired by the addition of soft mud or small stones stamped down underfoot. The kind of road he was on now, damaged by the vehicles of the past, could not be repaired by present methods. He recalled seeing a great middenheap of old petrol cars, rusting behind a broken fence. Where had that been? Truth to tell, he didn't really know where he had been or where he was going. It seemed pointless even to have a destination now, for everywhere was the same.

He was brought back to the present by the emergence from behind a building of one of his visitors from the night before. To his relief it was the tall man, the friendlier of the two.

'So you've come to see us.'

'Good morning. My name's Jonas.' He again offered a handshake, and this time it was accepted.

'Leo. Let's get moving, shall we?'

Leo led the way to the nearest of the square buildings. A doorway led to a flight of concrete stairs, chipped and stained and evil-smelling. At the top Leo hammered on a solid-looking door; there was a short delay, and a voice called out,

'Who's there?'

'Leo. Let me in.'

Jonas heard the sound of a heavy bolt being drawn back, and then another one. Finally the door opened and Leo shouldered his way in.

After a moment's hesitation, Jonas followed. In the gloom he could just make out a group of people seated on the floor, their backs against the walls. The windows were covered with some thick material that was clearly intended to keep out the wind, but it also kept out the light.

'This is Jonas,' said Leo.

A woman's voice said. 'What do you want?' She didn't move to greet him and nor did any of the other people in the room. They remained crouched on the floor, staring. Jonas supposed they must be Leo's family. He couldn't find a reply to the woman's question.

Leo didn't seem to think a reply was needed.

'Come on,' he said. I'll show you some more.'

As they left, the bolts were slammed shut immediately behind them. Leo led him downstairs to a damp room with a pitted concrete floor and, with something of a flourish, approached the deep sink opposite the door.

'See here,' he said, twisting the tap. A trickle of brownish water issued forth, pooling in the sink alongside flakes of rust.

'Hm. Some days it's better than that.'

Jonas felt sorry for the man's embarrassment.

Leo tapped the wall, ignoring the flakes of plaster that flew off. 'That's strong, that is. That won't blow down when the wildstorms come again.'

He seemed oddly proud of the place, despite the decay and the dirt and its general sordid appearance.

Jonas was relieved when they were back outside in the open air. He took in a deep breath and wondered if this was the moment to take his leave, but Leo urged him on, leading him back along the main street and up and down the side streets; they were all depressingly similar, as were the dismal and damaged buildings that rose above them. To make conversation, Jonas told his companion of how he had hoped to offer himself as a teacher, to pass on some of the skills he had learnt.

Leo listened silently, and then, as though Jonas hadn't spoken, he waved an arm around possessively.

'We have everything we need here: doors with locks to keep people out, rooms where we can keep our belongings safe; water that pours from taps, most of the time, anyway. And - '

He stopped abruptly in front of a building in even worse repair than the housing blocks, nodding to the two men who seemed to be guarding it, and pushed open the door. It must once have held glass panels, but now only shards of the stuff remained, hanging precariously in the steel frame.

Jonas followed, cautiously. Rows of rusting metal cabinets lined the walls. Shelves of crumpled packets and boxes stood in the centre. There was a sort of humming sound, and Jonas realised that it was electricity; he had rarely experienced it himself, and he found it unnerving.

Leo raised the lid of one of the cabinets and a light came on inside. It appeared choked with ice, but he thrust in a hand and pulled out a box, marked in smudged letters: *Cod Loin.* He showed it to Jonas triumphantly, and to Jonas' puzzled look he said, 'Fish! White fish.'

Then the light went out and the humming faltered. Leo said, 'Oh, it happens. It'll be back on in a few days.'

'So where does the power come from?'

'There's an old wind farm up on the hill. It works most of the time. I think the blades need oiling or something.'

Jonas gave a polite nod. He'd heard about the wind farms. In fact, he realised that he had heard them, heard the eerie sound the wind made as it sang through the blades. He had wondered what happened when the wind didn't blow.

'Stay for a while. Eat with us.'

Jonas looked at the box in Leo's hand and sighed as he remembered the dancing points of light on the stream back in the Woodlands, as it tumbled and teemed with fish; the smoke that drifted across the camp as he and Will cooked their supper on the days they made a catch, stretching out afterwards beneath the trees; no locks or fear of strangers then. He explained that he had to be moving on.

'I'll walk back with you, then,' said Leo, nodding again to the two guards. His manner became confidential as they left the village behind. 'I did wonder, when we saw you last night, if you were actually heading to the...' He looked around, although they were out in the open and no-one else was in sight. 'If you were heading to The City.'

So they had heard the talk here too? Jonas shook his head. 'No.' He paused, choosing his words carefully.

'Most people aren't even sure it exists.'

'Well I believe it exists all right. In fact, I know it does.' The man lowered his voice even further, so that Jonas had to lean in to catch the next words. 'Some people were here a few days ago. They have proof that it exists: someone has come out of there and is willing to show the way.'

So Big Brendan had been spreading his mischief here too.

The cooler weather and intermittent clouds that had hidden the sun at the outset of his journey had given way to unrelieved, burning sunlight. The track he was following had widened out, and he covered himself with a length of cloth to keep off the glare and protect himself from sunstroke; there was little shade along this road, and he missed the sight of the trees as well as their shelter. Time seemed elastic, stretching and shrinking as the days rolled by, until he felt lost in a kind of timeless present where he kept walking because what else was there to do?

He was lucky that his darker skin didn't burn and felt sorry for those people he sometimes met whose skin, pale to start with, had reddened and burned until it was blistered before even beginning to darken. His mind went back to his first meeting with Rosie: he seemed to be remembering details he hadn't noticed at the time: how unusually pale she was, how straight her back. He recalled the moment he had grasped her wrist to save her from Big Brendan, how soft her skin was. He knew he had never seen anyone like her, a feeling that had grown stronger, a feeling that there was no room for in the present circumstances. He pushed those thoughts aside; it wasn't that, though, that occupied him now: it was that she really was different: there was no sign of reddening or blistering on her arms or face. She was as pale as Robin and Alison's new-born baby, paler, in fact. How was that?

As the track widened out he began to encounter a few small knots of people. Mostly, they overtook him, being less encumbered than he was. Everyone was travelling in the same direction. Taking a rest at the side of the road one afternoon, he found himself joined by a number of others who had also worked out that it was a good spot. He found there were people he recognised, and even if they didn't speak, he felt less alone.

A few days later, once more on the road, he was startled to be clapped on the back by someone.

'Well, if it isn't the teacher!'

'Leo! I thought you were settled in your concrete village, with the food preserved in ice?'

'I thought so too, but, well, when I heard that so many people were heading for The City, I thought I might see what all the fuss was about.'

'What about your family?'

Leo shook his head.

'Nah. Too scared.'

Before Jonas could find a reply to this, another voice broke in.

'Jonas! We wondered if we might catch up with you!'

Turning, he saw the unmistakeable fiery hair of Ginger, who called out to someone else to come over. His friend Tommy appeared and greeted Jonas warmly, joining him and Leo at the side of the road.

'Ah, yes. Well, I walk fairly slowly, you know, with the cart...' Anyway, what about your dad?'

'Oh, him? Old stick-in-the-mud! Never stopped talking about The City, but when it was time to go, decided he wanted to stay where he was.'

After a short rest they agreed it was time to move on, and Jonas was content to walk with Tommy and Ginger, and Leo. They continued together in silence for a while, but as Jonas tired, he said, 'Don't feel you have to keep pace with me.'

They expressed reluctance, but Jonas could see that he was holding them back and urged them on.

'OK. See you at The City.' It had become the standard way of bidding farewell amongst the travellers. He wondered if it actually had any meaning.

Now Jonas watched their backs receding into the distance. Being able to greet people by name, after so long, and to be recognised and greeted himself had given him a warm feeling, and he was sorry to see them go.

As he walked, the number of people passing him increased. Quite a few stopped for a chat; most with the same gleam of hope in their eye. Who was he to disabuse them? And really, what did he actually know? His meetings with Rosie seemed almost dreamlike now.

Two women drew level with him, both with bright copper curls and skin that was noticeably blotchy and blistered. Sympathy made him wince.

'How far have you come?' asked one of them.

'I don't actually know,' he replied, smiling.' It feels as though I've been walking forever.'

'Are you heading for the Hexadome?' asked the other.

'I've not heard that name before. Is that the same thing as The City?'

They nodded, and the first one added, 'It's what The City really is; its true identity. That's what we believe, anyway.' She paused. 'My sister and me…' she nodded at the other woman, 'We lost all our family.'

'The sickness is still around, you know, whatever they say,' said the other.

'So,' the first resumed, 'We thought we might as well. Nothing to lose…'

'And some say that if you reach the Hexadome you will be cured of all illness…'

Her voice faded in his ears. The heat had weakened him and now he felt his legs beginning to give way. It was a long time since he'd had any food or water.

'Are you all right?'

'What?' He was holding onto the cart now. 'Just a bit thirsty.' The words came out through parched lips.

'Oh, we passed close to the river not far back, didn't we Cissy?'

The other nodded. 'Have you got any sort of container? I'll run back and get some water for you. You look after him, Shelley.'

Jonas sat down abruptly. He was more dehydrated than he'd thought. He waved a hand in the direction of the cart. 'There are things in there.'

Shelley said, 'Can you move? If you go round to the other side of your cart there's a bit of shade there.'

He moved with an effort, and lay propped against the cart, watching her as she chatted about this and that. Clearly she was doing this to keep him awake; it felt odd. Wasn't he supposed to be the one…? In a distracted part of his mind he could see how badly the sun had burned

93

her skin. He found himself wondering about the best treatment. Aloe vera would have acted quickly, but it was hard to find… His eyelids drooped.

Cissy returned with the water in a small jug and looked relieved as he drank, carefully, thanking her with a weak smile. She sat watching him, tugging unconsciously on the charm that hung about her neck and tucking it back inside her tunic.

'I'll rest for a while,' he told them. 'Don't feel you have to stay any longer; I'm all right now, really, thanks to you two.'

As they remained, watching him uncertainly, he remembered something and scrambled a little unsteadily to his feet.

'Wait a minute. I have something in the cart…' He was already rummaging about. 'I know it's here somewhere…Ah, here we are.'

He pulled out a twist of oilcloth and held it out to them.

'Honey and oatmeal paste. It's for your skin. It will soothe the burns. Not as good as aloe vera, but it should help.'

When they were reassured enough to leave him, he waved them on their way. What might have happened if they hadn't stopped? Careless of him to let himself get dehydrated, though. Suddenly he felt better in spirits as well as in body: the power of human contact. Cissy and Shelley had seemed genuinely pleased with the paste, too, applying it to their arms and necks there and then, telling him, in an effort to thank him, that it had already soothed the pain. It had felt so good to be cared for, and good to be able to offer something in return. That was surely how the world needed to be from now on.

Jonas fell into a doze, to be woken some time later, and none too gently.

'It's him! He was with her. Get him!'

The big man standing menacingly in front of him was a black shadow against the setting sun, but he knew the voice instantly, even without the second voice echoing Big Brendan's words.

'Get him! Get Him!'

There were about eight or nine of them, all with the same maniacal gleam in their eyes. He found himself pulled roughly to his feet. Big Brendan wasted no time on niceties.

'Where is she?'

'Who?'

'Don't mess with me. Her. Your friend. Rosie.'

Well of course: they wanted her to tell them how to reach The City. He thought quickly.

'She left me. Probably on her way home by now.'

'And where would that be?'

Jonas waved an arm vaguely in the direction of the setting sun. He hoped that was wrong.

One of the others stepped forward. 'Never mind her. She's gone. This one will do.' He thrust his face so close to Jonas that he felt himself gag on the man's filthy breath.

'Yeah,' said Big Brendan, with his customary snarl. 'He can tell us everything we want to know.'

Chapter Nine

Suddenly there were footsteps running, voices, panic in the air. People filled the small space.

'You need to get out of here! Can't you smell it?' The man jerked a thumb back over his shoulder. 'It's coming from over there. Run!'

He was followed by others, all equally panic-stricken, some with roughly-tied bundles on their backs, others with small children clutched in anxious arms; all running, fleeing the terrifying, roaring monster. Overhead he heard the clatter of birds' wings … somewhere a vixen screamed, a wolf howled.

Big Brendan and the others turned and lifted their faces, sniffing the air, but Jonas was already on the move; too late to save the cart: possibly too late to save themselves. He heard the tell-tale sound of cracking branches, felt the waves of hot, dry air.

The big man took a few steps in one direction, then changed his mind and moved the other way. Panic had paralysed him. Reluctantly, Jonas turned back, raising a finger to gauge the direction of the wind.

'This way,' he hissed at Big Brendan and his equally stupefied companions. 'You can't outrun it: you have to move sideways out of its path.'

With a last, lingering glance at his cart, Jonas ran. The others would have to take their chances. As he ran, the smoke reached his lungs and he began to cough. He heard Big Brendan somewhere behind him, his voice a childlike whine.

'They don't have to put up with this in The City.'

Jonas stifled the desire to turn back and thump him. Somewhere to his left he saw the reflection of the fire, turning the river into a dancing ribbon of yellow and red.

'Come on,' he yelled. 'Over there – water.'

He was coughing and panting and the water seemed to recede as he ran towards it. Big Brendan had finally understood and was following him. Jonas couldn't see any of the others for the billowing smoke, but could dimly hear their feet as they crashed aimlessly about in terror.

The plunge into the water shocked him. It was deeper than he'd realised, but now that he was wet, his clothes were wet, he was safe for the moment. He waded to the further shore, pulling off his scarf and soaking it, wringing it out before draping it around his head and shoulders, holding it across his mouth. There was a sound of more splashings and cries as others hit the cold water. At least some of them were safe, although why he should care… It angered him that Big Brendan and the others were so focused on reaching The City, so consumed with anger, that they were willing to hurt others to get there. Jonas had been lucky to escape from them; now could he escape the fire?

It had been the heat, of course. Days like today were known to spark the tinder-dry brush, and from there the fire licked inexorably up the trunks of the trees. Tomorrow this would be yet another blackened ruin of what had once been beautiful and filled with life. A sudden gust recalled Jonas to the very real danger he was still in. The ground on both sides of the river was alight; eucalyptus trees on the far bank, the leaves full of oil, had ignited like kindling, and the fire was still spreading. Well, it couldn't spread into the river. The only thing for it was to stay there, following its course until… until what exactly?

As the kites soared above the landscape they looked down to where some of the green and growing things still stood apart from the flames. The tree ferns had once disappeared from these parts for thousands, perhaps millions of years: the kites did not keep count. But the tree ferns knew, somewhere in their ragged, fibrous stems, they knew that they had been here long before anything else. Dimly, they recalled the arrival of the pine forests and the flower-bearing fruit trees; they had seen the dinosaurs come and go. When the great fires raged, they were the survivors, the first to recover, thanks to the moisture-retaining secrets of their stems. Growing alongside streams and rivers, they flourished.

A sudden, swirling gust of hot air brought screams from whoever was behind him in the water, but Jonas realised in that moment that the wind was changing direction. He blundered on round the next bend, and a beautiful sight met his eyes: grass, green and untouched. This must be a place where the river overflowed during storms; this patch of earth would not burn, nor would the tree ferns that stood untouched by the hungry flames.

Heaving himself up, he made it as far as the riverbank before throwing himself down on the grass, exhausted, coughing and retching, but safe, alive, unharmed. It wasn't long before he began to shiver. Standing was painful, but he forced himself upright, forced himself to move forward. A wide track lay ahead, and there, unbelievably, stood his cart. He must have come round in a circle. To his relief, there was no sign of Big Brendan and his henchmen. He had been completely outnumbered and they had been prepared to beat out of him information he did not possess, but it wasn't him they really wanted, was it? It was Rosie. She was in danger. How could he help her?

His lungs were hurting as he inspected the cart; it smelt strongly of smoke, but there was no damage. Once he'd pulled out a change of clothing he checked the wind direction again, and found himself a place, well away from any trees and in the shelter of some rocks, where he could spend the night.

The next day he made little progress. His limbs ached and the soft ground made the going tricky. How far had it spread, back there? Suppose it had gone all the way back to the place where Robin and Alison and little Jonas were innocently going about their business? The plastic sheeting most people used for their shelters would go up in seconds. He tried not to think about it.

Ahead of him, the flood plain widened out, and as he drew closer he could just distinguish shapes that resolved themselves into little groups of people. A small crowd had made a temporary camp there; like him, refugees from the fire. The idea of a few days' rest was appealing, and before long he found a small space on the edge of the group where he and his cart could stop. He scanned the crowd, anxious in case Big Brendan and his cronies were amongst them, but to his relief there was no sign of them. Instead he caught sight of the copper-headed sisters, waving to them and receiving a wave in return. He felt once more warm inside to be recognised by someone; to be no longer completely alone.

Over the following days he chatted to people, showed them some of the things he'd been making, and explained to them how they could weave the reeds from the river's edge to make baskets or rugs. Cissy and Shelley were engaging companions and seemed to know everyone, and through them Jonas soon found himself included in the lively conversations taking place here and there.

There was much talk of the narrow escape they'd all had from the wildfire, but the main topic was inevitably the Hexadome; that was the name most of the people here seemed to prefer for it. To his relief, no-one he spoke to was as fanatical as Big Brendan's lot, and he had a few interesting fireside discussions that went on late into the night. That was where he spotted two more familiar faces, Jim and Harry, who remembered him from the settlement where he had befriended Rosie. They were still inclined to give Big Brendan the benefit of the doubt, but they freely admitted they didn't really know what to expect when they reached it.

To his surprise, Granny Tabitha was there too. He moved over to sit beside her, and received a friendly hug.

'No, of course I think Big Brendan is wrong,' she said, as they discussed the destination of their journey. 'I think the Hexadome is a place of peace, don't you?'

'When you talk about the Hexadome, it could be an entirely different place from the one Big Brendan describes; The City, as he calls it. Could they be different places? Perhaps there are two of them?'

Tabitha thought for a while. 'Maybe they are different ideas of the same place: different visions. The Hexadome is surely a place of light and beauty and green and growing things; it must be. It's what we all need, so we can rebuild, make a better world. It can't possibly be a place of weapons and death.'

Someone else, seated on her other side, said, 'It's keeping the dream alive that matters, not what it looks like.'

'And is that where you're going?' he asked the other woman.

'Oh yes,' she said. 'We're all heading east.'

Jonas said goodnight to them then; he was still tired, and people were beginning to settle down for the night. As he headed for his spot by the cart he thought for a moment that he'd glimpsed Rosie in the firelight, but it seemed so unlikely that he assumed it was his own wish to see her again that was playing tricks with his mind.

Little by little, the people began to move on. They set off in ones and twos, family groups, little huddles of acquaintances who had become friends in their shared hour of need. Eventually, Jonas decided it was time to move on too. He said goodbye to Cissy and Shelley - they were staying on a little longer - and to Tabitha, who seemed to have made friends with quite a few people. Harry and Jim were packing up too, and Leo had left days ago; having once cast off the security of his concrete village, he was eager to keep moving. Rosie, if it really had been her, was nowhere to be seen.

The kites, looking down dispassionately at the human confusion below, could have told them how much further they had to travel. It was a short distance for a powerful pair of wings, but for the creatures below, their heavy movements graceless, confused, seemingly without purpose, it seemed never-ending.

Jonas was on his own again, although it didn't look that way. Other people were constantly catching him up with a friendly wave and a few words but his progress with the cart was slow, and they all eventually overtook him. He had once been alone and accepting of his lot, but being in the Woodlands had shown him the joys of friendship, and now, preoccupied with an inner struggle, he was more alone than ever.

He had left Old Will with a sense of purpose even if he had no very clear idea of what that was, and in the months since then he had been exposed to so many contradictory views, so many different circumstances, that his thoughts were all confusion. Woven through all of this was the realisation of how much he missed Robin and Alison and their child, the child they had named after him, as though he was someone who mattered. And then there was Rosie...

'Jonas!' At first, he ignored the voice. It was just too much to hope for.

'Jonas! Hey, wait for us, Man!'

It was as if by thinking he had conjured them up; it took his breath away. They were the last people he expected to see, and the people he most wanted to.

Robin came right up to him and hugged him warmly, with Alison not far behind.

'Shall we sit down in the shade?'

Robin urged him to the side of the track where the ruins of some former dwelling gave shelter. 'Here, let me give you a hand with the cart.'

'What?' He was still stunned.

'I don't think you can leave it there, in the middle of the road.'

They found a place some distance from the road, hidden away; other people had lived there once, when the world was a different place. As soon as they had manoeuvred the cart into position, they settled down to exchange news. It seemed the fire had reached their settlement, as Jonas had feared. They had been on the point of leaving, anyway; things had never really been the same after so many left. Jonas described his own escape, and was wondering whether to mention Big Brendan and the others when Alison, who had been searching in one of their bags, announced triumphantly,

'We have fruit!'

She began to share it out.

'No, I couldn't, I...'

'Eat, Man. You look all in.' Robin's tone suggested there was no refusal, and indeed Jonas was grateful. He hadn't eaten much these last few days; it had seemed like too much trouble. Robin was cradling their sleeping baby, and Alison began to unpack another bundle, bringing out the cradle Jonas had so lovingly carved before the baby's birth. For the first time he felt a pang of longing for the past, not the family home he'd left without regrets, but the more recent past, that time of contentment in the Woodlands. Alison took the baby from Robin and carefully placed the child in the cradle without waking him.

'Now, eat that melon before it drips all over you!'
Her smile was warm and maternal, and Jonas enjoyed the comforting sensation, so long missing from his life, of being taken care of by another human being. It was almost as if he were a child again himself.

When he awoke next morning, the sun was well risen. Alison was sitting a few metres away, feeding the baby, and Robin had just come striding back to their makeshift camp.
with a bowl of water in his hands.

'So, where are you heading?'
'To be truthful, we're not really sure. There didn't seem much point going looking for our families again, and the camp wasn't the same any more. People were just passing through, all headed east, so we joined them. It seemed safer to travel with others, anyway.'

Jonas and Robin were sitting on top of crumbling concrete blocks that had once been part of something: an unknown person's life had been lived inside this place when it was still standing; or perhaps it had been a place of work; unknown actions carried out for an unknowable purposes.

Jonas shook his head. 'I've no idea where I'm going either. I seem to keep meeting up with the same people, though, so we must all be going somewhere.'

'Have you seen Big Brendan again?'

Jonas nodded. After a pause, he said, 'Still spouting his talk of finding The City and storming it – and after Rosie too, because he thinks she can lead him to it.' He told Robin how he'd been threatened by him. 'And at the same time, half the people I meet seem to think it's something else completely.'

'Yes, I've heard some of that. I suppose it would be good if it turned out they had some of the old medicines, and maybe a way of making shelters that withstand the wildstorms.'

'Yes, those are the good things from the past, but I don't think they're what Big Brendan and some of the others are interested in.'

'So what is it that's bothering you?'

'Oh, I don't know. When my family all died and I was on my own, I had to learn, well, how to be on my own. I was contented, being in the Woodlands with Will. He was on his own too, and he taught me so much: not just how to make things and mend, but being with him helped me to start to look forward, think about how the world could be in the future.'

'And that's a good thing, isn't it?'

'Yes, but if we are really going to create a future for whoever's left, we need to look forward, not backwards. We need to discover things for ourselves, things that make sense in the world as it is now. And to do that I guess we have to understand, to accept, what the world really is like, now.'

'What about things like medicines?'

'Well, yes, obviously it would be good to have those, and the skills that go with them. Realistically, though, we have to decide what we're going to do here and now.'

He paused, wondering how to explain his still unformed thoughts. 'My grandmother was a doctor - you know, trained in a hospital, back then, when there was still some of all that left...'

They were both silent for a few moments, paying their respects to the recent past that might as well have been millennia ago.

'She knew all about the medicine of her day; she used the machines, the techniques, all the things that are now gone. But as things started to fall apart, she also found ways to adapt.' He laughed. 'To go forward, she turned to things of the past. She taught me about the herbs and ways of healing that had been around far longer than the Anthropocene.'

Robin flinched involuntarily. Few people dared to use such an inflammatory word nowadays.

By unspoken agreement they stayed where they were for a few more days, all of them grateful for the time of rest from travel. Alison and Robin busied themselves by turns with the baby, while Jonas scouted the area for anything that might prove useful. They were clearly not the only people to have passed this way: discarded animal bones and scorched patches of grass told of other travellers passing through.

With nothing in particular to do one morning, Jonas idly picked through some of the smaller bones; they had dried out quickly in the heat, and as Jonas ran his thumb over one of them, he found its shape oddly pleasing. This was something that could be used; but what to make from it? Just then he heard the baby cry out, and he knew what he wanted to do. He set to work with one of the knives he had salvaged at the last middenheap, but it was blunt. Annoyed, he redirected his energy to solving the problem, searching amongst the contents of his cart for the piece of the grinding stone he had brought from the Woodlands.

As he shaped the bone with the sharpened knife, he realised that the stone itself might be useful for smoothing the bone once he had carved it into shape. The use of a little animal fat further softened the edges, and after careful washing he was satisfied.

Alison and Robin were delighted with the gift. It was perfect, just what the baby needed! It seemed he was teething yet again, and now he could find relief by biting on the plaything Jonas had made. Pleased with his efforts, Jonas began to collect more and more of the bones, and in his mind experimented with designs for different objects that might be of use to others. It soon became his habit, each evening while they were there, to carve various small objects. He remembered the plastic combs he and Robin had found on a middenheap; perhaps combs made of bone would be more pleasant to use?

On the morning they were finally ready to set off, Jonas packed and repacked the cart several times. Robin came across to see if he needed a hand.

'That's going to be heavy to push, Jonas. Are you sure you need all that stuff?'

Jonas groaned. 'That's the problem. How do I know? I don't know where I'm going or what I'll need.'

'So perhaps now is the time to decide?' His friend's voice was gentle.

Jonas shrugged. 'That's just it. I don't even know how to decide.' He sighed. 'I started off with this vision of helping people, you know, teaching them the things I've learned from Old Will, all the practical things; and the things I learned from my grandmother about healing. And then things changed: all these rumours about The City: remnants of the old world. People started looking back to the past again, hoping they could rebuild it.'

'But you know that won't happen, don't you? You've said as much yourself.' Robin placed himself squarely in front of Jonas. 'The world has changed too much. But that isn't your responsibility at this moment. All you have to decide is whether you're going to stay in one place or keep moving. If you stay in one place, you can build up stores of useful things; if you keep moving, you have to find a way of travelling light and using what you find on the way.'

Jonas shook his head. 'That's still too much, too big.'

'You don't have to decide today. But if you decide to stay in one place, you need to find the place. This won't do.'

Jonas looked at him in puzzlement.

'Well,' said Robin. 'How many people have we seen since we've been here? None. If you decide to stay somewhere, it needs to be a place where people are settled already, or with people who are travelling to find a place to settle.'

The little group walked steadily on, continuing to follow the sun's rising for want of any better plan. One evening, when they had stopped to rest a little way back from the track, Jonas was holding the baby. He smiled a lot now, and Jonas was thrilled that he sometimes gave him a beaming smile in between frowns as he chewed on the bone plaything. He was beginning to make new sounds too, no longer the heart-rending wail of a hungry newborn, but little cooing sounds. Jonas talked to him as he had talked to no-one since his youngest sister had died. He spoke a mixture of nonsense and philosophy.

'So what will you make of this strange world when you grow up?' he asked the baby one day, and was rewarded by a responsive cooing.

'That's right,' he said in delight. 'That's how you hold a conversation: we take it in turns to speak.'

The child looked at him, waiting.

'Go on; it's your turn now.' Jonas smiled as he spoke, and the baby responded with another series of gentle sounds, morphing from gentle cooing to an excited babbling.

The conversation continued for some time, without Jonas being aware of Robin's presence behind him.

'You're a natural.'

Jonas blushed. 'How long have you been there?'

'Long enough to see how good you are with him.'

'Well, I guess I have known him since before he was born.'

Alison appeared from behind a rocky outcrop, where she had been preparing food.

'It won't be long, now.'

She turned to Jonas. 'Would you like me to take him?'

As Jonas was handing the baby over, the sound of voices startled them. Back down the track, a small group of figures could be seen. They seemed to be arguing amongst themselves.

'That's odd.' Robin stood to meet them. 'I wouldn't expect people to be just passing through this place.'

Their visitors' words began to reach them.

'It was you that lost track of her...'

'Oh yeah, and if it hadn't been for you...'

There were three men and a couple of much younger women. Jonas wondered idly if they were a family, although by now family was a loose definition. They stopped in front of them.

'Hello,' said Robin. He had evidently decided to be the spokesperson. Jonas was happy to let him. He'd had enough encounters with strangers, especially strangers looking for someone, as this lot clearly were.

'Nice little hidey-hole you've got here,' said one of the men. 'Anyone else with you?'

'No, just us.'

'You seen anyone?'

'Not for a while. Not since we pulled off the main road.'

One of the young women stepped forward, appealing directly to Alison.

'We're looking for someone. A woman.'

Alison smiled. 'I'm the only woman here.'

Little Jonas began to gurgle his little baby sounds, and the stranger smiled wistfully.

'We've lost our families... lost everything. S'pose most people have. But then we heard about the Hexadome; you know, how everyone's heading that way, the Search and all that, how it's all going to be all right, back to how it was before...'

'The Search?'

'Yes. You must have heard of it? Everyone's trying to get there. To find the place of peace and light.'

'The thing is,' one of the men who had not yet spoken broke in, his voice a discordant contrast with the young woman's. 'Thing is, there's this woman, she knows the way; knows all about it...'

The first man interrupted. 'Damn it, we saw her, we spoke to her. People said she was leading the Search. But she disappeared, gave us all the slip!'

The young woman was still smiling at the baby, amusing him by swinging the small wire shape that hung around her neck; then she tucked it back inside her dress and looked at Alison with silent appeal in her eyes.

'She just disappeared. It was somewhere round here. She can't be far.'

'OK,' said Robin. 'Well, we haven't seen her. We haven't seen anyone. But if we do, where will you be?'

The young woman looked at the man who, Jonas now reckoned, must be her father. He replied, 'Carrying on up this road; heading east. What else?'

'Right. If we see her, we'll tell her.'

They left then, looking suspiciously at Jonas' cart as they did so.

'That's where I keep my tools and things,' he said. 'I've got all sorts in there. I could show you how to weave a blanket, or make a rug, or a stool with proper joints, or how to carve a comb from bone, or…'

The man rolled his eyes.

'No thanks.'

Robin and Alison stood watching as the group departed the way they had come, heading back to the main road. Jonas sat down again, his legs trembling. When enough time had elapsed, Alison said, 'That was clever, Jonas. I think you bored them into submission!'

'Not the type to be interested in learning new skills,' added Robin, with a laugh. 'Well, I hope they don't find her, because…' He stopped, seeing Jonas' expression. 'What is it?'

Jonas was staring at the cart. The ropes he had tied so carefully the day before were no longer how he had left them. Slowly, he walked across, glancing round to reassure himself that there was no one in sight. He pulled the corner of the canvas back where the rope had been loosened.

'How long have you been there?' he asked, as Rosie stretched her cramped limbs.

Alison's response to Rosie's appearance had been practical: she fed her. Robin was busy with the baby, and Jonas was left to wonder what to do.

'Did you hear? They were looking for you.'

'So are a lot of people,' she replied.

'I was nearly beaten up by Big Brendan and his gang because they were convinced I knew where you were.'

She shrugged. 'Well, you did get involved with him back at the camp. You can see why he thought you might know.'

'I told him you were heading west.'

'I wonder if he believed you?'

She stood to take her bowl back to Alison. She was still limping slightly. Jonas noticed that her dress was scorched on one side.

'So you were caught in the fire too?'

'And I got out.'

'Look, Rosie...' He stood before her. 'Why don't you stay with us. You'd be safer, and we could hide you...'

She looked around at the bare landscape, the bleak outline of the hills in the distance.

'Here?'

'No, we're planning to move on.'

'Ah. So you think I'd be safer with a couple with a baby and a man with a cart? That no-one would notice me...?'

Exasperated, he let out a groan.

'Oh, have it your own way. But at least let me give you the poultice I prepared for your ankle.'

She disappeared in the night, as Jonas had known she would. They gathered their few belongings and set off again, back down the track to the main road, back to join the crowds heading east.

Chapter Ten

The road stretched ahead. As more and more people headed that way, so it became widened, trampled firm with the tread of many feet. The settlements they passed were no longer makeshift camps, but had all the appearance of villages, permanent places where people had developed - or found again - the skills to build, with stone, with wood, or with whatever came to hand. By the old standards, of course, they were primitive, and yet there was something hopeful about them to Jonas' mind. There were attempts at farming, too; in one village, pipes and channels had been used to take water from its source to the strips of land where rows of growing things could be seen, nosing their way tentatively through the crumbled earth.

The people were mostly welcoming, pleased to barter food for whatever the travellers could offer in return. They craved news of the wider world, and especially of the Hexadome, or The City, or whatever anyone cared to call it. More than anything, though, they craved novelty, new faces, new people to talk to.

Young Jonas was growing and becoming heavier. He had long outgrown the cradle, which had been passed on to another family. He needed to crawl, to sit on the flattened grass, to play. The endless walking and stopping each night had been wearing for Alison and Robin, and although Jonas offered to place the child in the cart, he could see they were not keen. His thoughts turned to making things; surely it must be possible to construct a small cart, just right for a baby? But they hadn't passed anywhere they might find materials for some time, and anyway, he would need to stop longer than one night to make the thing.

They walked, sometimes in silence, sometimes deep in discussion. On one such occasion Robin asked, 'Do you ever find yourself longing for the past?'

Jonas thought for a moment. 'Which past? The past of our childhood when everyone was dying around us, from sickness or battle wounds or despair? The past before that, the one our parents and grandparents talked about?'

'Which past was real?'

'All of them, I suppose. The past our grandparents talked about was a past that had some good things about it. It had allowed my grandmother to train as a doctor when she was young, and there had been proper hospitals then, even if medicines were in short supply...'

'They believed in things then, too, didn't they?'

'My grandmother and her generation believed that the world could still be saved.' He gave a sad smile. 'But the others - the ones who took power and held on to it no matter what - they believed that money, position, possessions were all that mattered; that the world's problems could be solved through technology, no matter how grotesque it became.'

Robin looked around, taking in the trees and the sky, the wheeling kites. 'You know, despite everything, Alison and I have been happy. We get by. We have each other.'

Jonas barely breathed the words. 'Even though... Skylark?

Robin threw an arm around his friend's shoulders. 'We had her for a while; we loved her...'

They came to a small village in a pleasant spot, a short way from the road. A number of their fellow travellers decided to stay for a while, and although he was keen to continue the journey, while being at a loss to explain properly why, Jonas recognised that his friends needed a proper rest. The people of the village were friendly, and there were other families there. He could see how well his friends fitted in. While Alison was comparing notes with the mother of another small child one evening, Jonas wandered off, talking to people, trying to find out what there was to find out.

There were few people of his own age, and anyway Jonas had always got on well with the older folk, like his grandmother. He stopped now in front of a shelter that seemed to be home to quite a large family.

'You're a young fellow,' said the frail-looking, elderly lady sitting outside, her shoulders hunched. 'Are you one of the Seekers?'

'The Seekers?'

'The Seekers. The Seekers of the Hexadome.' The old lady's expression clouded. 'Oh dear...' Her voice sank to a whisper. 'You're not with the PA, are you... the People's Army?'

He reassured her that he most definitely was not.

'So who are the Seekers? I've heard people mention The Search. Is that the same thing?'

'I guess that's another name for it.'

'I don't really know anything about it, though I'd like to hear more.'

'Well, the Seekers believe that we can travel east and find the Hexadome.' Her face was alight. 'Oh, it's a wonderful place: a dome, or maybe many domes, all with light streaming in, and inside it's all green with growing things...'

'Big Brendan says it's the fortress at the end of the journey, and for him it's not a place of peace and light; anything but. He talks about weapons and defences and fighting.'

115

His companion looked sad. 'Oh, Big Brendan. You've come across him, have you? Him and his ideas about the People's Army. I'm sure they've got it wrong. You have to believe if you want to find the real Hexadome. Look.'

She reached for the twisted thread that hung about her neck, pulling it up from her clothing until he could see what was on the end of it. A small hexagonal shape, crudely worked in wire, lay on her palm. Jonas realised that he had seen this sign before.

'And do you? Believe?'

She nodded. 'I certainly don't believe that those awful corrupt people from the old SAR regime are still in control there.'

'So what is in there?'

'Well, it depends who you ask. Some say it's like a garden, protected from the outer world and filled with goodness and light, and that once there, all their troubles will be over. Others say it's where all the birds and animals went; you know, the ones we don't see any more.'

'And you? What do you think?'

'I think I'd go there like a shot if I could.' She looked away over Jonas' shoulder, into the distance, her eyes misted with tears.

Jonas wasn't sure what to make of this. Who were these people, these Seekers? Were there many of them, and how long had they been around? And what would happen if they came face to face with Big Brendan or any of the PA?'

Wandering round, still talking to people, he picked up reports of the People's Army, although it seemed the name was something of an exaggeration. Small bands of angry people had passed through the village, recruiting for the PA without great success. Few of the villagers, settled in homes they had made for themselves, had any stomach for such a thing. Jonas also gathered that the PA were unpopular because of their habit of demanding food and supplies without offering anything in return.

As he walked about the village, Jonas found himself torn between several courses of action. He desperately wanted to stay with Robin and Alison, to watch baby Jonas growing and changing each day; he wanted to find out more about the mystery that was Rosie; he wanted to fulfil his, as yet unknown, sense of purpose.

Gazing up at the graceful flight of the red kites, high above the troubles of a ruined world, he wondered what they could see: were they watching the drawing together of many groups of PA supporters, like rats to a granary? Could they see the Seekers growing in numbers, all headed in the same direction? He wondered what would happen when they met at journey's end, and whether there was anything he could do. In the end, he felt he had only one choice. Sadly, he returned to the others. Robin looked up at his arrival.

'You've decided to leave.'

'I'm not sure how you knew, but yes. There's so much happening; I just feel I have to be there, somehow.'

Alison reappeared from somewhere, the baby balanced on her hip.

'And Rosie might need your help,' she added quietly.

After yet another parting, which hurt no less than the last one, Jonas was off. He was not alone in travelling on the road, even if he was alone in his thoughts. Some of the people, the ones walking more slowly, sang songs, smiled, greeted fellow travellers. These, surely, were the Seekers. At times, he was disturbed to see other groups, walking faster, their faces set; he shivered, thinking they must be part of the PA. He didn't see Big Brendan among them, but he recognised the same angry style.

The kites, from high above the land, knew nothing of numbers, but they observed the straggling line of human creatures, all travelling in the same direction. There were fewer of them now, though; in ones and twos and small groups, some were stopping, staying behind when the rest moved on.

One evening Jonas found a pleasant little clearing some way off the main road, well hidden by the surrounding undergrowth. He was more than ready for some time to rest and just be. As the light began to fade, he occupied himself with making a shelter in front of a tree whose downward-sweeping branches provided a perfect framework, with the broad trunk as the back wall. Over this he draped the sheets of strong polythene he'd been carrying; he could no longer recall which of the many middenheaps had yielded those up, but he had known instinctively that they would be useful. There was space at the back of this improvised tree house to store his bedding and a few pots and pans, and he placed one of his strong reed-woven rugs in front for a sitting place. It was almost as though he were playing house, like his young sisters used to. He shook himself and retreated from the memory; sometimes remembering was as bad as thinking.

Instead, he got busy setting his cooking fire, and while that was taking, he went to fetch water from the spring he'd heard bubbling away just beyond the clearing. Then, still in need of distraction, he embarked on a complete audit of the contents of his cart, lining up the various medicines he had been preparing throughout his travels. He re-tied the bundles of herbs; then checked the dried leaves of nepeta and rosemary, the basil and dill. He arranged carefully the powdered arrowroot, the curls of white willow bark, the seeds of poppy and cumin, and placed them carefully in the little wooden chest Will had made for them.

Distracted by these activities for a time, he still found his mind running over recent events. Part of him believed that Robin and Alison were so much part of his life now that he was bound to see them again. Naming their child after him had to mean something, didn't it? Part of him wondered what on earth he was doing on this strange journey. He knew he wanted no part in the People's Army, although he had an interest in seeing where they went, what they would do. But was he a Seeker? That too seemed absurd.

He settled down for the night, and to his surprise, slept until morning. It was just after breakfast, as he was settling down to think about his choices, that he was startled by the sound of someone crashing through undergrowth.

'Rosie! Are you all right?'

She was shivering.

'Here, put this around you. I'll build up the fire.'

He dropped the woven blanket loosely over her shoulders, afraid to wrap her in it, afraid to touch her. She looked up at him with a feeble smile of thanks. As he busied himself with the fire, guiding the small dry sticks into its heart, he felt concern: the shivering meant she was ill. It was a warm day with not a breath of wind.

'I'll be back in a few minutes.'

He went down to the stream to fetch water in the battered bucket that he'd mended long ago, under Old Will's watchful eye. Thinking about Old Will kept him calm. When he returned, Rosie had thrown off the blanket and in those few short minutes had gone from cold to hot. Even from the other side of the clearing, he could see the unhealthy shine on her face and neck. He dipped a cup into the bucket and gave her sips of cool water.

'Have you ever had this fever before?'

She looked afraid.

'You think it's the old sickness, don't you?'

He shook his head.

'It's a fever, and we can do something about that. You need to lie down, over here, away from the fire. We can get your temperature down.'

He helped her to stand. She didn't object. Amongst his belongings near the tree was a pile of sheep's wool, gathered from the spindly hedgerows along the road. It was soft and absorbent and would make an easier bed for his patient than the bare ground. Once down there she threw herself restlessly, first to one side, then the other, hardly aware of his presence. He went over to the cart and pulled out a cloth, then fetched the bucket closer to where she lay.

'Rosie!'

She turned on to her back and looked at him without recognition, but he explained anyway.

'I'm going to sponge you to bring down the fever, cool you down. Do you understand?'

He wasn't sure that she'd heard, but he began anyway, dipping the cloth and wringing it out as he methodically sponged her face, her neck, her chest and arms. The heat rose to her skin again each time and he repeated the actions over and over. He moved on to her legs, and wondered if he should risk removing her dress to sponge her whole body. He had crossed an invisible boundary, and he was afraid, but then he remembered with piercing clarity the times he had helped his mother do this for the little ones.

'You must act quickly,' she had told him. 'Never mind the embarrassment, whoever it is. If it is just a fever,

120

there won't be any further symptoms and they'll be fine in two or three days.'

'And if there are other symptoms?'

She had looked away then. He knew what that look meant – and before long he knew what the other signs of the illness were. Little Sarah died of hunger before the sickness could get her, but the rest died, one by one, gasping for breath, until it took his beloved mother too. He thought he had wept all the tears he had left as he dug their graves, wondering all the while who would dig his. Why then had he been spared? He knew the disease was carried from person to person, and he had been daily in its presence, yet never suffered a day's illness.

Throughout that day and into the night, Rosie suffered alternate bouts of sweating and shivering. Jonas stayed awake to watch over her, fighting against his body's demand for sleep. He dozed a few minutes at a time, always returning to full wakefulness the moment the rhythm of her breathing changed. As the morning sunlight filtered through the trees, she opened her eyes and looked without seeing him. He spoke soothingly, as he had spoken to his little sister the day she lay dying.

'It's all right, Rosie. You're here with me, in a quiet place.' Her eyes searched his face, but he didn't know if she was hearing him.

'You've been unwell, but you're going to be all right.'

He laid a tentative hand on her temple, stroking gently, making soothing noises. Gradually her eyes closed and her breathing steadied. Once he was sure she was sleeping he got up and busied himself, opening up the little wooden medicine chest. He set a pan of water over the fire and measured out a dose of dried nepeta leaves. His grandmother's words came back to him: all those clever scientists in their expensive laboratories, all that money and squabbling about who owned the rights. Too bad they had not known back then the curative powers of this little plant, and all the others growing wild out there.

As he waited for the boiling to take effect, he wandered around, looking to see what other treasures the clearing offered. Flat white mushrooms marked the boundary of the clearing, their tops glowing faintly in the twilight like so many lamps placed to light the gloom. There was something else white, too. He moved closer. Feverfew! Alison had remarked on its prettiness back in the second camp, but now it would have another function. He took up several clumps. Then he found ribwort, less showy, but good for making a paste to soothe sore skin. He took some of that too. If he had stayed in the camp, he could have planted it, planted many of the herbs that could be used for healing: a herb garden, like his grandmother's. Well, that was not to be; not yet. He would make up some of the paste while he was here, and once Rosie began to recover, he would brew some tea from the leaves of the feverfew. Returning to the fire, he continued with his preparation of the nepeta liquid, adding a little of his precious store of white willow bark to ease the aching she would surely feel later.

The sun was high by the time Rosie woke. He offered her a few sips of the distilled liquid and she took the cup, pulling a face as the medicine touched her tongue.

'I know,' he said. 'It tastes pretty disgusting, doesn't it? But it will do you good. Trust me.'

Again she slept, but that night the shivering took hold again, and despite the fire and the blanket he was forced to lie beside her to offer his own body warmth. It was barely enough. Towards the middle of the night she shuddered so violently that had to he put his arms around her in a firm grip until she calmed and slept once more.

But Jonas couldn't sleep, despite his exhaustion. He lay there closer than he had been to any human being since he was a child. Her hair lay in a tangle across his face, and he left it there, fearful of disturbing her if he moved to brush it aside. For the first time he was aware of her fragility, and for once he knew himself strong. She began to mutter, the meaning incomprehensible, but the tone urgent.

'No... we can't... we must... I don't know, I don't know...'

Later more words came.

'Yes, all right, I'll join you... there has to be a better way.'

Then a series of names which he couldn't make out. And then, 'No, I have a mind of my own. I'm not your little Shanti any more...'

On the second day it was Rosie who woke first. Rosie – or Shanti? As Jonas struggled into consciousness he found her looking at him with clear eyes. He sat up at once, wiping away the tears of relief.

'You had a fever,' he said. 'I had to cool you by sponging you down, and then you were so cold that the only way I could keep you warm was...' he gestured to indicate her sleeping position.

Rosie nodded. 'Thank you,' she whispered. Looking down, she saw that her dress was missing.

Jonas flushed. 'I had to take it off to cool you. Then it was, well, it was very sweaty, so I washed it. It'll be dry soon.'

She accepted his explanation without comment, and he offered her one of his tunics, then busied himself with tidying up the camp, repairing the fire, putting some broth to heat. He kept his distance – giving her space was how he put it to himself. Later he administered another dose of the foul-tasting medicine, vaguely surprised as she accepted it from him.

'Do you feel you could eat?' he asked.

She nodded, and he brought her a bowl of broth and a little bread. Neither of them spoke of the first time he had offered her bread.

As she ate, she asked, 'Where did you learn to make medicines?'

'My grandmother was a healer; she passed some of her knowledge on to me, and I watched as she prepared medicines when my brothers and sisters were ill.'

'Where are they now?'

He shook his head. 'All gone.'

'I'm sorry.' She placed a hand on his arm for a second.

'It's... it's something you learn to live with. Besides, who hasn't lost someone in these last years?'

She acknowledged this with a nod. After a while she said, 'Do you think I could wash in the stream? I'm pretty disgusting after all that sweating.'

'Stand up first and let's see how steady you are on your legs: we don't want you being swept away!' He was smiling, and she managed a weak smile in return.

She returned from the stream looking refreshed in her clean dress. Jonas thought she still looked pale, even paler than usual, but there was a light in her eyes now that had been missing before.

'How do you feel?'

'Better than yesterday!' She seated herself in the centre of the clearing, spreading her wet hair in the warm sunlight and attempting to untangle it with her fingers. 'I've lost my comb,' she said.

'Wait.' Jonas went over to the cart and rummaged around for a while. 'Will any of these do?'

He held out to her a selection of combs: one of blue plastic, another of wood, and one carved from bone. She took the bone one.

'This is beautiful. Is it old?'

'Not really. I used to make a lot of them, sitting alone at nights. They've been useful for exchanging for things as I travel.'

'What do you want in exchange from me?'

'Nothing but to see you get well.' To lighten the tone, he added, 'And to see how well it works on your tangles.'

She smiled, one of her less defensive smiles, and began to comb. Before long she stopped, dropping her arms to her sides.

'Are you all right?'

'Just a bit tired. Would you...?' She held the comb out to him.

He had often combed out his sisters' hair and knew how to do it without tugging at the knots. Carefully, he held the hair a lock at a time, beginning with the knotted end, and working his way back until he could comb smoothly all the way from her head. She seemed to find it soothing, and after a while there developed a comfortable sort of rhythm to the actions.

'I thought your lot didn't believe in plastic,' she said.

'What?'

'One of those combs – it was made of plastic, wasn't it?'

'What did you mean just now when you said 'your lot'?'

'I don't know what you call yourselves. I just know that there was a strong movement against the use of plastic and fossil fuels and space flight and... Well, in the… in the… where I come from… there is almost nothing *but* plastic.'

He noted her hesitation in naming the place she came from. He made no comment but responded to what she had said about plastic.

'Well, yes, of course you're right about plastic. It's been known for generations that it's harmful to the environment when it's discarded, but if it can be reused or repurposed in some way, then that has to be better than throwing it away.' He sighed. 'That was one of the mistakes of our great-grandparents' generation: always making new things and throwing the old ones away.'

'So in your philosophy new is bad and old is good?'

'Well, that depends what the new things are.'

She looked at him quizzically.

'I mean, what was new then is now old to us, if we're talking about going back to the age of technology. But it's not as simple as new versus old, is it? This is a completely different world for us; we need to find new ways of living in it.'

'And one of your new ways is by using old things?'

'Yes, and by rediscovering even older ways of doing things.'

Neither spoke for some time. Jonas was trying to find a way to reopen the communication he felt they had begun to establish earlier.

'So, what about your family?' he asked, finally.

'My family?'

'Yes. I've told you about mine. I wondered what yours is like.'

She turned to face him so abruptly that the comb was whipped out of his hand and hung there, caught in her hair.

'Why would you want to know about my family?'

'You don't need to… if you don't want to…'

She sighed.

'No, I'm sorry. It's not your fault. You don't know…'

'But I do know your real name.'

She stared at him and he saw the hunted look in her eyes.

'Shanti. That's right, isn't it? You said it in your sleep. No-one calls their child Shanti, unless…'

She looked away, as if making a decision, and then took a long, deep breath.

'Yes. My full name is Shanti Alexander.' She got up then and began pacing. 'Now you know,' she said at last, still not looking at him.

Jonas sat for a moment, stunned, before getting to his feet to face her. He had gradually accepted that she had some sort of connection with The City, but that she could be a member of the hated Alexander family, the regime that had caused so much harm, so much suffering…

He took a deep breath. 'So they named you after the Shanti Accord! A child of the Regime. Is that it?'

She nodded, mutely.

'We used to call it the Shanti *Apocalypse* Regime when I was a child. We didn't know what the letters SAR stood for.' His voice sounded harsh to his own ears. 'Or the Shanti *Armageddon* Regime.' He looked at her in disquiet and would have spoken further, but she rose to her feet, staggering, and Jonas leapt up and caught her as she swayed.

'It's all right,' he said, the healer in him coming to the fore. 'Rest now, talk later.' He steered her to the shelter. 'I'll be just outside.'

The sun was beginning to sink towards the horizon. Jonas had prepared some meat for the pot and was taking advantage of a few minutes' peace and time to think, sitting with his back to the shelter, when he heard the sounds of someone stumbling carelessly through the trees at the far side. Whoever they were, they were not worried about meeting others. He waited, his eyes fixed in the direction of the noise.

Two men checked as they found themselves in the clearing. Jonas felt his heart sink.

'You!' said the big man. Even in the failing light, Jonas could not mistake him.

'So we meet again.' Big Brendan's expression was less belligerent than previously. He was tired, thought Jonas.

He gave a polite smile. No sense meeting trouble halfway. 'Hello. Please, take a seat.' He rose and indicated the three-legged stools he'd taken out of the cart earlier. 'I can offer you fresh water to drink now, or some supper later if you care to wait.'

The tall man glanced at his companion, who growled something Jonas didn't catch. It wasn't Joe Farmer, and Jonas wondered absently where Big Brendan's shadow was.

'You been here long?'

'A few days.'

The other man stepped forward, his eyes raking the surrounding trees. 'We're after that pale bitch. You know who we mean?'

'Who?'

'You know. She gave us the slip because of you.'

'Oh… the *pale* girl.'

'Yes, *her*. Have you seen her? We were sure she came through the woods. Couple of days ago.'

Jonas' apparently genuine puzzlement must have been convincing. He shook his head.

'I've seen no-one.'

The shorter man turned away, tugging at his companion's arm.

'Come on. We're wasting our time.'

As they were leaving, Jonas called after them. 'If I do see her, what should I do?'

The short man spat on the ground.

'Hold on to her, you fool! She's escaped from The City – she knows the way there.'

It was a moonless night. Jonas was sitting in the opening of the shelter, whispering over his shoulder. Behind him, inside, he could just hear Shanti's breathing. They had eaten in silence and it was only now that Jonas judged it safe to talk.

'So let me get this straight.'

'What?'

'You know what. You are part of the Alexander family...?'

'Yes.' She sounded on the edge of tears.

'You are a member of the SAR.'

'Yes.' It was the merest whisper.

'And Patrick Alexander, the leader who abandoned the people who voted for him...?'

'He was my great-grandfather.'

'And so the present Supreme Leader is...'

'My grandfather.'

Jonas gave a low whistle. 'No wonder you didn't want to talk about your family or where you came from.'

'Do you blame me?'

In the continuing silence he thought he heard a small, strangled sob. Then she said, 'Jonas, for pity's sake: I didn't choose my family.'

Jonas was silent for a while longer. 'To think how hard it's been to believe the place is real, even after what you told me back at the middenheap that day … and all the time, people going mad with longing… so many stories.'

'Don't be angry with me.'

Her voice was so small then. He had never heard it like that before. He turned round then to face her. She was the faintest outline in the starlight.

'I'm not angry… just confused. You've been so against the place, so against other people going there… but if what people are saying about the place is true, why would anyone choose to leave?'

She didn't reply. She had heard something, and so had he.

'Just keep perfectly still.'

The sound of someone approaching the campsite was unmistakeable now, Jonas wanted to laugh: they were clearly trying to creep up on him without being heard, but it was something Big Brendan was entirely unsuited for.

'Hello again,' he said, trying to keep his voice calm. 'There is still some stew left if you're hungry…'

'The girl,' growled Big Brendan. 'What have you done with her?'

'I told you last time: she left me. Did you say she's come from The City? Really?'

Big Brendan was only too glad of the chance to enlarge upon his favourite subject. He repeated much of his previous rants: the corruption, the unfairness, the need to fight them to regain what rightfully belonged to him and to people like him who were prepared to take the risk…

Finally, after he had yawned so many times that his jaw ached, Jonas said,

'It's late, gentlemen, past my bedtime. Do you want to bed down here for the night?

'Nah, you're all right. Come on, Toby. Let's go.'

As they reached the edge of the site, Big Brendan turned.

'Don't forget: if she turns up…

'I know: hold on to her.'

They were gone more quickly than they arrived. Jonas yawned, for real this time. If only he *could* hold on to her. He crawled inside the shelter. As he had expected, Rosie - Shanti - was long gone. She must have crept out under the plastic at the back.

Chapter Eleven

So Jonas travelled on. What else could he do?

The weather was hot and cold by turns. The leaves continued to crinkle and fall. Sometimes people passed him on the road; sometimes he travelled alone for many kilometres. The landscape changed: it was no longer flat, and the undulating terrain made for hard going with the cart. He took a few days' rest to prepare himself for a determined effort. The weather was hot again, hot and humid, and he made sure he had plenty of water in the cart; that was a mistake he wasn't going to make again. Then he gritted his teeth and set off.

The red kites, absent from the skies above the middenheaps, for there was nothing to interest them there, were back, doing what they had always done. If they had given it any thought, they would have found perplexing the uncertainty and indecision that afflicted the strange creatures below, plodding on their two feet in the wake of the others who had passed that way. But it was nothing to them.

One day Shanti appeared alongside him. Her sudden appearances and disappearances no longer surprised him, but they spoke few words and for some time she would not meet his gaze. He couldn't understand why she was heading in the direction of The City after all she had said about the danger, and he thought that perhaps she didn't know why herself. She kept her travelling cloak close about her, and none of those who passed seemed to recognise her. The two of them walked in silence, while the other small groups of travellers chatted amongst themselves.

They camped that night with others within a small circle of trees, bedding down around the fire. Shanti lay a short distance from Jonas, and he couldn't help remembering the night of her sickness, when he had lain along with her, sharing his body warmth.

Suddenly, he was alert. There was a noise, something or someone moving stealthily behind the outer trees. He cleared the space between him and Shanti in a heartbeat, and was already poised to strike the intruder and pull Shanti out of harm's way when he saw that she had dealt with the problem herself. The man was cursing fluently, bent double over his groin as Shanti's booted foot landed a perfectly aimed kick.

'Are you all right?'

He knew they were safe; the interloper, whose height and bulk clearly identified him, was unlikely to hang around after being humiliated by a young woman.

Shanti replied in mock admonishment, 'Still rescuing me, Jonas?'

The old Shanti was back.

As they set off next morning, she wrapped herself in her cloak again. Her skin was already turning pink and she seemed in pain. A column of travellers stretched ahead of them on the road. They were at the rear, Jonas labouring under the weight of the cart.

'Two pairs of arms better than one?' she said, attempting to take one of the handles.

He shook her off. 'I can manage.'

'Look, Jonas...' she got as close as she could, whispering in his ear. 'Please trust me.'

She laid her hand over his as he gripped the rough wood. He liked the gentle feel of her touch, but was still feeling wounded from her refusal of his help the night before. The weight of her admission of who she really was hung between them like a curtain.

They became aware of a commotion up ahead. Shouts of 'over there!' and 'lie down' were carried on the wind that had suddenly blown up. The sky was darkening rapidly, and now they could see clearly the corkscrew shape, twisting and twirling and getting bigger all the time. It reminded Jonas absurdly of the spinning tops he had carved for the children, back at the second camp.

'Help me with these ropes,' he roared above the noise.

Together they pulled the ropes tight across the top of the cart, and then Shanti pulled him to the ground in front of it. They lay, arms shielding their heads and faces, as the force of the tornado swept over them, sucking the air from in front of their faces. He heard the cart rock and, turning, saw it lift until there was clear space beneath the wheels. The next moment the air seemed to set it back down as though, having had its fun, it was moving on to some other game.

In the wake of the storm there was absolute silence for many minutes. Awful thoughts went through Jonas' mind until he began to hear the tremulous questions from those on the road ahead, repeated over and over:

'Are you all right?'

'Yes. You?'

'Are the others all right?'

Next day Shanti was gone again, and Jonas was once more alone.

Time seemed to lose all meaning as the days and nights followed each other; he kept on walking. One day he had made a considerable distance, but by evening he was exhausted. The air had become unbearably heavy, full of unshed moisture. His hands were wet with perspiration and he constantly felt his grip on the cart slipping. His tunic was glued to his back and he could feel the moisture trickling down between his shoulder blades. At last he could go no further.

The land had been rising steadily for some time and he suddenly found himself close to the edge of an escarpment: there could be no further travel in that direction. More carelessness! He should have taken greater notice of his surroundings instead of being so lost in his thoughts. He would have to rest before he could even think about what to do next.

Leaving the cart he crossed the final space leading to the edge. Even up here, exposed to the elements, there was no breath of air. His gaze swept the landscape, taking in the network of tracks that criss-crossed the plain below. In the distance he could see a place where two of these roads converged.

Allowing his gaze to travel back from there, he found he could make out small knots of people, moving slowly, with gaps in between, heading for the meeting place of the roads. They must surely be the Seekers. He cursed himself as he realised that that was where he should have been. From up here, they looked a pathetic lot, strung out along the road like a broken necklace. Over the course of their journey their numbers had been swelled by newcomers and reduced by illness or exhaustion. Still, his heart leapt to think that there were still people whose faith in their vision of a better place, a better way of living, kept them going despite all. Perhaps they were simply determined to reach it on behalf of those who could not.

As he watched, he realised something else: on the other road, also heading for the place where the two roads met, was another group of people. They were less scattered than the others, and although he was too far away to make out individuals, the man at the head of the group was all too familiar. A big man, turning and waving the others on with an impatient gesture, his belligerent gait discernible even at this distance. Were they on their way to join up with the other members of the much-vaunted People's Army, or - he laughed aloud - was this the sum total of it?

Another thought struck him. The Big Brendan group, further from the place where the roads converged, was moving more quickly than the exhausted Seekers. There was every chance they would reach it at the same time. What would happen then? He didn't see Big Brendan having much truck with ideas of peace and light.

Well, there was nothing he could do from up here; in fact, there simply was nothing that could be done wherever he was. In any case, he must look to his own safety now, for this was an exposed place to be caught in the storm that was surely coming.

At first it was a low, indistinct rumble, then louder, closer, only to fade teasingly away. He moved back a little from the edge, his gaze still on the plain below. The yellowing sky lent an eeriness to the scene. There came the crash of another, much louder roll of thunder, making him jump. Suddenly, the air began to stir; the treetops, minutes ago so immobile, began to sway and toss their heads; the water in the river below boiled and heaved. Jonas went back to the cart to wait it out, then changed his mind and made a dash for the trees. The storm broke.

Much later, when it was over, he sat up and looked around. Beside him the slender trunks of beech trees lay at crazy angles; broken branches littered the ground; others hung perilously above his head, creaking threateningly. As he moved, he shook off a layer of leaves and twigs that had almost covered him. He was wet through.

Stepping out from his hiding place he looked around for his cart, thinking to find a blanket to dry himself. The temperature had dropped considerably, and his lungs gratefully breathed in the freshened air. But the cart, the cart that had accompanied him since leaving Old Will in the Woodlands, that had been his home, his workshop, his place of safety, was no more than a heap of timber and buckled wheels. Remnants of his life on the road lay strewn around: the heavier pots, his grindstone, some of his tools. Further away lay his blanket and travelling cape, too wet to be of any comfort. He shivered as he stood forlornly wondering what to do. Then his thoughts turned to the people below.

As he looked over the edge, he gasped. The scene was utterly changed. Where there had been a grassy plain and roads and a river, now there was a vast, spreading, moving force. In the stillness, he could hear it: water, water that gushed from somewhere just below his feet.

The crowds had been scattered, that much was clear, but from this distance he couldn't make out quite how badly affected they were. It looked like fewer people, but that could have been because they were huddling together. The road ahead of both groups was obliterated by the spreading body of water.

There was nothing for it but to start walking.

Hours later, back on flat ground, Jonas sat and ate the last of the provisions he had retrieved from the wreckage of his cart. The blanket was still damp, and he had no means of making a fire. In any case, everything was so wet that there was nothing left to burn. He couldn't survive alone out here with nothing; the only thing to do now was to join the crowds he had watched from above.

It was a long slog, and he was tiring again as he rounded the cliffs at the base of the escarpment. He would have missed the mouth of the cave altogether, had it not been for the unexpected glow from within. Cautiously, heart beating, he approached.

'Jonas!'

Was his mind playing tricks?

'Jonas! Oh, thank goodness!' Her voice broke a little. 'I saw you up on the top. I was so worried…'

Wonderingly, he entered the cave. The questions could wait. She took his blanket from him and spread it before the fire, then draped her own travelling cape around him.

Later, after food, she curled up beside him.

'Am I awake? Am I really seeing all this? How did you…? The fire? The food?'

'The fire is easy to explain. I was shown how to do this by a man who kept on rescuing me. Now it's my turn to rescue *him*.' She said this with the gentlest of smiles.

He remembered how she had watched him setting the fire, back in his camp, back when he had the cart.

'I've lost everything, Shanti,' he said, using her real name awkwardly for the first time.

'No you haven't.' She gave his arm a squeeze.

With a change of tone she added, 'I didn't gather or catch my own food, though. Have you heard of the Seekers?'

He nodded.

'Well, some of the Seekers have been keeping me provided. They're treating me as their leader. They think I'll lead them to the Hexadome.'

'And will you?'

She averted her eyes. 'I really don't want to... and I don't think it's the right thing to do, not for them anyway.'

To his puzzled look, she replied, 'They have such a powerful dream, some of them. It would be so heartless to destroy it.'

'And would it destroy it for them? If they saw the Hexadome?'

She nodded, sadly. 'What they believe in is good, and the Hexadome has become a symbol of that for them. But if they saw it, knew the real story, what it represents, yes, I think it would destroy their dream...'

'Are dreams really that easy to destroy?'

She left that question unanswered. Shifting her position, she turned to face him. 'The main problem is that Big Brendan and his lot are also heading this way.'

'Yes, I saw them from up on the edge.'

'What were you doing up there anyway?'

He thought for a moment. 'Being lost? Trying to find myself, maybe?'

She looked at him steadily for a few moments before replying.

'Well, I don't know if you've found yourself yet, but you've found me.'

She stood then and went to fuss with the fire. Her back was turned to him; he thought he heard her say, 'And I'm so thankful,' but told himself it was probably wishful thinking.

When he awoke, stiff from sleeping on the floor of the cave, there were voices, several of them. He couldn't make sense of their words, but at least they didn't sound aggressive. Seekers, then, come to tend their leader.

He raised his head and the words became clearer.

'We're sending out scouts,' someone was saying. 'If they can get round the flood, we'll find somewhere we can regroup, set up camp.'

'Then we can rest a bit while we make our plans.'

Another voice, more hesitant than the others. 'You do know where the Hexadome is, don't you?'

Jonas didn't hear Shanti's reply, so she must have nodded. In any case, the others seemed satisfied with her response.

The waters subsided almost as soon as they'd risen. They left behind mud and silt, and little trace of the road, but the Seekers did what they'd been doing all along, and headed east. As Jonas joined them, he was welcomed warmly by many familiar voices. The copper-haired sisters were there.

'Jonas! You made it!' said Cissy, flinging her arms around him. Shelley appeared moments later.

'Look,' she said, holding out both arms. 'Your ointment worked really well. See?'

Jonas smiled. 'I'm so glad.' It felt like the best thing that had happened in days. He was comforted to realise that, while his carefully gathered herbs and pots of salve might have been lost, at least, thanks to his grandmother, the knowledge of plants and roots was firmly lodged in his head.

'How are you two, anyway?'

'Well enough,' said Cissy.

'You decided to join the Seekers, then?'

'Yes, it made sense. The only thing that did make sense in the end.'

Shelley added, 'What's life without hope?'

They became aware that those ahead were slowing down. Jonas left the sisters and moved forward to see. Shanti was up there somewhere, and to his joy he spotted Alison and Robin, too deep in the crowd to see him, but there would be time for a reunion later. Robin was carrying young Jonas on his shoulders, and the child was gazing around, eyes wide with wonder.

Right near the front of the line, seated on a fallen tree, was Tabitha. He greeted her warmly.

'Where's Sam?' he asked.

Tabitha sighed. 'Who knows? Gone with the People's Army for all I know.'

'I'm sorry to hear that, Tabitha. I wouldn't worry too much though: from what I can gather, it isn't really much of an army.'

Just then Tommy and Ginger appeared, and there were more greetings and hugs.

'I see you've met our granny,' said Tommy, laughing.

'No, she can't be...'

'Nah, not really.' Ginger gave him a friendly nudge. 'We just decided to adopt her.'

Another thing to make his heart leap. Jonas found that he did love human beings after all. He carried on working his way to the front of the column, all the time looking out for Shanti.

'What's happening?' he asked when he caught up with her at last.

'We're stopping for the night.'

'Here?'

'Where else do you suggest?'

'Sorry. I just mean that it's, well, there's nothing much here, is there.'

'It'll do for one night. Can you pass the word back through the crowd for people to sit down?'

'I can do that, and then what? Tell them to lie down and go to sleep?'

'Yes, after we've eaten.' To Jonas' sceptical expression, she replied simply, 'You'll see!'

Within half an hour, he did see: he saw how the people responded to the instruction to sit down, grouping themselves in small circles; he saw how one by one they produced food from bags and pockets and bundles, sharing it out amongst the others in their groups. He saw how happy they were, despite being bedraggled and weary, and he began to understand why they had undertaken this journey to an unknown and unknowable destination. It was the doing of it, the travelling, the effort, that made sense.

His thoughts turned to Big Brendan and the People's Army, to their anger, their desire to have for themselves power and control and revenge, an outlet for their rage, and he sighed. He could almost feel pity for them.

'Jonas!'

He was brought back to earth by the sight and sound of his friends. Robin and Alison hugged him so tightly that the baby, on Alison's hip, started to squeal. Jonas took him and smiled a greeting, and the child responded, kicking his arms and legs in joy.

'He knows me!' Jonas grinned at his friends. 'He remembers me!'

'Course he does!' Robin took his arm. 'Come over here and eat with us.' He pulled him over to a group of people he didn't know. He stood hesitating as they made room for him.

'I have nothing to share,' he said, helplessly.

'But we have,' said a large, motherly lady, patting the ground beside her. 'That is how the Search works.'

Later, Shanti came to find him.

'I need your help.'

'Well, that's a first!'

'Oh, come on... you know I've always been grateful in the end. Anyway...' She drew him away from the crowd and they walked together for some time to the front of the crowd and beyond.

'And anyway... you were saying?'

Shanti took a deep breath. 'You know some of my story now. The first time I met you, on the road, I'd not long been out of... where I came from. I was scared half out of my wits.'

He nodded. That made sense.

'And I was very hungry.'

'Like I was, yesterday.'

'So now we've each fed the other.'

'So where does that leave us?'

Before she could answer, a small group of Seekers came and approached her respectfully.

'What are we going to do tomorrow, Rosie?' said one. 'Once the food's all gone?'

She smiled calmly. 'That's what Jonas and I are going to see about now. You can tell the rest to go to sleep and be prepared to move in the morning.'

They moved off and Jonas said, his eyebrows raised, 'Rosie?'

She shrugged. 'They trust me. They don't need to know anything more.'

'So when --?'

'Look, Jonas, please, won't you just trust me too? There'll be time for talking later. Right now, we have to make plans for tomorrow.'

It was noon. Shanti was leading him along the track that had begun to reappear ahead of them. It was sticky with mud and their progress was slow. They didn't speak for some time.

Finally, he asked, 'Do you know where we're going?'

'Sort of.'

Again, they continued in silence. When they reached the place where the two roads converged Shanti indicated a turning on the left. The path they took now was through woodland, overgrown in places; thorns snatched at their clothes. At length, just as the moon was becoming visible, they emerged from the undergrowth. Straight ahead was a shape, silhouetted against the velvet sky. In the fading light they could just make out the honeycomb panels of the dome. It stood less than a hundred metres away. Jonas laughed aloud.

'No! You have to be joking.'

It was the size of a small tent.

He turned to Shanti and saw that she was laughing too.

'No, of course not! This is just a... wait until later and you'll see. But come on – we need to get organised and then get back to the others as soon as we can.'

She moved quickly forward. The dome had a door to it, with a hexagonal pane of glass fixed in the upper portion. Jonas tried to see what lay beyond, but the glass was of the opaque kind. Shanti spoke into it, giving her name, and the door opened in response.

'They can see out from the other side,' she said to Jonas in explanation. She stepped through the door and Jonas, after a moment's hesitation, followed. No sooner were they under the dome than they seemed to be in some sort of passageway, lit from above by an invisible light source. He saw no sign of whoever had opened the door.

The passageway continued, unfeasibly long given the size and shape of the building.

'Shanti... ?'

'Shh! Later.'

At last the passage widened out into a space so unlike anything he'd seen before that his mind struggled to grasp what he was seeing: the building itself, its incomprehensible contents, and now, approaching them, a group of people, human beings like him, and yet not like him. He might later reflect that the main difference was that they were clean and well-fed, but for now he saw only that everything about them was strange: they moved differently, held themselves differently. Like Shanti, they were tall, pale like her too; even the fabric of their garments was the same as hers. These people were her kin. He was used to being alone, but he had never before felt that he didn't fit, didn't belong, that he was the wrong person. He felt he was seeing himself through Shanti's eyes for the first time. In some part of his mind he wanted to turn and run. It was only the thought of the Seekers, hungry and forlorn, waiting for them to return, that stopped him. He turned and looked at Shanti in complete bewilderment.

'I'll explain later,' was all she said.

Without warning, she broke into a run towards the strangers and threw her arms around a young man standing at the front of the group. He embraced her warmly in return. Jonas felt an unexpected tightening of his chest.

'Oh, Keegan, there were times when I thought I'd never see you again! Let me look at you.' She stepped back, squinting at him, looking him up and down. 'Oh, it's so good to see you again.'

'You too. We were worried.' He looked up. 'Who's your friend?'

She turned then and beckoned Jonas forward.

'I promise I'll explain everything later, but look, this is Keegan. He's leading the advance party.'

'Advance party?' His words came out oddly, like someone waking from a dream.

She shook her head. 'Later.' To Keegan she said, 'This is Jonas. I trust him with my life.'

Keegan stretched out a hand, and, bemused, Jonas took it. The other man's handshake was warm and firm. '

'It's good to meet you, Jonas.'

Jonas nodded.

'You look as though you could do with some sleep.'

It was only when he awoke the next morning that he saw his surroundings clearly. Despite his misgivings, he had slept a sound and dreamless sleep. At first, he could make no sense of where he was. The straight lines and smooth surfaces puzzled his senses. He was lying, not on bare earth, but on some sort of platform, and he was warm and dry. Then it all came back to him: the strange, dome-shaped structure, the welcome Shanti had received from these people; the tall young man called Keegan.

One of the other men from the previous evening appeared at the doorway.

'I hope you slept well? Come and have some breakfast.'

Jonas followed him along another tunnel to a large room, all with the same hidden lighting that looked a little like daylight but clearly wasn't. There was a long table in the centre of the room, and Shanti was already there with some of the others. They broke off their conversation to welcome him, and Shanti moved along the bench to make room for him. The breakfast he was offered was like nothing he had ever eaten before. For a moment he hesitated, but Shanti was eating the same food, and reassured him that it was safe. He began to think again of the Seekers, still in the muddy field, cold and bone-weary, as he had been, before Shanti had rescued him. He had to trust her; he did trust her, but it was harder now, as he looked around the table at these people who so much resembled her, with their pale hair and skin untouched by the sun. Then he noticed that her skin had begun to darken, so that she was no longer quite like the others. He gave his mind a shake: she had experienced all this in reverse when she first appeared in his world. She must understand how he was feeling now.

Someone on his other side said,

'I hope you were comfortable last night? You must have been exhausted.'

The enquiry was kindly enough, but Jonas swept the pleasantries aside. 'Look, please, will you tell me what's going on?'

One of the others, he hadn't caught his name, said, 'I'm sorry, Jonas, we realise that it's all a bit... confusing. Shanti has told us how much you have done for her, and we're grateful. You trust her, don't you? Then you can trust us.'

Jonas ran his hands distractedly through his hair, which was growing long. 'But who are you? What is this place?'

Chapter Twelve

It was Keegan who spoke first.

'We call ourselves - well, I'm not sure we call ourselves anything really, but, well, I suppose we are the advance party, like Shanti said.' His voice carried the same inflections as Shanti's.

'Advance party from where? From what? From The City? From the Hexadome?'

A look passed between Keegan and Shanti.

'Ye…es.'

Jonas was unnerved. Were they hiding something?

'So what are you all doing here? Half the population wishes they could get into the place, and yet Shanti is glad to have got out of there. Apparently.'

'There are a lot of people who want to get out, believe me. When we found the tunnel that leads here, we had no real idea of what was outside, beyond the small dome. Shanti undertook to well, find out a bit more by going out to explore what the world is actually like, as opposed to what we've always been told.'

'And now you've had a look at us, you don't like what you see and you've decided to go back?'

Shanti moved closer to him. She looked upset.

'Jonas, please, don't be angry. It's not like that. We're on your side.'

'Are there sides?'

Keegan leaned forward now. 'Oh yes, there are sides. It's us, the rebels, against the SAR back there. And you have given your support to Shanti.'

Jonas tried to absorb this, as Shanti spoke again.

'We've had to plan for our escape very carefully. Look, Jonas, there isn't time now for the whole story, but I promise we will tell you everything as soon as there is. For now, we need to help those hungry people out there, where we left them.'

'So what do you suggest?'

'That we bring them here, while we arrange supplies.'

'I still don't understand what this place is.'

Keegan spoke again. 'We're using it as an outpost for the movement. It was a kind of temporary HQ for the scientists who set up the Hexadome –'

'So the Hexadome really does exist?'

Keegan glanced at Shanti again. 'Oh yes, it exists all right.'

'And…the movement?' Scientists?' His head was spinning with it all.

The man next to Keegan - he introduced himself as Vector - took up the story.

'The scientists of the previous generation wanted to create somewhere self-contained, somewhere where the earth's legacy could be preserved; but they still needed access to the outside world, at least until they could make themselves self-sufficient. They were bringing in plants to stock it, and materials of various kinds for maintenance. There were underground tunnels back to base, but this place gave them somewhere they could stay overnight when they needed to, and keep their specimens safe.'

He shifted round in his seat to face Jonas. His pale blue eyes had a very direct gaze.

'When they built it, the small dome was really just the endpoint of one of the tunnels. The dome design was needed for the plant specimens, and I think they also hoped it would deflect attention away from the tunnels if any of the Remainder got curious. And, afterwards, when they sealed themselves inside the Hexadome, this was forgotten.'

'The Remainder?'

'Sorry, yes. The Remainder, the Outlanders... the people who were left... outside, after...'

Jonas nodded. 'OK.' This was no time to take offence.

'We think the SAR wasn't even aware that it exists. They were focused on their own preparations.'

Shanti was on her feet now. 'Shouldn't we be on our way?' she asked nervously. 'I can fill Jonas in a bit more as we walk.'

The way back didn't seem as far as the trek there, and Jonas was conscious of how much difference a good breakfast had made. The mud had stiffened overnight somewhat, too, and they made good progress as they walked, side by side.

'So that was the kind of food you were brought up on?'

'Yes. Nutritionally balanced, protein enriched, part of a balanced diet. Completely unrelated to real food in the real world, as I've now discovered.'

She patted the bags she carried slung across her shoulders. Jonas, carrying matching ones, had glimpsed the pale yellow substance they contained and tried to relate it to the kind of course bread he was accustomed to.

'It tasted OK, although I'm not sure what it was,' he said, guardedly.

'It's the kind of stuff they developed back when they used to send astronauts up to the International Space Station.'

'Is that what it was like, living in the Hexadome? Being on board the Space Station?'

She didn't answer.

Jonas found his mind going to the unfortunates trapped up there in orbit when the disasters struck, with no means of returning home, endlessly circling the once fruitful earth. Perhaps they were the lucky ones? He tried another question.

'Is there really room for all the Seekers in that place?'

'Oh yes. The tunnels are very extensive. In fact...' she glanced around, as though afraid of being overheard. '... In fact they link up to, well, close to, the Hexadome.'

'And that's good?'

'Oh yes. Firstly, the tunnels make it possible to borrow electricity from them.' She chuckled. 'They have no idea, just keep working the system harder to keep up with the demand.'

'And secondly?'

'Secondly?'

'You said 'firstly' so I thought there must be a 'secondly.'

'Well, yes, the second thing is, it allows some of the advance party to come and go. We have a regular supply chain set up; that's where the food comes from, and tools when we need them. And it's given us a base to work from.'

They continued walking, while Jonas tried to take all this in.

'Isn't it dangerous? I mean, if your people are coming and going, isn't there a danger of getting caught? I assume the SAR doesn't exactly approve of your activities?'

She gave a harsh laugh. 'You can say that again! Fortunately, we have help from dissidents on the inside. Oh...' She stopped, looking round. The track petered out. 'Are we going the right way?'

Jonas glanced right and left. 'Where's the sun?'

They agreed that the sensible thing to do was to turn towards the south, and before long they recognised the outline of the escarpment in the distance.

'So,' he said, once they were confident that they were heading in the right direction, 'Your idea is to bring all these people here? Isn't there just the slightest chance they'll notice it's not the actual Hexadome?'

Shanti ignored his attempt at humour. She took a deep breath. 'If they are determined to travel there, then they at least need to rest and get supplies before they set off again.'

'And are you going to guide them there? You keep saying you don't want to.'

'No, I don't want to. But it may be the right thing to do.'

They continued their walk in silence. After a while Shanti asked him what was wrong.

He looked at her incredulously.

'How can you ask me that? I'm being asked to believe that a whole lot of you are rebelling against the SAR - the regime you are a part of *by birth* - that you've escaped, recolonised an old escape route…'

He was surprised when she slipped her arm through his, but liked the warmth of it against his skin; it was comforting.

'I know,' she said. 'It's pretty much how I felt when I first got here: so much to take in. I'd never seen the world as it really is, never looked up at a tree, felt the wind in my hair… I do understand, Jonas.'

He doubted that, but there was so much he still wanted to ask her.

'There must be, what - a hundred, a hundred and fifty hungry people out there. Maybe more! How are you going to feed all of them? This bread stuff is only enough for a few bites each.'

'I told you: there's a supply chain. We've got people on the inside delivering food and other equipment.'

'This is getting more and more weird. I --'

They both stopped dead. The sound of voices was carried to them on the slight breeze that had blown up. And there was something more: footsteps.

'That can't be the Seekers already, can it?'

'The PA.' The look of concern on her face reflected his own. 'We'd better hurry.'

It was fortunate that they were by now not far from where they had left the Seekers. Most of them were already on their feet, waiting patiently. The word was passed from the front of the column to the back, along with the supplies of bread, and they set off, with a welcoming cheer for Jonas and Shanti. Someone started singing, and it was soon taken up by the whole group.

As they began moving, Jonas whispered, 'So, how far away do you think they are, the PA? We heard them quite distinctly.'

'Yes.' Shanti was looking worried. 'If they continued along the original road they'll be getting closer all the time.'

'So we'll meet when the roads meet...'

It was hard going for the Seekers, especially those at the back of the column, who must walk where dozens of other feet had already trampled the ground back into thick mud. Several of them slipped over, pulling their companions with them, and then there was a delay while those behind them waited for them to right themselves and clean off the mud as best they could. Shanti and Jonas decided to walk at the rear of the crowd to encourage the slowest walkers.

'So, tell me, why did you decide to leave? You and the others?' It was still not really making sense. 'I mean, if the Hexadome really is what you say it is...'

Shanti stopped and faced him; she took a deep breath. 'Look, there just isn't time right now - '

'You keep saying that! But there's something you're not telling me, something really fundamental. The regime you describe, the plastic and the artificiality, the food – that just doesn't sound like a place where growing things are nurtured.'

'No, you're right. The place I'm talking about is not the Hexadome. The SAR made other plans when…'

'When they saw what was coming to the rest of the world…' It was unusual for him to betray bitterness in his tone.

'Jonas, I wasn't born then!

'Neither was I! But it still affects me…'

They remained facing each other, their bewildered expressions reflecting the gulf that still remained between them. Shanti was the first to speak.

'You are quite right. The place Keegan and Vector and I were brought up in was not the Hexadome. The people who describe it as a city are nearer the truth. It is all the bad things I've already described to you, and I will tell you more about it when there's time, I promise.

'But to answer your question about why we want to leave: there's been a movement building in the past few years, especially amongst my generation. Once we - some of us - realised we'd been lied to…well, people felt angry to be so cut off from the real world, deprived of light and sound, to be living where everything is artificial.'

'If that's how people feel, why don't they just come back out?'

'Because the people in power repress such ideas; they present a picture of a totally ruined world unable to support life outside. They've persuaded most people that they are living the ideal life; everyone just conforms. Or they did…'

As they neared the small dome, Jonas and Shanti had moved up towards the front of the column, and they stopped talking as it came into view. Jonas saw the look of incredulity on the face of those nearest.

Keegan and one or two of the others came out to greet them, and once the column of ragged and weary people had passed through into the passageway, the entrance was shut behind them. Jonas was fascinated by the glass panel that showed clearly what was on the outside, the same panel that was opaque when looking in.

'But you must have had that sort of thing in the Outlands,' Shanti said.

'The Outlands?' He let that go. 'Yes, probably. Before my time, though. Technology was already all falling apart by the time I was born.'

Shanti sighed. 'So much to learn.' She looked at him, and he saw himself mirrored in her eyes. 'For both of us.'

Just then, Vector appeared from the end of the corridor to announce that food was ready.

'It's amazing,' he said to Shanti, as they filed past. 'What these people have done to survive. And so clever, their ingenuity…'

'Yes, said Shanti, giving Jonas an apologetic glance. 'We wouldn't survive five minutes out there without their help; but they're people, Vector, just like us, not some other species.'

They were walking towards the room with the big table. Many of the Seekers were seated on the floor, leaning gratefully against the walls; a few were at the table, and places had been left for Shanti and Jonas.

Jonas was hesitant. 'What about the others?'

'Don't worry, we've found room for all of them. Remember this tunnel goes back a long way.' Keegan stood as he spoke, gesturing Shanti and Jonas to the spaces on the bench beside him. 'And I promise you, they've been given food.'

The magic window in the door showed that the weather outside was not favourable for a further journey that day, and anyway, it seemed a good plan for the Seekers to spend the night resting.

'I'm sorry there aren't beds for everyone, but we'll make them as comfortable as we can,' Keegan said. 'At least they'll be warm and dry in here, and while they rest we can put together provisions to help them on their journey.'

A rota system was swiftly organised for the Seekers to use the bathrooms, gleaming rooms with taps and drains like those Jonas had been shown in the concrete village; here, however, everything was sparkling clean, and the water flowed smoothly, clear as a woodland stream. Some of the advance party were dispatched back to the far end of the tunnel system to fetch further supplies for the Seekers to take with them.

Amidst the noise and bustle Shanti and Jonas found a small alcove off the main tunnel where they could talk and gather their thoughts.

'So, once they're fed and rested, they'll be setting out again, towards the Hexadome.' Jonas wasn't sure whether he was making a statement or asking a question.

'Yes. You can see that nothing is going to stop them.'

'So, have you decided: are you going to lead them there?'

'I don't want to.'

'So you keep saying.'

'But I think I might.'

'And when they reach it...?'

'What?'

'Will some of your people – the dissidents, I think Keegan called them – will they be there to meet them?'

'It's a little more complicated than that.'

There was silence for a few moments.

At last Jonas asked, 'Are you going to explain?'

Shanti gave him an imploring look. 'I don't think I can, not right now.'

Jonas groaned. 'I'll just have to accept that, I suppose.'

After a pause he said, 'What about the PA? Do you think we should scout around, see if we can find out what they are up to?'

The next morning, as Jonas and Shanti prepared to set off to track the PA, the Seekers gathered to see them off. Some of them asked Shanti directly if she would lead them.

'I'll be back for you,' she said.

They walked for some time in silence, heading for the place where the two roads met. This time they went cross-country, skirting the base of the cliffs. The cave where Shanti had welcomed Jonas to her fire after the loss of his possessions showed nothing now but a black emptiness. As the sun rose ahead of them, Shanti pulled her cloak over her bare arms.

'I understand now; you'd never been exposed to direct sunlight before.'

She nodded.

'If I still had my cart I could have given you a paste to soothe your skin.'

Shanti opened her mouth to reply, but a sudden noise stopped both of them. From the escarpment to their right came the sound of rocks, tumbling and skittering down the cliff face. Clouds of dust came with them, and from the dust something was heading towards them, the pace alarmingly fast.

Despite herself, Shanti clung to Jonas.

'It's all right,' he said, laughing. 'Look!'

The black and white shadows, with their back-swept horns, resolved themselves into four-legged animals.

'What is it?' She remained where she was, gripping his arm tightly.

'Goats,' he said. 'Mountain goats!'

The animals careered past them as if the two human forms were invisible. Jonas wondered if this was a good time to tell her that he had often hunted them for food, but thought she might find the idea repellent.

They decided to aim for the area they had come from, some distance before the place where the roads met. Reaching it, they saw that the floodwaters had largely receded into the riverbed, although it was still swollen and moving fast. On the other side cliffs rose to mirror those behind them.

Shanti stood listening. 'I can't hear a thing.'

Jonas strained his ears. There was no clue as to the whereabouts of the PA. 'What should we do?'

'If they kept going - don't forget, we took a detour – they'll be ahead of us by now, don't you think?'

'So, this way, then?' He indicated the road ahead.

As they walked, the gap between the two escarpments narrowed and the land began to fall away. They were now in a lush valley, the river widening and slowing. Glancing up at the cliffs on either side, Jonas tried to trace in his imagination the water that must once have been a gurgling stream, patiently carving its way over the millennia through the layers of rock and soil to become the broad, meandering flow that lay at their feet.

The sun was less fierce now and the air moved down the valley to cool them and to send scurrying the fluffy little clouds that made him think of the duck-down he had once used to make a mattress for young Jonas. That peaceful time in the Woodlands with Old Will seemed a lifetime ago.

Shanti was asking him something.

'Sorry. What?'

'What are those?'

He looked to where she was pointing. 'Apple trees! And fruiting…Come and see.' He led her to what might once, long ago, have been an orchard. The trees they gazed at were not the twisted and gnarled remnants of the past, though; they were young and vigorous and laden with fruit.

'Oh,' he breathed, awestruck. 'These must have grown from the seeds of the old ones.' He picked an apple, firm and shining and exuding its fragrance even as he touched it. 'The earth renewing herself, Shanti.'

He gave it to her and took another for himself. He bit into it, and she copied him, hesitantly.

'Yes,' she said, smiling.

He took her hand and led her to the water's edge. 'Take your shoes off,' he urged, removing his own. 'Come on!'

Again, she was hesitant, but before long she was wading in, and they began to splash each other and shout aloud for the sheer joy of the new sensations.

'The earth is beautiful,' she said, with tears in her eyes.

They lay down on the soft grass and dozed in the late afternoon sun, until at last it was time to move on.

It was raining, not the sudden harsh rain that followed thunder, nor the rain that fell relentlessly from low, dark clouds, but the soft, caressing rain that Jonas remembered from his early childhood. His parents had been great believers in being outdoors – just as well for him, as things had turned out. While their house still stood, they had left it each day to walk or run or play. It was the childhood little Jonas would never know.

He turned his face upwards, breathing deeply, to feel the rain on his skin. Shanti watched him curiously, and then did the same.

'This rain feels different.'

'Yes, it used to rain like this sometimes when I was very small. I loved it.'

A wistful expression came over Shanti's face.

'Of course I never felt the rain at all as a child.'

Jonas tried to take this in. 'Did you ever see it?'

She nodded, slowly. 'I think so, sometimes. When I was very young.'

'You think so?'

'Rain was never spoken about. Water was a commodity, to be accessed, distributed, measured.'

They looked at each other, wondering the same thing: could either of them ever possibly understand how different things had been for the other?

'For us, the elements were the enemy. Wind was to be either avoided or controlled, but never experienced. Until I came out here, I had never seen that wind can do other things.'

'Other things?'

'Make the trees dance; whip up little needles of light on a lake when the sun shines...'

He looked at her with great sadness then. For the first time, he began to see how hard it must have been for her to let him get close.

'And...' She hesitated.

'Go on.'

'And it makes me feel alive. Really alive.'

Jonas found himself thinking sadly about the destructive power he had seen in the wind, especially when the fires had raged; and how could he forget that his cart had been lost to its power?

As if reading his thoughts, she said, 'Oh yes, I know wind and rain can still be the enemy, but in the Outlands you have found how to work *with* the elements rather than against them.'

Was that true? It was how it should be, certainly.

'Do you remember the way you were showing people how to create fire where and when they wanted it, back when I first met you? And how carefully you doused the fire afterwards? You worked *with* nature, but you always respected its power.'

'How do you... your people... make fire?'

'I don't think we...they... ever do. There is still electricity; to heat and cook and keep people cool, to entertain them, to measure and control the environment... When I was a child we were completely insulated from the outside world; the real world.' She paused, remembering.

'What?'

Shanti gave a wry smile. 'We had things we called 'windows.' They showed the sun rising, the night setting in, a few rows of dead trees. We had a rhythm to our lives, of a sort: day and night. But the windows weren't real; they were just moving pictures.

'It must have been a shock, when you got out and saw what the world really looks like?'

'I was terrified!'

Jonas shook his head in disbelief. 'You were always so sure, so strong. Except that first time.'

'The first time?'

'When I met you on the road. You looked so hungry and exhausted, but when I offered you food...'

'I know. I'm sorry.' She paused, remembering. 'We'd been warned since early childhood that the Remainder...' She smiled apologetically at him. 'Those who were left. We were told they - you - had descended into a bunch of savages, animals almost. And, of course, we believed that the old sickness was still out there - out here - and we'd had it drummed into us that, well, that it was death to have any contact with any Outlanders.'

'And now?'

'Now I know better.' She took his hand, resting her head briefly against his shoulder.

'There they are! Down there!'

The shout from the clifftops echoed from side to side of the valley, startling them out of their moment of peaceful contemplation. There followed the roar of many voices, the clattering of metal on metal, and then the sound of rocks crashing and rolling as determined feet forged a way down the cliffside.

Jonas and Shanti looked at each other.

'I guess we've found the PA.'

She smiled. 'I guess we have.'

'So, this is it,' he said between clenched teeth. 'Ready?'

'Ready,' she replied.

Chapter Thirteen

They made an odd contrast: the crowd of shouting, weapon-wielding men and women, all movement and noise, and the two young people standing silent and still beside the river.

Something about their stillness must have unnerved the crowd. As they approached, they slowed, lowered their makeshift weapons, and finally came to a halt a few metres away. Their faces were still contorted with the effort of scrambling down the cliff but behind that there lurked a kind of puzzled satisfaction at having tracked down their quarry.

Jonas prepared to speak, squeezing Shanti's hand, but it was she who spoke first. Her voice held its usual calm softness, yet carried easily over the space between them.

'So you've found us. What is it you want?'

There was a brief pause. Big Brendan was used to getting his word in first, to blustering and to shouting down opposing views. He was confused to be simply invited to speak. Besides, he had been primed for a chase. The mob had set off angry, a hunting party filled with blood lust. Now, faced with this unaccustomed situation, Big Brendan simply stood, breathing heavily.

One of the others filled the awkward silence.

'We know who you are,' came a voice from the back of the crowd.

'Yeah,' growled Big Brendan, who had recovered a little. 'And you're going to take us to The City.'

A supporting roar rose from the crowd. Jonas and Shanti remained where they were. It was clear to both of them that they could neither fight nor fly from this mob.

'Why would we do that?' Jonas asked.

Big Brendan took a threatening step forward. 'You keep out of this,' he growled. 'This has nothing to do with you.'

Shanti moved forward too. She was icy calm.

'Why do you want us to take you there?'

'Stop wasting time,' Big Brendan turned and spat on the ground. 'The deal is, either you take us there or else…'

He drew a finger across his throat, making a gurgling noise. Shanti didn't flinch.

'Well if you kill me you'll never get to The City, will you?'

Big Brendan registered this slowly. His face reddened with fury and he turned towards someone behind him in the crowd, gesturing with his head. For one terrible moment Jonas thought he was going to carry out his threat, but it seemed the other man had understood the order to be an instruction to take Shanti and Jonas captive. Within minutes they had their hands bound and were being dragged towards the cliff path.

The camp was as makeshift as the weapons, a temporary shelter for a self-appointed army on the move. They were not separated from each other as Jonas had feared they might be, and after the initial precautions to ensure they didn't escape, they were left pretty much to themselves.

From their position on the ground they watched as Big Brendan strutted and preened, the hero of the hour. People came repeatedly to clap him on the back and tell him they had known he could do it. Later, as things began to quieten down, some of them came across to stare at Shanti; her paleness puzzled them, but also reassured them that she was different, alien; they could with a clear conscience storm the place she called home.

Jonas wondered if they would be offered food, or at least water. He thought back longingly to the brief time they had spent in the green valley, with its tranquil river, and wished he could have swum in its cool waters. More than anything, he longed to be alone with Shanti once more, her hand in his, her head against his shoulder.

'Hey, Dreamer, wake up!' She must have spoken so softly that he had failed to hear her.

'Sorry.' He turned so that his ear was close to her mouth.

'I said not to look so worried. I'm going to tell them I will lead them there, but not as a prisoner.'

He was confused. Did she really mean to lead them there, more or less willingly, or was this some trick? And if a trick, what might they do to her when they discovered that she was leading them astray? He was uneasily sure he knew the answer to that.

'Jonas, stop looking so worried. I know what I'm doing.'

'You're taking a terrible risk. When they find out you're not leading them to The City…'

'Oh but I *am* going to lead them.'

His sense of shock winded him. 'Really lead them? Actually take them to the…?'

'Yes.' She rested her head against him; their hands were still bound. 'Please trust me. I can't tell you yet… it's safer that way. For you. I told you once before – people need to see it for themselves if they are to let go of the myth.'

'And that's another thing I don't get. You've told the Seekers you'll lead them to the Hexadome, and the PA you'll lead them to The City. Are they the same thing? Do they both even exist?'

'They are all part of the same thing, I suppose. When my great-grandfather -- '

She broke off; a familiar figure was approaching them, carrying chipped cups of water.

Shanti lifted her bound wrists. 'Thank you, but...'

The man hesitated, then pulled out a knife to cut the rope. It looked as if it had been recently made from some sort of plant fibre, and was so loosely twisted that it was already beginning to unravel. Jonas found himself absently trying to work out a way of improving its manufacture. When Shanti was free he held up his own hands and the man, somewhat grudgingly, cut him free also, but as they were trying to persuade him to free their legs, a coarse shout rang across the camp.

'Joe! Over here – NOW!' Joe didn't need to be told twice when it was Big Brendan calling.

'Coming, Boss.' He leapt up nervously and ran. His boss had never liked to be kept waiting.

The ground was hard and the night was hot, and Jonas had no trouble staying awake. When he was as sure as he could be that everyone else was asleep – crucially he could hear Big Brendan snoring like a wild hog – he pulled out the knife that Joe Farmer had left behind in his rush to obey the big man's orders, and began severing his own bonds. It was an easy task: really, whoever had made this rope had a lot to learn. Then he leaned over and whispered in Shanti's ear.

'Are you awake?'

He could just make out her smile in the darkness.

'I am now.'

'OK. I've got a knife. The rope's easy to cut – I've done mine already. We need to work out how to get away as soon as yours is cut.'

'And how far do you think we'll get?'

Jonas groaned. He hadn't foreseen opposition.

'No, seriously, Jonas, they're not going to harm us. If they do, they'll never find The City. Look, realistically, how far do you think we'd get without them finding us? We can't go back down into the valley, it's wide open, and there's no tree cover up here for miles.'

He knelt there in complete indecision, the knife suspended.

'I suppose you're right,' he said at last. 'I still don't trust Big Brendan as far as I could throw him.' He gave a harsh laugh. 'Which, given his size, is no distance at all...'

Shanti aimed a clumsy kick, her legs still roughly tied with the fibre rope.

'Could you just get on with cutting the rope, please?

'What's the point, if we're not going anywhere?'

'Well, I'll be a lot more comfortable, for a start. This stuff's really chafing my skin.'

Jonas got to work.

'So what's the plan?'

'Yes, I've been thinking about that. *You've* got to go...'

'Without you? No!'

'Wait. Listen: while you're here, they've still got a hold over me. You're the one who's in danger. Once you're gone, I'm perfectly safe.'

'But you've already said there's not much chance of getting clear.'

'Not with both of us. But if you go, I can cause a diversion, give you more time.'

He looked at her doubtfully. Although she couldn't see his face clearly, she must have picked up the tension in his body. As he finished cutting through the last rope, she raised a hand to his cheek in a swift caress and repeated what she'd said earlier:

'Trust me. Please?'

Jonas tucked the knife into his belt, standing cautiously. She stood with him, drawing him behind the provisions store.

'I think, really, I've always known I have to take them there; it's the only way to put an end to this. Meet me there when this is over.'

She stood on tiptoe to plant a soft kiss on his cheek.

'Now go!'

Big Brendan woke in his usual bad temper, but after a few minutes remembered what had happened the previous day. A slow smile spread across his weather-beaten face, and he stood up, scratching. That was the trouble with sleeping out in the open. He examined the bite marks on his legs with disgust, calling to mind the village they had stayed in for a while, with its secure doors and taps that ran water. The regret soon vanished, however, as he turned his mind to the place they were going. He didn't know exactly who she was, this pale creature, but he knew he could use her to his own ends to smash the system. As he headed over to the place set aside for the latrines, he mused that he could probably find other, additional ways to use her for his own ends, and grinned to himself.

When he got back to the open space in the centre of the encampment he met with a scene of uproar. Joe Farmer was on his knees in the centre, sobbing and quivering. Various other people were dashing here and there, pieces of equipment were scattered all over the place: the whole scene resembled a disturbed ants' nest. Looking up at his approach, Joe got up and tried to run, but tripped over his own feet and ended up prostrate at Big Brendan's feet. Big Brendan gave him a kick.

'Get up, you useless pile of shit,' he said, with his usual delicacy. He gave him another kick for good measure.

Joe was opening and closing his mouth, fish-like, in an attempt to find words, any words at all, when Big Brendan's attention was suddenly drawn to what was not there.

'Where in thundering hell are they?'

His roar was heard two miles away, as Jonas could have attested, if asked. He had done as Shanti insisted, still doubting the wisdom of it, and knew he had a good start on them, but his mind was still back there with Shanti and the brief kiss she had bestowed. No time to think of such things now, though. He took a deep breath and forced himself on.

High above, the red kites continued their wheeling flight. Below them all was churn and change, but up there, up amidst the mysterious currents of air where they kept their watch, there was calm, a kind of stillness even as they moved.

Joe Farmer reckoned he was lucky to have got away with his life, at least for now. Big Brendan's attention had switched suddenly away from him to the cause of all the chaotic activity. He was standing staring at the frayed ends of the ropes. There was no telling what would happen when he found out whose knife had been used! But that was for worrying about later.

Ten minutes later, Big Brendan was still worrying away at the ropes, as if staring at them might reverse what had happened. No-one had yet dared approach him, although some of the men had made a half-hearted attempt to go after the escaped prisoners.

Finally, Big Brendan came to his senses, or what passed for his senses. 'What are you waiting for?' he yelled at the assembled company. 'Get hold of your weapons you bunch of useless half-wits. Follow me!'

He raised his arm in what was intended to be a kind of battle signal and roared, 'Follow meee...!' as he led the charge.

They had gone no more than a few hundred metres when Big Brendan stopped so suddenly that the man behind him cannoned into his back, and the man behind him into his, and so on. Walking serenely towards them, silhouetted against the morning sun, was the unmistakeable figure of the pale girl.

'Oh, are we leaving?' she said, when she was near enough to be heard.

Big Brendan, inarticulate at the best of times, spluttered and spat on the ground. Shanti looked at him haughtily, which made him angrier still. He flung his pruning hook spear to the ground and groaned, loudly.

Shanti walked on past him, as if nothing out of the ordinary had happened, and entered the camp. Some of the women were there, paused like statues in the act of preparing breakfast.

'Oh, yes please,' she said to one of them. 'I'm absolutely starving.

When the atmosphere had calmed a bit, and everyone had been fed, Shanti seated herself near Big Brendan and the group of cronies that passed for his war counsel. This was not so different from how her grandfather ran his governing body, after all. She recognised the set-up. A blindly convinced leader, ideologically driven, with a few hand-picked, fawning supporters. No need to consider the facts; no question of wondering whether the system worked for the good of all. No, in his world, as in Big Brendan's, it had always been a question of knowing the goal and aiming at it, no matter what the cost.

'So?' she said. She was unaware of the look of utter contempt she wore, but it reduced Big Brendan to incoherence.

'What... I don't get it... what...what was all that about?' he stuttered, finally.

'Do you mean why did I object to being tied up and held prisoner? I should have thought that was obvious.'

She paused. Over the years of being at odds with her grandfather she had found that silence was often an effective weapon. It gave the other party so little to go on.

Joe Farmer, anxious to reingratiate himself with Big Brendan, repeated his leader's question - if anything, even less coherently.

'Yes, but what, I mean, why, I mean what? What was all that about?'

'Oh shut up, Joe.' Big Brendan was back in control, inasmuch as he was ever in control of anything. He turned his attention back to Shanti. 'What are your demands?'

'Demands? I have no demands.'

The big man began to grind his teeth, a sure sign of trouble.

'Now...' Shanti was almost enjoying herself. 'When are we setting off for the Hexadome?'

Big Brendan said nothing. The Hexadome? That was Seeker claptrap. He wasn't sure what trick she was playing, but he wasn't going to be caught out if he could help it.

'Look.' She leaned forward, businesslike. 'You want to go there. You don't know where it is. To be honest,

I'm not sure everyone here even believes it exists, but they're following you anyway because some hope is better than none.' She looked around at the crowd, all spellbound; this was the best entertainment they'd had for as long as most of them could remember.

'I think you'll be disappointed, to be honest, but if you are determined that it's what you want, then, yes, I'll take you there.'

She stood up then, a commanding presence amongst so many dispossessed people, worn down by the hardships of a life she had never known. She found it in her heart to feel sorry for them.

'You take us to The City.' Big Brendan's voice was gruff.

'I'll take you, but I will not go with you as a prisoner.' She swept away to the corner she had made her own at breakfast. That should have given Jonas time to get far enough away; in fact, they seemed to have forgotten all about him. But that was something Shanti was not going to do, not ever.

Chapter Fourteen

If Shanti was surprised to see how well provisioned Big Brendan's people were – at least in terms of food, if not weaponry - she didn't express it; nor did she ask where the rest of the PA was, and what their plans were. Joe Farmer, finally reinstated after his blunder in letting the prisoners go, was guilelessly boasting about the way things were managed under Big Brendan. At this moment he was explaining how they had fed themselves on the journey, and his bravado was beginning to falter.

'Easy as anything,' he said, as he walked alongside her on the first day's march. 'Old Brendan don't do things by half! Those people in the villages – no guards nor nothing. Like taking food from a baby…'

Shanti shuddered. She could easily imagine Big Brendan doing just that.

'So we got everything we need --'

'Will you stop rabbiting, Joe.' Big Brendan's voice rang out from somewhere behind them. 'I said keep an eye on her, not talk her to death.'

Some of Big Brendan's cronies laughed at that, and Joe Farmer blushed. Being constantly humiliated by Big Brendan was beginning to take its toll.

Shanti looked around. She could make out, from up here, the path she had taken with the Seekers. She estimated that they were about a day's journey ahead of the place where the roads met. For the first time since leaving her home behind, she wished she had with her a communication device so that she could speak to Jonas. Would he do the obvious thing in her absence and lead the Seekers back to the road and onward, through the valley where they had spent such a magical time? It was almost too painful to remember that now.

Jonas, meanwhile, was regretting that he had agreed to be separated from Shanti. He would have to trust her sense of having a higher purpose, even though her reasons remained unclear to him. In her absence he would have to do the thing she had hinted at, the one thing that might put a stop to all this Hexadome-City fever. He would have to lead the Seekers.

The way back to the small dome seemed much further as he travelled without Shanti, and he was weary and apprehensive as he approached it. It was Keegan who let him in. The man was pleasant enough, but a mystery. He was clearly someone who mattered a great deal to Shanti: she had hugged him and shed tears of joy when they were reunited. Where did that leave him? Down in the valley she had rested her head on Jonas' shoulder, taken his hand, kissed his cheek, but could he be certain she would weep tears of joy to see him again?

He might have expected recriminations for returning without Shanti, but Keegan only said mildly, 'Are you all right?' adding, after Jonas had given a brief account of events, 'Well, that's Shanti, always the risk-taker!'

There was a pause. Jonas could think of nothing to say. Finally, Keegan asked, 'Anyway, what do you think we should do now?'

They batted various ideas' back and forth, finally concluding that they should hold to the original plan and get the Seekers back on to their original road.

'Of course, they were expecting Shanti to lead them to the Hexadome,' Jonas said. 'She didn't say she would, not definitely…'

'No, she wouldn't. Say, I mean.'

Jonas looked at Keegan expectantly, but he didn't elaborate; instead, he said, after a pause, 'So you must do it.'

'I was rather afraid that would be the case, but I don't know the way.'

'Then I'd better come with you.

'While Shanti leads the PA there.' He groaned.

Keegan threw an arm across Jonas' shoulder.

'Don't worry about Shanti. She's tough. You'll see her again.' He held Jonas' gaze for a long time as he said this. 'Now come and eat.'

Next morning everyone was awake early. They began to assemble outside. The older children were running around playing tag, tripping each other and generally irritating the adults. Some of the little ones were wailing while their mothers desperately tried to calm them. The members of the advance party were in and out, sorting provisions, reassuring the Seekers that all was well, that Shanti was safe, that Keegan and Jonas would lead them now.

'We should eat well before we leave.' Keegan's voice carried a ring of authority. 'We have a long day ahead of us.'

They had been walking for some time. Despite himself, Jonas found he liked Keegan. There was something very open about him. He talked about his childhood.

'When you're very little, of course you believe what you're told, but then certain things didn't quite add up. We started asking questions...'

'What sort of questions?'

'Well, we worked out that some things disappeared, you know, old, broken down pieces of

176

furniture, general household waste, but no-one would tell us where they'd gone. And then sometimes there'd be new things, but we never saw where they were made, or who made them. When we looked out of the windows, we could see the light, the sky going dark at night, but none of that light ever made its way into any of our rooms. And we'd been told since we were tiny that the Remainder were out there, but there was no sign of anyone when we looked out of the windows.'

'What you're describing, it's not the Hexadome, is it?'

Keegan shook his head. 'No, and I hope you never have to see the place where Shanti and I were born.'

'OK. Go on. You were telling me about what it was like...'

Keegan gave a quiet groan. 'By the time we were emerging from childhood we'd explored every part of the place, apart from the forbidden zones. But then one day we discovered a hidden...'

He paused.

'A hidden what?'

Keegan hesitated. Jonas wondered if he thought he'd said too much.

'You see, I'm not sure how much my sister has told you, but...'

Jonas stopped walking. 'She's your sister?

'Didn't she say?' Keegan seemed amused. 'Typical Shanti!'

At that moment one of the Seekers caught up with them, to say that Tabitha and some of the others really needed to rest, and there was a child with a cut toe.

'That sound like a job for you, Jonas.' Keegan had already heard about Jonas' skill in treating minor injuries. As he set off with the Seeker, Keegan called him back.

'I've told you: don't worry about Shanti. She's tough. She will find us.'

Big Brendan had replaced Joe Farmer at the head of the column. Shanti wasn't sure it was a change for the better. Although he was no longer as openly aggressive towards her as he had been, he assaulted her all the way with questions she had no desire to answer.

'You still haven't told me how you know,' he said, at intervals.

'No, that's true. I haven't,' she replied each time.

'So, how do you?'

After a while Shanti became bored with this.

'Maybe I don't.'

He wheeled round on her. 'You bitch! I've a good mind to...'

She stopped walking, turned and faced him.

'To what? Ruin the only chance you have of finding it? I told you back at the beginning that your ideas were dangerous, that you were mistaken about it, but you carried on, with your People's Army and your rage for revenge...'

She watched his face, his thoughts passing transparently across it.

'So will you turn round now and tell all these people who've been following you while you trash their villages and steal their food that you don't have a clue where you're going?'

Big Brendan opened and closed his mouth.

'No, I didn't think so! You have no choice now, Brendan, no choice but to trust me. Shall we carry on walking?'

To Shanti's relief, he remained silent for a while, leaving her space to think about Jonas.

Jonas and Keegan kept up a brisk pace as they led the Seekers towards the meeting place. Refreshed from a good night's sleep and food they hadn't had to forage for, the Seekers were mostly able to keep up with them. They had been walking for several hours when Jonas suggested they needed to stop for a proper rest. Infants needed feeding, small children were weary, feet were sore. He had been moving backwards and forwards through the line, talking to people, reassuring them. There were many of his old friends from the months of travelling.

Towards the back, but hobbling gamely on, was Granny Tabitha, assisted by Ginger and Tommy, who had clearly been quite serious about adopting her. Cissy and Shelley had made their way to the front, intent on questioning the enigmatic tall man who had appeared with Jonas when they were all lost and starving.

As he wove in and out of the crowd, Jonas greeted Harry and Jim and a number of people he'd met on some of the halts earlier in the Search.

Leo was there too. He looked a bit quiet.

'Are you OK?'

Jonas' question seemed to startle him.

'Yeah, I guess so.'

Jonas waited.

'I mean, I'm OK, but I keep wondering about the family, you know?'

Jonas nodded sympathetically and they continued to walk in silence for some time. At last he said, 'At least you know where they are, and that they're safe.' He resisted a shudder at the memory of the dismal, fearful place where he had met Leo's family.

'I wish they'd have come with me. Maybe I'll be able to go back and fetch them, you know, afterwards?

'Yes, why not?' Jonas gave him what he hoped was a reassuring smile and then moved on as someone called him from further back in the line.

Shanti was also thinking about her family as she walked at the head of Big Brendan's collection of self-styled warriors. She knew that Keegan would be all right, but she wished, as she had wished so many thousands of times, that they had not lost their parents so young, and so tragically. It was her parents' unquestioning loyalty to the First Generation that had, ironically, sown the seeds that led her to begin questioning the SAR.

Since leaving, she was still trying to assimilate all she had learned about the Outlands, and especially about the Remainder. Of course, they were not the semi-feral people she and her contemporaries had been warned about. Unlike her own, these people did not heartlessly condemn their peers to exclusion, or worse. Out here, she had, for the first time, experienced real kindness, even from people she did not know. She smiled as she recalled her first meeting with Jonas, the unknown young man with the wobbling handcart. How sensitive he had been when he offered her food, sensing her fear. The food had been, well... it had fed her when she was near starvation, and she was grateful, but it had been a shock. Later, in the camps, she had been astonished to see how food had to be acquired – trapped or foraged – and then cooked laboriously over a fire. It hadn't taken her long, though, to not only become accustomed to it, but to enjoy it: real food, for the first time in her life.

Of course, the dirt and general lack of hygiene had bothered her at first, but she had become used to that too. Most of all, she had exulted in the freedom to disagree, to challenge another's views, as she had challenged Big Brendan's at their first meeting. Perhaps she had been too unguarded, and what she had seen as Jonas' interference had annoyed her at first. It had been strange and disquieting to find that a stranger was prepared to offer her help freely and for no other reason than because he was concerned for her safety.

The courage it had taken to leave had made her reckless at first, but in there, the place she had left, she had at least known what the dangers and consequences were. Jonas' actions had made her aware that she knew nothing about life in the Outlands. She should not have assumed that what she was taught in her lessons on the Anthropocene was necessarily true, and she was appalled that the SAR could have considered themselves superior to the Remainder, could have believed that they were somehow fitted to take what was left of the old civilisation and leave the rest to fend for themselves.

The cult that had formed around her great-grandfather no longer filled her with pride in her bloodline; she felt instead shame that her own survival had been at the cost of so many other lives. It had been humbling to see how these people, this 'Remainder' of what had once been a thriving nation, cared about something more than themselves. They had a purpose beyond mere survival, beyond holding on to power at all costs. She had watched how they created community, believed in something worth striving for, a dream of... what was it they said? Peace and light.

Then she had encountered Big Brendan, and seen the other face of people living in the natural world, seen the anger and rage that could turn to violence. And somehow, here she was, leading them, if not exactly to The City of their imaginings, to a place where the reality of what they would find there would no doubt double the anger and frustration they already felt.

Furthermore, it would not be long before they were back on the original road, and if Jonas was doing as she expected he would, the two groups would soon meet and travel side by side to the one place on earth she didn't want to return to. The Seekers would face disillusion when they reached the goal of their search; the PA would no doubt vent their anger and frustration on everyone in sight, and she would be responsible. In the end, perhaps she was no better than her grandfather; surely she could have done better for the people under her care?

It was mid-morning of the third day since Jonas had parted from Shanti. As the roads converged, he felt his pace and his heartbeat increase. The Seekers found themselves walking faster to keep up with him. A small copse of bedraggled trees within the angle made by the roads kept the two groups from sight of each other until the last moment, but they could each hear the other. Keegan, who was walking next to Jonas, placed a warning hand on his shoulder, as if he might forget himself and the seriousness of their purpose. Despite that, as the others finally came into view, with Shanti walking undaunted alongside the bulky figure of Big Brendan, it was all Jonas could do not to run ahead and drag her away from him.

For several moments there was nothing but silence as the two groups looked at each other, and then suddenly it was broken. It was Granny Tabitha, of all people, who moved towards the ragged ranks of the PA.

'Sam,' she said, simply, as she faced her son. 'It's so good to see you.'

The mud-stained figure who shuffled out of the line of Big Brendan's men was almost unrecognisable to Jonas. The irritable swagger had disappeared; he looked smaller, like a rag doll with the stuffing gone.

Then Tabitha was on the move too, and they met at the exact point where the tracks converged.

'Ma!' He dropped his bundle with a clatter to fling his arms around the old lady, with a fierceness that almost knocked her off her feet. 'How did you make it here?'

By this time Tommy and Ginger were at her side, looking anxious.

'Boys,' she said. 'I'd like you to meet my son. This is Sam. Sam, this is Tommy… and this is Ginger. They've been looking after me.'

There was a pause, and then Sam tentatively offered his hand to the two young men and said, in a small voice, 'Thank you for looking after my mother.'

Within moments, members of each group were crossing the space between them, greeting friends and family, sitting down together, swapping stories of their journeys. Rugs were spread, food packets were unwrapped; in some cases, tears were shed.

Jonas ached to throw his arms around Shanti, but there were practical matters to attend to.

'How far are we from the river? These people are going to be thirsty.'

'We passed a stream on our other side, just before the roads met. They can go and drink there.' Then, her voice quavering very slightly, 'It's good to see you.'

'You too.' He risked a brief kiss to her forehead.

'Jonas…'

It was Keegan calling from somewhere within the shelter of the trees. As the sun reached its zenith more

183

and more of the crowd had found shelter beneath their shade. Making his way towards him, Jonas caught snatches of conversation. Sam was telling his mother and her fiercely protective companions that he was ashamed of things that had happened on the journey.

'We were so tired, Ma, but Big Brendan wouldn't listen. He kept us moving on – said we had to rendezvous with the rest of the PA. Then, whenever anyone said they were hungry, he led a raid on the nearest settlement... we stole food, Ma, stole it from under the gaze of women and children.' He looked close to tears. 'I kept thinking: suppose someone had done that to my children? Or to you? We want justice, don't we, from them in The City? But that isn't the right way to do it.'

Jonas bit his lip. Well, that was one small, good outcome from a bad situation. If only others among Big Brendan's followers would reach similar conclusions. Passing the little knot of people grouped around the big man, however, Jonas' elation fell. The talk there was still all of revenge and weapons, and the tone was fierce and angry.

Further on, he noted Joe Farmer seated next to Leo, with Cissy and Shelley, and Harry and a group of very serious-looking Seekers.

'You see, as Brendan says...' Joe leaned forward earnestly, 'Once we take control of The City, we can use it as a base for contacting all the other PA groups, the ones who haven't got here yet.'

Leo looked unconvinced. 'Have you seen any of the others?'

'Well, no, not personally, but...

'And anyway...' This was Tommy, temporarily separated from Tabitha. 'I've seen Big Brendan and his – what do you call them, soldiers?'

'Warriors.'

Tommy gave a short laugh, and Joe turned red.

'Warriors! OK, *warriors.* How are they going to defeat a bunch of people who will have seen them coming from miles away, up there in their fortified position - '

He was interrupted by Cissy. 'But that's not what the Hexadome is.' She looked around at the other faces in the little circle. 'It's not a place of war. Why would you think that?'

Joe fidgeted uncomfortably.

'Well, of course it is. It's where the Regime are. What else could it be?'

Cissy looked steadily at Joe.

'But everyone knows it's a place where things still grow; where the birds and animals are kept safe, where the sun doesn't burn and the river flows...'

Joe stood up abruptly. 'What are you talking about? Of course that's not it!' With every utterance his tone grew less certain. 'I'm not saying it wouldn't be good if it was,' he added, wistfully, 'But it's not... of course it's not.'

Someone asked Leo what his opinion was.

'I've no idea. I'm just following everyone else...'

Jonas felt he had heard enough and moved on. He tried to form some picture in his own mind of what they would find when they reached their destination. How could the Hexadome be at the same time a Stronghold? Some of the things Shanti said only served to confuse him further. The small dome was indeed made of hexagonal panes, like the charms hung around the necks of many of the Seekers, but he struggled to reconcile it with what she had told him of her childhood. He had set off from the Woodlands without any formed purpose, and as he travelled, his purpose had become simply to become part of something bigger than himself, and to do some good, if he could.

Finally, reaching Keegan, Jonas said, 'OK. What do we do now?'

'Perhaps we should ask Shanti?'

'Do you know where she is?

Keegan turned aside: there, at the foot of a tree, almost hidden by its downswept branches, Shanti lay on the bare ground, fast asleep.

'I told you she'd be OK, didn't I?'

As they waited for her to wake, the two men tried to make sense of the present situation. The absurdity of it struck both of them: the Seekers and the PA – or this small section of it – intermingled and indistinguishable at this point on their journey. They were travelling to the same place, yet their expectations were worlds apart.

'Can you tell me what they'll find?'

'Not what they're looking for, that's for sure.'

'Neither side?'

'No.'

'Why were you and Shanti and the others so keen to leave?'

Keegan looked thoughtful, as though trying to find the words. In the end he just said, 'I'm sorry; it's a really long story. I will explain it to you when we have the time, I promise.'

Reluctantly, Jonas accepted that he would have to be satisfied with that for the present. He asked, 'Now that you've seen how the rest of us live, do you wish you'd stayed there?'

Keegan shook his head, vigorously. 'Never.'

In the end, the groups had to agree that, since they were travelling in the same direction, the only sensible option was to travel together. Big Brendan protested, loudly. He was not happy about sharing his moment of glory.

'The People's Army should lead the way, and if the other lot can't keep up with us, then too bad.'

'What about the rest of the PA?' Despite his best intentions, Jonas couldn't resist the taunt. 'Where are they?'

As usual, Big Brendan blustered. 'They're there already, waiting for us. Obviously.' He turned to the crowd. 'Come on. Time to get moving.'

'Yeah. On their way from all over the country. Obviously.' Joe Farmer must have thought he was helping, but his tone was noticeably subdued.

Some of their supporters gave a weak cheer. No-one moved.

Shanti, awake now and somewhat refreshed, emerged from the trees, shaking leaves from her hair.

'It's up to you,' she said to the crowd. 'We've come this far.'

There was considerable murmuring, and then someone from the back of the crowd – Jonas couldn't tell if it was a Seeker or a Warrior – spoke loudly enough for everyone to hear.

'OK, come on. Let's go. Together or separate, what difference does it make? What else are we going to do?'

For the first time, Jonas realised how much all of these people – Seekers and Warriors - had needed this journey; it had given them purpose. He felt a shadow of fear at the thought that it would end. He and Shanti had still had no chance to talk properly.

The road stretched ahead over a flat landscape. The earlier speculation had given way to a heavy silence as they trudged without seeming to get anywhere.

'Are you sure this is the way?' Big Brendan asked, shifting his bundle of makeshift weaponry from one shoulder to the other. 'I mean, there are no landmarks: you could be mistaken.'

Shanti fixed him with her level, pale blue gaze. 'This is the way.' She looked about her. 'This could be the road the Romans took, more than two thousand years ago. They always took the most direct route.'

'The who?'

It was no surprise that Big Brendan didn't know who the Romans were, but Jonas' home, while often lacking in food and comfort, had been overflowing with books, mostly those of his grandmother. He wondered, absently, what had happened to them.

'I didn't realise you knew about, you know...'

'The history of this country? Well, I wasn't taught about it as a child, that's for sure, or at least a very edited version. But once we found the forbidden records, we tried to learn as much as we could. I loved the way the Romans built their roads to go straight to their destination, refusing to acknowledge any obstacles.'

Jonas said, 'But they weren't going where we're going, were they?'

Shanti gave him a sideways glance.

He ploughed on. 'I mean, they weren't like us, going backwards. They were heading towards the future.'

He was still brooding when Shanti said, so quietly that he had to bend his head to catch the words, 'And so are we, Jonas, even if it's not what we planned for. Can we talk later? Properly?'

They lapsed into silence, as did most of the people, conscious that they were approaching their journey's end.

The land continued, flat and brown and featureless, and as they walked the column became elongated, with Big Brendan and his followers edging forwards.

Shanti, who was at the very front, stopped to allow the rest to catch up. She waited, looking back at the ill-assorted group of people, as they tried to take in the sight that met their eyes.

Ahead of them on a slight rise, silhouetted against the crimson streaks of the setting sun, stood what might have been the object of their journey.

Big Brendan pushed his way roughly to the front. His jaw hung slack, his eyes blazed.

'What trick is this?'

'No trick. We are almost at our destination.'

'Almost there? So what is this?'

'Keep calm and I will do as I said I would: I will lead you to whatever it is you are seeking. If,' she added, facing him squarely, 'If you are still sure it is what you want.'

Big Brendan turned on his heel, almost flattening Joe Farmer, who squealed in alarm.

'Get out of my way,' Big Brendan snarled. He headed off into the crowd of his supporters, all clamouring for an explanation.

After some animated discussion, he returned to Shanti.

'We've decided: we need to stay here for a while; wait for the others.'

Shanti raised her eyebrows. 'The others?' She looked around. From where they stood they could see for many kilometres.

'The others?' she repeated.

Big Brendan spoke through gritted teeth. 'The rest of the People's Army.'

In the silence that followed, Big Brendan's face slowly registered the beginnings of a realisation that there were no others. The People's Army had always been a fantasy. Whatever he might have heard, Big Brendan had been the only one angry enough to act on the rumours; the only one to arouse in others an echo of his own rage.

A little way off, Jonas stood quietly, registering the Seekers' much quieter dismay. They believed they had reached the end of their journey, the place they had heard about and dreamed about and walked so far, for so many months, to find. They had believed they would find a place of light and warmth that would somehow lead them back to a vision of the earth that had been destroyed. What lay before them was no such thing.

Chapter Fifteen

In that wild, deserted landscape the jagged shapes that sprawled along the skyline loomed black and threatening; they contradicted nature, the natural world, the only world their generation had really known. Despite themselves, the Seekers could do nothing but marvel as they stared at the dark shapes before them, reaching up unimaginably high into the evening sky. This had been made by human hands; yet it was human hands that had destroyed the world as it had been. They had been searching for something that would help restore the old world, but this remnant of what had been wrong with that world was not it.

As for Big Brendan, even he could see that this was no fortress. Like the rest, he stood still for a long time, looking. Then the old Big Brendan took over; he wheeled round to face his dejected followers, indistinguishable now from the rest of the crowd.

'This will be the easiest battle ever!' he roared. 'We don't need anyone else. This place is a ruin! We will overcome them in minutes! One hand tied behind our backs!

Jonas felt a shiver run over him. Not again, he thought, please, not again, never again. Better to stay grubbing around in the middenheaps, foraging for roots and herbs, than to begin all this over again.

He became aware that Shanti had taken hold of his hand. He turned and they exchanged a look, but he was unsure what it meant. She squeezed his hand; he thought she was trying to reassure him, but he wondered what reassurance she could in truth offer. He realised how little he knew about her, even now. Above all, he still didn't understand her reasons for leading such a ragtag group of people to this place. Then he wondered again at his own motives. Had he thought that this would be an object lesson, a way of teaching people that hankering after past glories would lead only to destruction? If so, how had he thought it possible? He felt weak, and found himself sinking to the grass. The others too were slowly sitting down, groaning as they noticed for the first time since setting out that morning how much they ached, how fatigued they were.

Jonas noted where Alison and Robin were, thinking he would join them later. Young Jonas was standing, holding on to his father's hands. He bent his knees, jigging up and down with delight, then lifted one foot and then the other, as if trying them out. He would be walking soon. All around them small knots of people were making themselves a space, inviting others to join them, opening up what remained of their supplies. The Warriors had largely abandoned their improvised weapons, and Joe Farmer had just finished stacking them together in one place.

As he watched, Jonas tried to draw comfort from the fact that the two groups were no longer separate; some of the little clusters contained Seekers and Warriors together, tentatively discovering that they were people, not so unlike themselves, perhaps. Certainly, they were all one in their puzzlement, their disappointment, their sheer exhaustion.

Joe Farmer was keeping out of Big Brendan's way. He had been yelled at once too often already that day. Seeing him wandering about alone, unsure how to make an unaided decision even about where to sit, Alison called to him.

'Come and join us, Joe. We have food and water.'

Before long, they were deep in conversation. Jonas made his way through the crowd towards them, catching the tail end of something Joe was saying. He was more animated than Jonas had ever seen him.

'...and, to be honest, I'd go back there, if I could, with the land beginning to come to life again, you know? Mum and Dad had saved enough seed. It had taken, too; should've been a good harvest - ' He broke off as he saw Jonas and began scrambling awkwardly to his feet.

'No, Joe. It's OK. Stay where you are.'

If his friends were prepared to take even Big Brendan's shadow under their wing, he supposed he could put up with him too.

'Did I hear you saying something about farming?'

A shy smile spread across Joe's face. 'Yeah. That's why they call me Joe Farmer. When I joined up with Big Brendan and his lot, I suppose I was always going on about the farm, so that's what they called me, see? Joe's my real name, though.'

'Why did you join Big Brendan, then, if the farm was so important to you?'

'Well, Big Brendan said that once we got rid of the SAR we'd get back all the land and the machinery and all the things we needed to get things going again. And I believed him.'

'And now you're not so sure?'

Joe Farmer shook his head. 'Look at that.' He turned to stare at the strange sight that lay before them. 'That's not what we were expecting, is it? That's not the SAR Stronghold, is it? Nothing like. It's not even the Hexadome. And if Big Brendan was wrong about that, then perhaps he's wrong about some of the other things he said.'

'And what about Shanti?' Alison spoke gently. 'She promised to lead us all there. Do you trust her?'

Joe shook his head back and forth in what looked like agony. 'I don't know. I don't know,' he moaned.

'Right, let's eat.' Robin's tone was decisive. 'One way or the other, we'll all know soon enough.'

He opened the pack they'd brought from the small dome and began doling out hunks of bread and something resembling cheese. As Robin went to hand something to him, Jonas stood up. 'No, it's OK, Robin. I need to get back to Shanti.' On a sudden impulse, he reached down and offered his hand to Joe, who, after a brief hesitation, took it. The two men shook, although neither was sure why.

Over at the front of the line, Jonas finally caught up with Shanti. They moved away from the others a little.

'Shall we sit here?' Shanti indicated a rocky outcrop.

He joined her. 'So?'

'So?'

'You must know what the people are saying? The Seekers as well as Big Brendan's lot?'

'That I haven't done as I said? That I haven't led them to the Hexadome? Or The City?'

'You've always said you didn't want to take them there.'

'And I also said that I would.' She smiled at Jonas' confusion. 'We're not there yet.'

'So where are we?' A dim memory surfaced. His grandmother had spoken of a city. The Old City, she'd called it. If *she* had spoken of it, then it might be real. 'Is this the Old City?'

She nodded.

'And the Old City is not the SAR Stronghold?'

'It never was.'

'But the Hexadome – it does exist?'

'Yes.'

Now he was more confused than ever.

Although the Old City looked close, that was an optical illusion; it was still at least half a day's travel away. They would not reach it this evening, and anyway, the sun was sinking fast; there was no point arriving in the dark. Jonas stretched out where he was, in the shelter of the rocks. Shanti lay down beside him.

The sound of birdsong woke him at dawn. Raising his head, he looked around; it seemed everyone had slept where they stopped, just like him. The open grassland had the appearance of a plaguefield, with bodies everywhere. He turned sideways to see if Shanti was awake, but the space beside him was empty. Why should he feel surprise? He suppressed his deepest fears. Surely not this time?

He stumbled away from the group – still no-one else stirring – in search of fresh water and a place to relieve himself. He would never normally have slept without checking that those things were available.

Soft footsteps behind him made him swing round.

'Have you come looking for me?'

He choked back his relief.

'Don't flatter yourself! I'm looking for a place to pee.'

She laughed at that. 'Try over there.'

He hesitated.

'Go on! I'll still be here when you get back, right by the water. Scout's honour.'

'What does that mean?'

'No idea. It's what my Grandfather always said when he was making a promise. Now go on, before you burst!'

They didn't return to the others right away, but sat beside the stream for many minutes, chatting idly, avoiding the unspoken questions that hovered in the air.

The Old City lay before them. It shone in the late morning light, bright rays reflected from its surfaces. But it was not like the light that danced when Jonas and Will fished in the stream for the sparkling trout. It was a cold, hard light.

Wearily, the crowd got to their feet, shook themselves out, and prepared for further journeying. Big Brendan shouted orders for his Warriors to collect their weapons. He seemed completely unable even then to let go entirely of his hope that the rest of the PA would join them; he begged Shanti to wait just a little longer.

Shanti stood up. She shook her head and raised her voice so that those nearest her could hear. 'Come on. We still have quite a journey ahead of us.'

Big Brendan fell into step alongside her. He began again.

'They'll be here, the others. We should give them time to catch up.' He looked round as though expecting to see the hordes of People's Army troops appearing out of the West.

'I really don't think they're coming, Brendan.' Her voice was kind, kinder perhaps than he deserved.

'But, I...I'm not... I don't...' He was unable to articulate his disappointment; perhaps it was shame that he felt, or maybe just confusion.

Now they were closer they could see the enclosing wall, the forbidding gates of the Old City. The people advanced slowly, like so many sleepwalkers. Soon, only a short distance separated them from the entrance. Then they stopped.

Shanti had already explained, with the help of Keegan, that they must pass through the Old City if they wanted to reach the Hexadome. She had assured them that they would be safe until they reached the dome itself.

Not one person had asked, 'What then?' They had come too far for that.

Big Brendan squared his shoulders. This should have been his big moment. He should have been delivering a stirring speech, urging his followers on, but instead he was as overawed as the rest of them, Seekers and Warriors alike.

Finally, he seemed to shake himself from his trance. The shout, ripped painfully from his throat, must have caused real physical agony.

'Go on! What are you waiting for?'

He turned to face them, trying to pick out the faces of the people who had followed him from amongst those of the others.

'This is where it all started,' he declaimed. 'This is where the rot set in; where the power was stolen from the people. This is where our rights and freedoms were taken from us, bit by bit, until we had nothing.'

The crowd was listening now, all eyes fixed on Big Brendan. He was right, Jonas thought, from what little he knew of those times. No-one had acted to prevent what was happening, and then what was happening became something that no-one could prevent.

The big man turned and made eye contact with as many as he could; for a moment he appeared to falter; then the old Big Brendan reasserted itself. He raised an arm. Jonas noted the vicious curved hook in his fist.

'Let's give them hell!' he roared, and the next second a crowd had erupted, each of them armed with a crude weapon. Some had old, rusted pitchforks; others had axes, or knives fixed to stakes, while a few carried heavy wooden clubs. They were mostly men, but among them were a few women, equally armed. Their faces were terrible to look at in the soft light of morning, and Jonas shuddered.

Shanti whispered something.

'What?' His eyes were fixed on what was happening ahead of them. He hadn't managed to make out her words.

'Have you noticed? There aren't so many of them now.'

She was right. He turned back to the crowd, and saw a number of the Warriors still there, Joe Farmer among them. The People's Army - a pathetic army now, as if it had ever been anything else - were muttering the old refrains, mostly about 'making the bastards pay for what they'd done' and claiming that the Old City was now theirs.

'Yes, we are here. The Old City is ours!' It seemed Big Brendan had remembered his speech and didn't want to waste it. His supporters cheered.

'This is our time,' Brendan continued. 'No-one is going to stop us. No-one! The machines, the technology, the...' he paused before the next word to give it emphasis. 'The *power* is ours now. The time of the elites is over. We will make the decisions. We will decide who gets what.' More cheering and shouting.

'Yes,' someone yelled. 'Make them sorry they were ever born!'

'We'll do that all right!' said Brendan, to further hysterical acclaim.

'Oh, get on with it!' shouted someone else.

The mob moved forward, broke into a run. The more peaceable elements of the crowd held back, afraid they would all be seen as the enemy. Perhaps they would be shot, as people used to be when they gathered in crowds to protest against injustice. Or gassed: didn't they do that too? The folk memory of those times lived on, alongside the longing for the internet and the oblivion of computer games that was still cherished by some.

They watched as Big Brendan and his supporters roared towards the entrance, then stopped, then finally disappeared inside. No sounds came from within the Old City. Finally, curiosity got the better of some of the less timid of those watching, and the crowd began to inch forward, Jonas with them.

As they stepped cautiously through the gates, Jonas saw that they were wide open, with no sign of being forced. There was no sound of shouting or even of footsteps; no clash of weapons. A wind had blown up from somewhere, lifting a litter of papers and dead leaves from the floor, wrapping them around their ankles, filling their eyes with grit. The buildings that surrounded them were so tall and sheer that the daylight was all but blotted out. The canyons that ran between them funnelled the wind, making them gasp and hold on to each other.

A sudden banging made them look upwards. A window frame, blown back and forth, a welcoming drum marking their coming. It stopped as suddenly as it had begun, and the wind dropped. Stillness filled the streets. They walked slowly onwards, into the shadowed spaces, gazing up at the empty windows and down at the rubbish underfoot. Not a sound was heard beyond their own footsteps. Doors hung open. The stench of rotting filled their nostrils, making them gag. Some covered their noses, others drew back. One or two ventured through doorways and returned, shaking their heads.

A woman gave out a squeal. Jonas thought it sounded like Cissy.

'Ugh! It ran right over my foot!'

'What?'

'A rat. I've never seen one that size before!'

Now they listened more intently; the sound of scratching reached them from the vacant buildings; bird calls sounded high above. The children began to murmur.

Jonas edged cautiously forward. The group fanned out behind him, began to spread through the streets. Voices were heard, echoing in the deep passages between the buildings; then footsteps. The remnant of the PA reappeared round a corner. Weapons hung loosely in their hands. Faces wore puzzled looks. Big Brendan was nowhere to be seen.

Shanti had continued along one of the streets, knowing, perhaps, or dreading, what she might see. A strange, muffled sound came to her, a little way ahead of where she stood. She followed the sound to a broken doorway at the foot of one of the buildings.

The unmistakeable shape of Big Brendan lay there, huddled against the hard wall. He looked broken, too.

Shanti knelt carefully next to him and placed a calming hand on his shoulder. Big Brendan shook it off, savagely.

'Are you happy now? I suppose this is what you wanted all along?' He wiped his face on his sleeve.

'I tried to warn you.'

'What?'

'I told you your ideas were dangerous.'

'Dangerous?'

'Can't you see? All this just makes you the same as them, the people who built the Old City? They were hungry for power too. They had a plan to grab what was left for themselves.'

'So? Is that fair?'

'No. And it's not fair when you do it either.'

He was squatting on his haunches now, sniffing intermittently.

'So?'

'So if you stir up anger and hatred, if you urge people on to violence, if you take what you want by force, then what happens to the people left behind?'

He mumbled something. 'Same as happened to me. When I got left behind.'

Shanti waited.

Finally, he spoke. 'I never had anything, worse than nothing. I had everything I ever had taken away from me.'

'Did you lose family?'

'Yeah.' He seemed about to add something. Again, she waited. 'Well, aren't you going to tell me that everyone lost people they loved?

'I could do, but it doesn't help to know that, does it? It doesn't stop it hurting.'

'What hurts is that the ones who died were the only ones who could have saved me.'

He was letting the tears fall down his cheeks now, quite openly.

'Tell me.'

Big Brendan heaved a shuddering sigh. 'My mother. My sister. They died.'

Another pause.

'But my fucking sadist of a father lived to torment me. Still alive for all I know.'

'So you got away?'

'Oh yes. I got away. Once he'd reduced me to a pulp. Inside and out.'

Shanti was silent. Big Brendan continued.

'It wasn't just him. My brothers and uncle too. As if having to scrape for a living wasn't bad enough, I was always the one given the dirty jobs, always the one they made fun of. I couldn't help my size, but they kept saying I was eating too much, that was why... Then we got the rumours about The City.'

He sat up, looking at her for the first time. 'Suddenly I had a purpose, you know? There was something I could do, something that would make people sit up and take notice. It was my chance to have what I'd never been allowed to have, to take the power away from them that didn't deserve it.'

'And you didn't stop to think that you might end up doing to the others, the people left outside, exactly what you'd had done to you?'

'Why should I? No-one cared about me. Except when they thought I could take them to The City. And now that's gone as well.'

He drew the back of his hand across his face, streaking it with dirt. Shanti noticed that he no longer had his weapon with him.

'Was it all just a story? You went along with it, making me believe you would take us there?'

Calmly, Shanti answered, 'No, the SAR Stronghold does exist, but it's not here; the Hexadome certainly exists, too, and I will take you there, just as I said I would. But I can't promise you'll find what you're looking for.'

The people had wandered about for some time, as Jonas tried to take in the sheer size and scale of the place. His legs ached from walking on the unyielding stone beneath their feet. Shanti reappeared from somewhere.

'So this is it? The place where the old governing bodies used to be?'

They were sitting in a patch of weak sunlight between two of the tall buildings.

'Yes, although that was long before I was born. By then they'd already retreated elsewhere.'

'How far is it now?'

'To the Hexadome? Not far.'

'You keep saying that. You seem to have been saying it for ever.'

'I know.' She reached for his hand. 'I'm sorry. It's hard for me too, you know?'

'You never wanted to come back.'

'No.'

'Bad memories?'

She nodded and he squeezed her hand.

'I'm here with you now.'

Very gently, he touched her face. They were silent for a few moments, holding their breath. Then Shanti stood,
tugging at Jonas' hand.

'Come with me.'

It was a long climb to the very top of the building. The concrete stairs, filthy with animal droppings and the dust of decay, rang with their footsteps in the silence. At the very top they paused to catch their breath and then Shanti led him into a room leading off the landing. It was all windows.

At first he couldn't make out what it was she was showing him; looking out made him dizzy. He could see, at his feet, Warriors and Seekers, indistinguishable now, like lazy ants, caught in the sunshine near the gates. Back in the direction they'd come from was the road, a broad, dark stripe of mud across the landscape. Shanti tugged his arm, urging him to look in the opposite direction. Jonas squinted, unsure of what he was seeing. Beyond the derelict city lay fields, largely scorched, but here and there showing patches of green. Further still was something else altogether: a vast spread of rectangles, like nothing in nature, winking blue and silver in the afternoon sunlight.

'Photovoltaic Cells. For powering the Citadel – the place you call The City.'

He tried to take in what she had said.

She added, 'Solar panels. Harvesting the sun's energy.'

Jonas stared at them as if hypnotised.

'Now look beyond…' She raised her arm to point, and then he saw it; in a dip in the landscape, there it was. The Hexadome was much as he had imagined it, like an upturned bowl, its honeycomb panels glinting, its massive size squatting firm and solid.

Back down on the ground the ants became people again, excited people who clustered around Jonas and Shanti, asking questions to which there were no clear answers. Big Brendan was nowhere to be seen, but a number of his supporters could be seen standing some distance away, grim-faced but uncertain. All the fight seemed to have gone out of them. Joe Farmer was deep in conversation with a young woman from among the Seekers. The two groups were mingling again.

Jonas shouted in Shanti's ear. 'This is hopeless! How are we ever going to get them organised?'

'Over there!'

'What?'

'Over there.' She pointed at what must once have been the plinth of a statue. 'Go on.'

Reluctantly Jonas climbed on to the plinth, but then he got down again.

'Shanti, I'm no leader. If this is going to work, we need Big Brendan up here with me. Can you find him?'

To Jonas' surprise, Big Brendan readily agreed to appeal for calm from the Warriors, and the weary Seekers were only too willing to sit on the hard ground and listen to what the two of them had to say. The plan to send an advance party to check out the Hexadome was acceptable to almost all, and it was agreed that Brendan and Jonas should each choose four others to accompany them. So it was that Joe Farmer and Veronica, the Seeker he'd been talking to while exploring the Old City, joined two of Big Brendan's Warriors, Jake and Bill; while Robin, Alison, Cissy, and Harry set off with Brendan and Jonas. Keegan would stay behind with the remainder, and Shanti really would, finally, lead them to the Hexadome.

Chapter Sixteen

They skirted round the vast expanse of solar panels, squinting in the reflected light of the sun. As thy reached the dip in the landscape they stopped and fell silent. Shanti met Jonas' eyes, and he gave her hand a squeeze. Veronica slipped her arm through Joe's; Cissy nudged Harry and pointed, but he was already staring, open-mouthed, at what she was indicating.

Slowly, they moved closer, all eyes fixed on the thing they had travelled so far to find. Even Jake and Bill were transfixed by the sight. With each step the Hexadome seemed to grow in size, until they were forced to tilt their heads back in order to take it all in. The sky beyond was a pure, deep blue, and somewhere a blackbird was singing.

Shanti and Jonas were at the back of the little group.

'Are you OK?'

She nodded, but he saw that she was biting her lower lip.

He said, gently, 'You'd better lead them in.'

Shanti nodded again and moved forward, slowly raising a hand as if in a dream state. A panel slid back, and she motioned for them to enter. The panel closed behind them, and they found themselves confined in a small space, barely big enough to hold them all. Shanti spoke in a soft voice, as if as much overawed as the rest of them.

'This whole place is a sealed ecosystem. That's why the airlock is there: to reduce the danger of contamination from the outside. We mustn't let any of the Hexadome's atmosphere escape either.' She looked round at each of them, as if to impress on them the significance of what they were about to do. 'You will be the first human beings to enter the Hexadome since the day it was abandoned.'

Only Jonas heard the slight quiver in her voice; the others were all too distracted by the anticipation of the moment.

The inner panel opened, slowly, slowly, and one by one they stepped forward. The soft whooshing noise as it closed behind them was followed by the sound of indrawn breath as they raised their eyes to the domed roof, impossibly high above them. The sunlight filtered gently through the honeycomb panels, turning the deep blue of the sky a softer shade. There were exclamations as they sniffed the air; it was full of the scent of green and growing things, more powerful than they'd ever known.

They began to move wonderingly forward and as their eyes adjusted to the light, the details became clearer. Silence fell on the small group once more, a calm silence, not like the menacing silence of the Old City; but one of awe and wonder. So much green! So much life! On either side of the path was unfamiliar vegetation, plants or trees they weren't sure which, dwarfing the human beings as they passed beneath their giant leaf-span. The air was hot, humid, and in places little spates of water droplets fell suddenly from the leaves, making them jump. They heard, without seeing, the whirring of wings.

No-one spoke for a long time, as they inched forward tentatively on the path that led gently down into the heart of the Hexadome. Then Veronica let out a shriek of excitement as a butterfly, delicate as paper, alighted on her hand, and the others crowded round to marvel.

'It's got tails on its wings!' Big Brendan was the most wonderstruck of them all. 'I've never seen anything like that. Look at the size of that thing! And the colours!'

Size and colour was all around them, in the trees and creepers reaching skywards, the plants beneath them, the flowers and fruits, and the giant dome enclosing it all.

'It's another world,' said Alison, her eyes misting. 'I have never seen any of these in my life!' The others murmured their agreement.

Jonas had continued to walk forward, drawn by the background sound he had picked up almost from the moment they entered; as he approached, it grew louder, until, rounding a bend he heard and saw the splashing of a great waterfall, and a cool breeze brushed his cheek. Beside the waterfall, steps cut into the rock ascended to a higher level, and before long the others had followed him until they were looking down on the water that gushed and tumbled into a deep pool below. As they watched there was a dizzying sense of something beyond themselves. At that moment anything seemed possible.

It was not long before they had lost all sense of time. Jonas began to recognise trees that might have been long-lost cousins of those he had seen on his journey east; he exclaimed with delight at the sight of medicinal plants remembered from childhood walks with his grandmother. This was the earth as it might have been.

Rounding a corner they found themselves blinking as the light became stronger. Here there were no trees, and beneath their feet were what Jonas would have termed fields had they been out in the world beyond the Hexadome. But could there be fields inside an artificial place like this? Whatever had once been planted here had fared less well than those in the humid zone they were leaving behind; what had once grown here had died where it stood, a ghost of what it had been.

Joe Farmer moved forward to inspect; this was something he knew about. For a few moments he stood looking down on the browned leaves and withered stems, before kneeling and gently running a handful of soil through his fingers. Looking at the others, he shook his head.

'Needs water,' he murmured. 'And organic matter. It could be made fertile again.' His voice sounded different; he was like a man who has found his place.

Still no-one spoke, but now the silence was turning to puzzlement. What was this place? What was it for?

Suddenly, Cissy uttered a cry of alarm. At the far edge of the field a figure was moving towards them, its motion spasmodic, uncontrolled. Shanti slipped a reassuring arm around the other woman's slender shoulders.

'It's all right. It's only an old agribot gone rogue.'

Now there was a buzz of conversation: questions and speculation replaced the silence. The agribot continued its progress towards them, a noise like angry wasps emanating from inside its chest. Close up it looked less human. Shanti moved to confront it.

'Shutdown!'

It took two or three repetitions before the buzzing quietened and it finally ceased moving. She turned back to the little group.

'Do you want to see the rest of the Hexadome?'

There was so much to see: walkways at the level of the trees, where things grew in huge containers, or spilt luxuriantly over the rails to form curtains of creepers down below; paths that twisted and turned so that they came suddenly one moment upon an area of arid desert where strange, fleshy growths clung to the stony ground, and the next they found themselves in a place where water seeped up and things grew, even there, in the heavy, marshy soil.

They came to a place screened from its neighbours, where rows upon rows of growing things clung to tall bamboo stakes. Some of the plants had grown too heavy for their supports and were beginning to droop; on others the leaves had faded to yellow, while others grew stunted in the shade of their more vigorous neighbours. Baby Jonas began to whimper, and Alison took him to the edge of the dome to soothe him, while the others wandered slowly around this new area.

Jonas stood still, gazing around him, unable to form coherent thoughts. Snatches of conversation flew past him.

'They're real plants, aren't they? Just like the others?'

'So big!'

'They're real, not plastic. Look!'

'This is what we've been searching for…'

'Plants, green, growing things…'

'Need a bit of attention, though…'

'We've found our true home…'

'Peace and light…'

'No weapons…'

'It's paradise.'

'It's just like the Old City…empty. No weapons, no army.'

This last was Big Brendan, gradually absorbing the reality of their journey. 'We came to fight an enemy that wasn't here.'

Shanti remained apart from the rest, standing by to let the others explore unhampered. Jonas walked back to where she was.

'They're saying they've found their paradise.'

'That's what *they* thought.'

'Who?'

'The people who made it.'

'Who were they? The old government? The Alexander Regime? Doesn't seem their style, somehow.'

She gave a thin smile. '"*They*" were the ones who saw what was happening; the scientists, the people with prophetic voices. They made this place to preserve precious things. Like Noah's Ark. Do you know that story? The Hexadome was an experiment to see if human beings could live the way nature intended.'

'So it was built before the disasters?'

'It was begun before then, but it took a long time to complete. It's not something you can hurry; it takes a long time for the ecosystem to build. At the same time, the government of the day was planning its own escape route. That's when they made the Shanti Accord.'

'Your great-grandfather?'

'Yes.'

'Did he mean it, the promise to the people? Or was it just a means of keeping them quiet?'

She shook her head and sighed. 'I've asked myself the same question so many times recently. I'd like to think Patrick Alexander was doing the best he could for a world he knew he couldn't save.' She paused, allowing her gaze to sweep around the wilting plants below their honeycombed ceiling. 'But I just don't know.'

'So what happened? Was it just abandoned?

'Oh, no. They kept it going, long after the Old City was deserted. My grandfather succeeded his father as Supreme Leader and began to recreate the structures of government. The scientists continued their work on the Hexadome, and then set up the experiment. They sealed themselves in here, away from the world – they would survive and improve on nature, discover a new way of living. Or that's what they thought.'

'So what happened?'

She spoke slowly now. 'What always happens to human beings. They thought they'd planned it all so carefully: the psychological tests, the food storage, the crop rotation. Only…'

Jonas waited.

'Only, in the end they found they couldn't really trust each other. The balance wasn't right; harvests failed. They needed to ration the food supplies.' She looked up at him and he saw that her eyes were luminous with unshed tears. 'People began hiding food away, taking more than their ration.' She paused. 'They died.'

There was a long pause. She seemed to be struggling to speak.

'Who died, Shanti?'

'My mother and father. They were the team leaders; they denied themselves for the sake of the team…but in the end, they all died.'

'I'm so sorry; sorry for your loss, sorry you had to come back to this place… Come here.'

She buried her face in his shoulder as he embraced her and he barely caught her next words.

'So that's why we were brought up by my grandfather.' There was an edge of bitterness in her voice, something he had never heard before.

There was a shout from the far side of the dome.

'Look, over here! It opens out: there's another dome through there!'

Jonas turned to look. Through the panes at eye-level he could see that there was indeed another dome, and beyond that another, a whole series of smaller domes clustered around the main one. Seen from this angle, they appeared to Jonas like bubbles on a washpail. The thought made him laugh. It was all so incongruous, so impossible!

Harry and Cissy were already through into the next space, closely followed by the others. They stopped and stared, confused by the contrast with what they had just left.

Jonas and Shanti followed more slowly.

'Sleeping pods,' said Shanti, bracing her shoulders and moving towards the group. They were walking cautiously towards the small, spherical units attached to a wall of metal beams. Some were unzipped, affording a glimpse of scattered belongings: books and papers, a small drawstring bag, boots and a hooded jacket.

'This is where the scientists lived. If you go round there, beyond the pods - '

The group moved on to the area Shanti indicated. Cissy exclaimed aloud with pleasure.

'A cooking place! Is this where they made their food?'

Shanti nodded.

The others crowded round the long tables, their surfaces smooth as frozen water. Harry ran a hand across the surface of one, while Veronica pulled out one of the chairs.

'It's so light!'

Jonas winced at the memory of the stools he had made with such pride. Now he saw them for what they were: crude, rough, primitive.

Shanti, sensing his thoughts, squeezed his arm.

'I prefer yours. They're real.'

The exploration continued as they moved from dome to dome. All sense of time disappeared as they stopped every few metres to examine and wonder at and touch each and everything they saw. There was puzzlement and some degree of alarm in one of the smaller domes; the rows of metallic objects that met their gaze stared back at them through dark, empty screens, while tiny lights and dials blinked slowly. There was nothing green in this space.

'The whole system was computerised,' said Shanti. 'It was supposed to order everything: what was grown, when, what feed the crops received, when they could be harvested…' She turned her head away so that only Jonas caught her last words. 'The people too; only it turns out that however intelligent the machines are, people can still cheat them.' Then she shook herself, raising her voice. 'If you go
through there you can see where all the fruit was grown.'

The little crowd moved obediently in the direction indicated. There were gasps as they emerged into the next dome, a much larger space. Before them stretched rows and rows of bushes and trees, plants tied to stakes, and others, twisting, curling and climbing. Having long since escaped the confines of the plots they'd been planted in they were now flexing their muscles up towards the top of the very dome itself.

It was not so much the sight of this, however, impressive though it was, that caused the intake of breath: dotted here and there along the rows, metallic arms paused in various positions, as though in the very act of picking the fruit. They looked like modified versions of the agribot they had seen earlier. It reminded Jonas of the story of Sleeping Beauty that his mother used to read to him. Whatever had happened here had happened suddenly, conclusively, all at once.

They looked around, taking in the fruit fallen to the floor, the budding apples and tiny oranges, other, unfamiliar fruit, swelling yellow and gold and red, the berries of so many different colours; and over it all the sickly-sweet smell that came from the boxes of rotting pulp, and an unmistakeable background sound.

'Bees!' Cissy shouted. 'I think. Does anyone know? Is that what they are?'

'Yes, said Joe, pointing upwards. A long shape hung there, shifting and flowing like a single living creature. Around it individual dots, black against the light, darted and danced in an unknowable pattern, a dance, a secret known only to their colony. 'I think they're about to swarm. We used to keep some, back home, until they got stolen.'

The little group continued to wander at random, and Jonas and Shanti found themselves in another screened-off section. Rows and rows of glass-fronted cupboards met Jonas' startled gaze.

'Oh!' he breathed. He turned to Shanti for confirmation. 'Can I look inside?'

She nodded, and he stepped forward, moving slowly along the row before selecting one and gently pulling it open. The jars inside were labelled.

'Aspirin! Antihistamines! Oh, Shanti! Vitamin D... rehydration salts... and bandages, sterile dressings, antiseptic... We could do so much good here, with these, and I could make and store my herbals and ointments in these jars, in these wonderful cold cupboards...' He turned and saw a look of deep sadness on her face. 'I'm so sorry. I should have thought what it would mean to you.'

She shook her head as if to wave away his apology.

'Come on,' was all she said.

The tour continued. They had come nearly full circle; the main dome was ahead of them once more, and they were slowing down as though by common consent, putting off the moment when they had to return to the others and decide what should happen next.

Jonas and Shanti were near the back, walking next to Big Brendan. He had been silent now for longer than she had ever known him.

'Are you all right, Brendan?'

He turned to her, his face contorted with the sheer misery of no longer knowing what to do or who to be angry with. He didn't answer Shanti's question, but turned instead to Joe, who was close behind.

'You know about growing things. Could anything be done here?'

Joe looked startled at this reversal of their former roles. He answered slowly.

'Well, if we can farm at all out there in the Outlands,
we can surely do something with what's in here.' He looked to Shanti for confirmation.

She hesitated for a moment. 'What you see now is the effect of this place being abandoned for many years. It has formed its own ecosystem; that's why so much has been preserved. I honestly don't know what would happen if people settled in here, coming and going…' Then she smiled. 'But it would be good to see you try.'

'We'd want to get rid of those tin men, though,' said Joe, with a tentative attempt at humour.

Shanti sighed. 'When the construction was completed, the whole place was sealed up, to keep the balance right, with the scientists sealed up inside too. To live like that there has to be absolute trust amongst them, otherwise the same thing would happen to them as happened to…'

',,,to the people who were here before,' said Jonas, wanting to spare her pain.

Cissy spoke up. 'We can't make a decision here and now, can we? We can't make a decision for the others, either. It's only fair that everyone gets their say.'

Big Brendan was among those who nodded in agreement.

As they headed back to the main door, Robin and Alison drew level with Shanti. Young Jonas was chuckling contentedly, from his seat high on his father's shoulders, as he made grabs with his fat little fists for the vines that hung just out of reach.

'So, who's in charge now? Where is the Regime?'
'Not here.'

'No, clearly. And not in the Old City either. So where? Where did you and Keegan come from?'

Shanti sighed deeply. 'It's such a long story, Robin, and in any case, it's all in the past. The important thing is that you, and your family, and these good people here, will be part of the future.'

They were now at the exit. While the others took a last, wondering look around, Shanti opened the sliding panel to the airlock and stood aside to let them pass through.

After the others had set off back to where the rest of the seekers and PA were camped, Shanti and Jonas hung back, each sensing they needed some time alone together.

'I was so afraid of that. That they would see it and want to stay.'

'Is that so bad?'

'Yes. The Seekers were right, of course: this *was* built to be a place of peace and harmony, but I'm afraid they won't be allowed to stay here in peace.'

To his unspoken question, she replied, 'We are very close to the Citadel.' She sighed deeply. 'When the

217

government saw what was coming and finally accepted the truth about what was happening...'

Jonas nodded, aware of how hard it was for her to speak of this.

'Well, they accepted the scientists' advice to build this place, but all the time they were making other arrangements for themselves. My parents were serious scientists, but when my grandfather succeeded as Supreme Leader, he was very different from my great-grandfather; he had no interest in the science, in conserving the past. All he cared for was power; power and his own comfort.

'Anyway, when the Hexadome was finally completed and ready for occupation, the people chosen for the experiment were all carefully selected; they went through strenuous fitness tests, medical examinations, rigorous psychological profiling. For my parents, it wasn't about propping up the Regime. It wasn't even primarily about the human beings who would live in here: it was about preserving knowledge, preserving what they could of the earth our ancestors had known, before it was too late. They were right, too, about the plants and the animals and the insects... they demonstrated how it was possible to preserve them, pitifully few, in retrospect, now we see how much has been destroyed, but at least...'

Jonas put his arm round her shoulders. She was shaking.

'But it was the human beings who ...' She left the rest unspoken.

'And... when the end came, in there?' He hardly knew how to ask the question, but she understood his meaning.

'They disposed of the evidence. The human evidence. They just left the plants...'

They stood together for several minutes, gazing speechlessly back at the mighty Hexadome.

A call pierced the air. 'Jonas! Shanti! Come on – we need you.'

Jonas started, and Shanti placed a restraining hand on his arm.

'Wait a moment.' Her voice was small.

He turned to her and saw that she was crying; huge silent tears streamed down her face like an overflowing lake.

Instinctively he wrapped her in his arms and allowed her to sob against his chest. He gave her time and asked no more questions.

Chapter Seventeen

Back at the Old City, the crowd had watched as Jonas and Shanti and the rest of the small group disappeared in the direction of the Hexadome, and before long they began to drift back to the place where they had been camped overnight. So much had changed since then, and the day held the hope of more change. The Seekers had reached only the edge of their promised land, and the Warriors had been forced to confront the reality of their own search. Together, the two groups that were now one waited in near silence for the small band of scouts to return.

The migrating swallows, massing in a dense cloud above their heads, could have imparted their own wisdom, for they too had made an arduous journey; like their human counterparts they had a destination in mind, a purpose, a goal. Each year they travelled great distances to seek warmth in winter, or shelter from the heat when the summer sun beat down on them; they went to find fresh sources of food, to find a mate, to bring up a new family. From high above the surface of the planet, they observed the mystifying movements of the earthbound creatures, who had nothing to show for all their journeying.

Jonas and Shanti walked slowly on, following a path that took them beyond the Hexadome and further away from the others. Ahead of them was a wide sweep of land where the earth was flattened.

'It looks as though someone's been preparing to build here,' said Jonas, remembering the smoothing of the ground he'd observed when watching people preparing to build, back in the camps and villages. It all seemed so long ago. In any case, the scale of this site was vast in comparison.

'Yes, I suppose that's just what it is, in a sense.'
Shanti had more or less recovered her composure, although she still looked shaken. Jonas felt it had cost her a lot to release her deepest feelings; he also hoped that it meant she trusted him at last.

They began to walk across the flattened earth. It made no sense to Jonas' eyes: the area in front of them was roughly circular, with short posts around the perimeter. On each of these was a small glass disc, winking and blinking with light.

'This circle is the only contact the Shanti Accord Regime – the SAR - has with the outside world.'

It took him a moment or two to fully take in her meaning.

'You mean they are living underground?'

She nodded, aware of the impact of what she was telling him. 'This is the place they were already preparing long before the Hexadome was finished. As the situation got worse, they speeded up the work: they thought they might be the only people to survive what was happening, at least in these islands. We still don't know about the rest of the world; as far as I know, contact has never been restored.'

'But they went ahead with the Hexadome...'

'Only because of the scientists; because of what they believed in.'

They continued walking around the perimeter of the circle; as they did so a kind of sigh rose from somewhere near the edge of the circle. Jonas looked round nervously.

'We must have walked past a vent shaft,' Shanti said. 'A place where stale air is pumped out from the Citadel.'

'So Brendan was right, in a way: the SAR is living in a fortress, a well defended one?'

'There is weaponry, and they would certainly use it to defend the Citadel, but their main defence is that they are living where no-one can find them. And of course most of the people are ordinary citizens; clerks, teachers, cleaners, manufacturers…'

Jonas stopped and turned to face her, his expression incredulous. 'So you are telling me there is a whole… what? A city, down there… people living in darkness?'

'Yes. Well, it's not dark: there is artificial light.' She looked up at the sky and sighed. 'It's not as good as the real thing, though.'

'That's where you were born? That's where you've lived most of your life?'

'We were allowed into the Hexadome to visit our parents a few times when we were little; to begin with, anyway, while they were setting it up. There used to be a passageway from the Citadel to the main dome. Then it was sealed, and we were back down there, with our grandfather.'

'You and Keegan?'

'Yes.'

Something dawned on him. 'That's why you are all so pale!'

'I suppose so. I know we look different from you.'

'And the sun isn't kind to your skin.' He took her hand, turning it about. Her arm was darker now, and raw in places where the skin was peeling.

'It's OK.' She shrugged. 'The worst thing about coming up into the Outlands was not really understanding what I was seeing.'

'No wonder you were confused – and afraid, too.' He remembered yet again her fear when they first met and he had offered her food. Then he smiled. 'But you soon lost your fear, taking on Big Brendan like that.'

'Oh, I had to. The idea of a group of unarmed people attacking the might of the Citadel... You don't know what they can do. The more people Brendan led here, the greater the danger.'

'Yet in the end, it was you who led us all here.'

'Do you think I don't know what I've done? I tried to resist it, but in the end it seemed better to show them the Old City... I hoped they would think fighting was pointless...'

'But you led us to the Hexadome as well.'

'I hadn't reckoned with the Seekers. I hoped the sight of the failed experiment would be enough for them, that it would turn them away, make them see that it isn't paradise...'

'Why did you leave the Citadel?'

'Oh, Jonas, that's such a long story.' She led him back, away from the circle of flattened earth, and they sat for a short time in silence on the soft earth.

'I'm sorry. I shouldn't have asked.'

'No, it's only right you should know. You already know some of it from Keegan, of course.'

She was sitting with her knees raised, her arms circling them, and her gaze far away into the distance - or perhaps into the darkness below.

'I was born and lived my early life deep underground in the Citadel. My grandfather had already succeeded our great-grandfather as Supreme Leader. I knew that I was the granddaughter of someone important; whenever he came into the room, everyone stood up, even my mother, who was his daughter. When my brother and I entered our schoolroom, our teachers stood and greeted us as if we were important adults, and sometimes the soldiers would salute us as we travelled around the corridors.

'It was a life of total control: the air we breathed, the food we ate, what we wore, what we learned, what we saw, all was controlled. We didn't know that at the time, of course, just as we didn't know that what we saw from our windows wasn't real. We were simply told that it was dangerous out there - out here.'

She smiled up at Jonas, ruefully. 'To think that I believed it was worse out here than down there!' She shuddered.

'Keegan and I were of the third generation to be born in that place. We missed our parents when they went to set up the Hexadome, but we were so used to doing as we were told that we accepted it without question. As we grew older, though, Keegan began to ask why we couldn't go outside to see the trees that we could see from our windows. He wanted to know how the water got into our taps and where the dirty water went to; what made our water come out hot from some taps and cold from others. How did the lights work? What made the screens light up when you switched them on? Then he started asking about who had been Supreme Leader before our grandfather's father, and where our parents had gone, and...He was told to stop asking questions, but he persisted, and one day he was no longer with me in the schoolroom. Grandfather told me he was being 'corrected.' I was really lonely without him.

'One day, during that time, Keegan's friend Gambit came to see me on the Recreation Level; we were allowed to spend an hour a day there. He checked there was no-one about, and then furtively handed me a note from Keegan. *Meet me on Horticulture. K'*

'And did you go?'

Shanti nodded, smiling at the memory.

'When I got there he was so excited. He said, "You've got to look at what I've found" and then he led me into a back room off the main complex, stacked with all sorts of obsolete computer equipment. He'd been tinkering with an old machine he'd found: he was really gifted at all that. Grandfather already had him marked out as a future chief of cybertech.

'He had got one of the really old machines working, and that allowed him to show me pictures of Outside. For the first time I saw our world as it really was – as it really is. There was so much more of it than we'd ever dreamed, and some of it was green, and the sky was sometimes blue, with little clouds scurrying along… There were old news bulletins, too, telling a completely different story from the one we'd always been told. We saw pictures of the Old City – deserted, just as we saw it today, but there was old film, too, of when it had been full of people and life. I asked him what it meant, and he said it meant that we had to find a way back there. "We can do it, Shanti!" he said. "We just need to begin educating the others. And we have to be very, very careful not to give ourselves away."

'After that, after Keegan's period of 'correction', he managed to appear completely reconciled to the ways of the Citadel, to our grandfather's regime. He was given more responsibility and that gave him more access to others. He began to tell people the truth, built up a network of trusted individuals, and in time they planned, well, what you saw. We started to find our way back to the world.

'It was only afterwards that we found out what had happened to our parents. That made us more determined than ever.'

In the silence that followed, Jonas was even more horribly aware of how difficult their visit to the Hexadome must have been for her that day. Tentatively, he asked, 'What was it like, that first time you visited, when you were little?'

She screwed up her face, remembering. 'Mixed feelings; it was beautiful, already becoming green, but ruled over by machines, or at least that's how it seemed to us. But we could see the sky through the hexagonal panels; not quite its natural colour, but the real thing for the first time, with clouds drifting. There were a few more short visits after that. Sometimes we heard the rain pattering, or could see that the wind was moving the trees. That must have sowed the seeds of our obsession with getting out, even when we were too young to understand what it was all about. Then it was sealed up, and the visits stopped.'

Jonas placed an arm around her shoulder, and she nestled into him. He had never felt closer to her, nor more sad. Resourceful as he was, he had no idea what any of them could do now. He thought of the Seekers, back beyond the ruined city, patiently waiting to hear what wonders the Hexadome held; the defeated Warriors, their purpose gone. He saw in his mind's eye his little namesake and the child's parents, the friends who had become so dear to him through their journeying together, and the others who had gazed with him in awe at the green and living place, frozen in time, that they had seen that day.

'You know the rest: last year Keegan and Gambit and Vector and their friends shared the discovery of the old records with everyone they trusted; the movement spread like a virus amongst the younger generation. They uncovered the old passageways, found the small dome, started to make plans for a full-scale evacuation; but they really needed to make contact with Outside, with the people who live here. Someone had to go first, and I volunteered.'

'You make it sound simple.'

'Oh, it wasn't, I assure you. It was terrifying. I was completely disorientated, my eyes hurt in the sunlight... I had known no other world until I came here.'

'Was I the first Outlander you'd met?'

She smiled, and nestled closer. 'Thankfully, yes.'

'And I gave you food that terrified you!'

She laughed now. 'It wasn't very easy to eat.'

He kissed her then, properly, for the first time. They were both silent for a while. Finally, Jonas spoke. 'I suppose we should be getting back to the others. There's so much to talk about.'

Shanti nodded and took his hand; Jonas pulled back.

'Are you going to tell them your story?'

'I'm not sure. Would that help the situation?'

He laughed. 'I don't know. We're not being very decisive, are we?'

'Better than making the wrong decisions, I guess.'

'Would you mind if I just have another look at this place? I want to fix it in my mind in case... well, I'm not sure in case of what, but, you know, just in case?'

'Sure.' She released his hand. 'I'll start heading back.'

After a few steps she stopped and turned round.

'Don't be long though, will you?

Chapter Eighteen

For a while Jonas wandered around the area beyond the Hexadome, trying to fix in his mind what he was seeing and what he had just heard from Shanti. His gaze swept over the circular area of flattened earth. All this had been here his whole life, and long before that, yet he had never known of it, never suspected, would never have thought to come here if it hadn't been for Big Brendan. And Shanti; Shanti who would now always be an essential part of his life.

While he was growing up, he had been completely consumed by what was happening in and around his family. He had learned, in a kind of abstract way, that there had been a Before, and that he was living in the After, but as life became harder each year he found himself focusing more narrowly on the Now. His life had opened up again when he made the decision to leave home, a home that was no longer home without the people who mattered, and he had found a kind of contentment in the Woodlands with Will until it was cruelly shattered by the arrival of Big Brendan.

As he studied the strange landscape, he began to make out subtle patterns in the earth: concentric rings, punctuated by smaller circles, and within those circles... something. He stepped inside the outer ring, moved closer to the nearest circle. Leaning over it he could see quite clearly that there was something inside it, something hard and metallic; the end of a pipe or tube... Suddenly his breath was swept away by an uprush of air. He moved cautiously to the next one, and at first there was nothing. Then again he felt the air, and again, and again. The whole circle seemed to be breathing.

What happened next was so sudden that he had no time to make sense of it. It was as though the earth had

228

opened up and swallowed him. He was in darkness, in some sort of enclosed room, small, metallic, and moving. It was moving downwards, and fast.

Even after the room came to a stop, it took Jonas' heart some time to regain its normal rhythm. His breath was still coming out in ragged gasps when one side of the space slid sideways and he had to turn his face away from the dazzling light that met him.

'I do believe we've captured an Outlander.' The voice was harsh, the accent strange.

A second voice addressed him directly.

'What is your name?'

Jonas hesitated. He remembered Shanti's fear of revealing her name, out in his world, and wondered for a moment if he should withhold his, in here. Then he remembered why she had; he had no such reason.

The second speaker approached, pulled him roughly by the arm into the light of the echoing space beyond.

'I asked you your name.'

'Why do you want to know?'

'There is a great deal we want to know, but let's start with your name, shall we?'

'My name is Jonas.'

'And who are you, Jonas?'

Jonas shrugged. 'I'm nobody.'

The other speaker paused, looked him up and down. 'I doubt that.'

Jonas waited. The silences were unnerving.

'You see...' The other man approached him now. He was even taller than the first man, and as he spoke he looked down at Jonas. 'You see, people who are nobody don't usually force an entrance into our Citadel.'

'Ah, well that's the thing. I didn't force an entrance.'

'Don't play with us. How else did you get in here?'

'I truly don't know.' He saw their looks of disbelief but continued. 'It was a complete accident. I was on the surface and then...' He gave another shrug, which seemed to annoy his interrogators further.

They spoke to each other now, ignoring him.

'So, what shall we do with him?'

'The punishment cell? Segregation Unit?'

'The Commander will want to see him first, though.'

'Then we'll take him to the secure room.'

Turning to Jonas the first speaker said, 'Come with us. Now!'

As they moved on into the corridor, a blast of something smelling unpleasantly of chemicals hit all three of them. It made Jonas gag. He coughed and spluttered.

'Decontamination,' said one of the men.

They walked along the brightly lit passageway, one of them behind Jonas, the other in front. There was little opportunity for him to observe his surroundings, and little to see if there had been. The passageway was long and it curved slightly, the only features a series of black dots on the ceiling and a pale green stripe along the wall. The unaccustomed artificial light hurt his eyes and gave off a low sound that troubled his ears. Finally they reached a place where the passage widened out and Jonas glimpsed a series of doors, all shut, that lined the space.

'In there!' His captor pushed on a door and indicated that Jonas should enter. The room was small and featureless. In his whole life he had never experienced confinement. It was a chilling experience.

They left him alone for some time. He wondered if that was part of the plan: time to think, to worry. What was happening above ground? What would Shanti think when he failed to join her? What of his friends: what had they told the others? What decisions were being made? If he focused on the people up there near the Old City he could avoid the claustrophobia of this bare room, and the awful fear that threatened to overwhelm him. No wonder Shanti and Keegan and the others had wanted to be free of this place! Everything about it felt hostile.

The room had a single glowing light in the centre of the ceiling. Clearly there was no shortage of electricity in here. But how much better it would be to see the light of the sun, to feel the stirring of the air in a gentle breeze. He remembered now how Shanti had told him, in that precious time just before the PA caught up with them, that she'd never felt the wind and the rain as a child, never felt the sun directly. At the time he had taken her to be talking about the Hexadome, but now he realised it must have been this deep and dismal place she meant.

The door opened and someone new came in.

'Outlander Jonas! Come with me.' The voice was not friendly.

More long passageways, more faintly humming lights, unnatural in the still, stale air. The floor beneath his feet felt hard as rock, yet it was smooth as still water. His shadow lay pooled at his feet; he wondered how long before he joined it on the ground.

The man, his guard - for what else was he to call him? - halted so suddenly that Jonas almost collided with his back. The guard's sharp tap on the door was followed by an even sharper 'Come in!'

Once in the room, the door closed behind him and the owner of the voice indicated a chair. Jonas couldn't help running his palms over its smooth surface before he sat. It was plastic of a quality superior to anything he had seen on the middenheaps, its legs perfectly balanced and stable on the smooth floor.

'You are interested in chairs?' There was sardonic amusement in the man's voice.

Jonas looked at him for some time without speaking. The man was pale, like Shanti, but his eyes were a much deeper blue. He wore the formal clothes of a century ago, like the people in old photographs his grandmother had amused him with as a child.

Finally, he said, 'Yes. I make them; stools, at any rate.'

'Not from this material, though?'

Jonas shook his head. 'I shape them from wood, cut down and seasoned. Oak is the best, but ash and pine are good too.'

'There are still trees to cut down?'

Jonas looked at him, wondering how to answer. What did this man know about trees? When, if ever, had he seen the world above ground? Jonas could almost pity him.

'I explained to the others: my entry here was purely accidental. I can't tell you how it happened because I don't know, but I would very much like to return to the surface.'

There was a shift in the atmosphere.

'It is not for you to make demands.'

'It was a request.'

'Well, perhaps. But for the moment you will remain here; you are very valuable to us.'

Jonas shuddered. That sounded sinister. He wondered if he was being held hostage against Shanti's return. Before he could pursue this thought, the other man sighed and leaned toward him, as if about to confide a secret.

'Firstly, there is much you can tell us about the state of the world out there. Our knowledge of it is of necessity very limited and we have little means of finding out about it. You are our opportunity.'

'You could come out and see for yourselves.'

There was another sigh, and the man gave a strange little smile. 'That is not possible.'

Jonas opened his mouth to ask why, but was prevented by the sound of hurrying footsteps in the passageway. One of his original guards opened the door abruptly.

'Apologies for the interruption, Commander, but we have reports from the Lookoutware that there are many more of them up there, and some have entered the Hexadome.'

The Commander raised an eyebrow. 'So it is the Hexadome they are interested in?' He gave curt orders to monitor the situation and turned back to Jonas.

'You did not come alone, then?'

'I came alone to this place. I don't think any of the others saw where I went.'

'Can you tell me why those other people came? What is their purpose in entering the Hexadome?' His tone was sharper now, and everything about him seemed on the alert.

Jonas sighed. Where to begin?

'I'll try to explain, but I don't know how much sense it will make to you. They came for different reasons. The Hexadome has become an object of mystical devotion amongst some people. Their lives are hard; many of those they loved have died. They are unsure of what to do with their own lives, and so they set out to find the Hexadome in the belief that it would heal them in some way. Others were angry, or restless; they believe you have everything they want and they think it unfair.'

He did not add that they wished to take it by force: now, in this stronghold deep below the earth, the idea was even more laughable than when Big Brendan first declared it.

The Commander had been leaning forward, listening carefully. He murmured, as if to himself, 'Oh yes; we had beliefs once too. And people who were angry.' He straightened back up and addressed Jonas. 'How did they know about the Hexadome?'

'Who knows? People have talked about it for years; rumours spread. Nobody knew for certain that it existed.'

'And what will they do, now they have seen it?'

'Different people will do different things. That's what they were trying to decide when I missed my way and found myself here.'

The Commander appeared lost in his own thoughts for some moments. 'Hm. I suppose - in a way - it is the same here.' He shifted in his chair and fixed Jonas with a ruminative look. 'I will tell you something: there is a growing restlessness amongst some of our young people. It's hard to know why: they are provided with everything they need and suffer none of the hardships you allude to. They have no knowledge of the world out there, other than that it exists and that it is ruined; yet still they persist in saying they want to see the Outlands for themselves.'

'I suppose it is in human nature to seek something beyond ourselves.'

The Commander gave a hard laugh. 'So our grubby Outlander is a philosopher!'

'We are human beings, as you are.'

'And how many human beings are there, out there?'

'We have no way of knowing. The means of communication were all wiped out in the disasters – as

234

you must know.' For the first time Jonas felt anger rising inside him, along with a frustrating helplessness; in that moment he came closer to understanding Big Brendan than he ever had.

'And yet you say that rumours about the Hexadome spread?'

'Yes, people do talk to each other.' With an effort he let the anger go. 'But we cannot speak to all the people, or even a large number, all at the same time. That has gone for ever.'

The Commander gave a rueful smile. 'In here too. Yes, you look surprised, but we have no means of communication beyond a very limited range. We know nothing of what happens beyond these shores…'

'So there is no way of knowing what is happening to people in the rest of the world?'

'Not from here. It may be that some of the satellites survived, that their signals still function…' He gave himself a shake. 'But all of that is beyond the point. We must deal with the world as it is.'

Jonas waited. He wanted to say that he and the Commander were from two very different worlds, and that one of them had dealt very unfairly with the other; yet he sensed that it was better not to antagonise him if he wanted his freedom.

The Commander spoke again. He seemed to be enjoying his time with Jonas, rather as he might spend time examining a specimen of scientific interest, or as a cat, toying with a mouse.

'Do you have any family, Jonas?'

Jonas briefly described what had happened to his family.

'Ah, the sickness. It still rages?'

'There are so many sicknesses out there it's hard to say what is what; sometimes disease comes from the filth of the middenheaps, where we must search for goods we can no longer make ourselves. Others are passed from person to person; still others are the result of not having enough to eat - '

'Yes, yes, I see.'

Jonas wondered if he had got under the Commander's skin at all. Did the man have *any* conscience?

'Look...' the Commander sat back. 'Let me tell you. When the land began to burn and flood, when the other, the manmade disasters struck – well now, the government of the day had decisions to make. They couldn't stand by and do nothing, nor did they have the means to save everyone. That was when my father was the Supreme Leader. He gathered his family and a few trusted aides and they chose to preserve what could be preserved from the world as it had been, preserve people of ability who could keep things going...'

Jonas sat, motionless, his face stony. His grandmother had always said the problem was a government that had acted too late – and totally lacked compassion.

'Yes, I can imagine what you think of us.'

The Commander paused, then gave his head a little shake, as if to clear it. 'Anyway, we kept going: new generations were born, inculcated with the ways of our lost civilisation. What we have in here, in the Citadel, is all that remains of that civilisation. The first generation had no idea we would have to continue like this for so long, but the Citadel was built to keep our civilisation alive for a future time. Do you see?'

Jonas ached to tell him that a new civilisation was already forming and growing beyond the Citadel; that it was keeping alive the values of hope and compassion; his instinct again told him to hold back.

The Commander fixed Jonas with a piercing look, his eyes glittering in the strange light.

'You have come at just the right moment, Jonas. You can help us.'

Jonas held his look. What was being asked of him?

'Yes. You see, as I said earlier, some of our young people are becoming restless; there seems to be some sort of unspoken connection amongst them: they refuse to conform, they question their elders…'

'How do you imagine I can help?'

'Well, put simply, you can talk to them, find out why they are so rebellious. You can tell them about the world out there.'

Jonas took a deep breath. 'What you mean is: you want me to make them realise that their lives would be much worse if they were living beyond the Citadel? That they are so much better off here? He paused. 'But that's hard for me to say; I mean, I really have no idea what their lives are like in here.'

The Commander stared at him for a while, his eyes narrowed. 'No, I suppose not.' He rose from his chair, opened the door and called down the passage for one of the guards. The guard arrived, panting slightly.

'Yes, Commander. Sir?'

'I want you to show Jonas around the Citadel. He would like to understand what life is like here.'

'All levels, Sir?'

'Yes, all levels.'

'What would be even more helpful…' Jonas was sticking his neck out, but in such a situation, why not?

'It would be really helpful if some of your young people were to show me round. Then we could talk as we go.'

There was a brief silence.

'It would help me to answer your question.'

The Commander grunted. 'Very well. Why not? Guard, go and fetch, let's see… Altair and Fortran. Yes, they would be best for this, I think.' He turned back to Jonas.

'I hope I have made myself clear. I want you to find out why they are like this, what it is they really want; and at the same time give them an idea of how impossible they would find life beyond the Citadel.'

Jonas' thoughts flew to Shanti and Keegan. He supressed them instantly. The Commander leaned forward. There was an urgency in his voice now as he spoke.

'This is a very serious situation; you must see that. If there is any hint of rebellion, we need to stop it before it spreads any further. A great deal depends on you, Jonas.'

Jonas remained silent. What could he say to that? Shanti and Keegan and all the others above ground might have said the same thing to him. It felt like treading a fallen tree across a raging river. His continued silence seemed to unnerve the Commander.

'I will tell you something else.' Now a new note crept into the Commander's voice. It made him seem almost human. 'I am beginning to fear that my own grandchildren are becoming infected by this foolish movement.'

He sat back in his chair, resuming his former manner. 'So, in conclusion, I am hoping you will be able to throw some light on this whole situation, and, quite frankly, help us avert a disaster.'

'That is asking a lot, Sir.' Jonas chose his words carefully.

All the Commander said was, 'Yes. It is.'

During the awkward pause that followed, while each held the other's gaze, the guard returned with two young men. Jonas stood politely while the Commander introduced them. They shook hands with no hesitation.

'These are two more of my grandchildren – and I them trust completely. They understand the rules.' He turned to address them. 'Jonas is our representative of the ruined world out there. I want you to show him the Citadel, give him a chance to talk to people, especially the young ones. He will, I am sure, be able to explain to them why any attempt to leave the Citadel would be inadvisable, to say the least.'

Jonas was following the two young men along the corridor. Like the guards, they were tall and pale, dressed alike in some soft fabric he couldn't identify. He was surprised by their lack of curiosity at being summoned for this strange task. Clearly they were not about to start questioning their elders. What was it the Commander had said? He trusted them completely. That would not make things easy.

One of them - Fortran, he thought - asked, 'Is there anywhere you'd like to see first?'

Jonas shook his head. 'I don't know what there is to see.' He became aware that his stomach was rumbling audibly.

The other one, Altair, said, 'Oh, where are our manners? You must be hungry. We'll start on the Food Level.'

They had reached one of the opening-out places in the passageway. Ahead of them stood a row of metallic doors with no handles. Small lights glowed to the side of each of them. Fortran went ahead of the others and pressed a button. Within seconds the door had slid open. It made Jonas jump, reminding him of his abrupt arrival in this place. He was ushered inside, and the small box began to move, leaving behind Jonas' stomach.

'Are you all right?'

They were seated at last at a table, one amongst what seemed to Jonas a vast number, in a large, echoing space. Quite a few of the other tables were occupied, and the people nearest to Jonas were openly staring at him. He could feel his companions' eyes on him too, but they at least were pretending not to look. He removed his hands from the table, suddenly aware of the dirt beneath his fingernails.

Sitting at a table to eat: that in itself was strange. And the knives and forks, gleaming cold metal; his grandmother had owned a set like that, but it had lost its shine and was rarely used.

Fortran repeated his question. 'Are you all right?' He glanced round at the other diners. 'Don't take any notice of them; they've just never seen an Outlander before.'

Now they were grouped around the table, away from the echoing passages, Fortran seemed friendlier. It had taken a considerable time for them to establish which of the numerous eating places they would choose. All was bustle and bright colours, the noise and constant movement as oppressive as the unremitting brightness of the lights and the conflicting aromas of the various foods.

Despite the smell of cooking, there was no sign of where or how their meal was being prepared. Finally, it was brought to them by two young men who lingered to stare at him until dismissed, a little sharply, by Fortran. After all the fuss and bustle, the food set before them was mostly pale in colour and tasted of nothing much, certainly not the richness of roasted fowl or smoked fish. After a few minutes, another dish was brought to the table; it was a surprise to see that it contained something with green leaves, although he could not identify it exactly.

Noting his surprise, Altair said, 'We'll take you up to Horticulture later and you can see where they are grown.'

'Hmm.' Fortran was frowning. Then he said, 'Actually, yes, Altair. Good idea,' and a look passed between the two young men that Jonas could not identify.

The food at least abated his hunger, and having eaten a similar meal in the small Hexadome, its appearance and taste were not too great a shock. Now there was time to look round. Between and above the tables were arched trellises, garlanded with garish greenery and unfeasibly colourful flowers. Altair noticed his glance.

'Plastic,' he said, with a laugh. 'And what workmanship. Beautiful, don't you think?'

Jonas gave a wan smile. Beautiful? The flowers were ugly, gaudy, and like nothing he had ever seen in the natural world. Looking at them again, he became aware that they were swaying slightly. A breath of air touched his cheek and he glanced round, seeking its source.

Fortran, again noticing Jonas' surprise, explained. 'Air is brought in from outside and purified through the filtration system; then it's pumped round, and when the CO_2 levels measure above a certain level it's pumped out.'

'As if there wasn't enough CO_2 out there already,' Jonas muttered. He recalled the circular tubes he had seen at the surface, exhaling like a living thing, and shuddered.

Altair made to stand. 'Anyway, if you're finished, perhaps we should get on with our tour of the Citadel?'

Before he could move away, a young woman came across from her own table to take the vacant place at theirs.

'Do you mind if I join you?' she asked.

'You already have.' Fortran glanced at Altair as he spoke.

'Hi,' she said, looking at Jonas and extending a hand. 'I'm Emmess. People usually call me Emmy.'

Jonas shook her hand, giving his own name as he did so. The young woman leaned forward, confidentially.

'We heard there were people on the Outside. They try to keep it from us, you know.'

Jonas couldn't think of a suitable reply.

Fortran gave her a warning look. 'Emmy! Don't…'

Emmy ignored him. 'How did you get in here?'

Wearily, Jonas explained that it was accidental. She gave him a knowing look. 'Well, you are welcome, no matter how you got here. Have they shown you the greeting?

'The greeting?'

'Emmy, not now.' Fortran was looking worried.

'Then can we talk later?'

'Yes, if you must. We'll be ending our tour of the Citadel up in Horticulture. Perhaps there?'

'OK.'

She leaned towards Jonas as she stood and whispered something he didn't quite catch, at the same time raising a hand and pointing towards the ceiling.

Politeness compelled him to respond with the same gesture. As he did so, he thought with a pang of the world up on the surface: would he ever again see the wheeling flight of the red kites or feel the wind in his hair?

'It means things will change,' she said, with a knowing look that he couldn't fathom, and then, more quietly, 'Onwards and Upwards!'

'Onwards and Upwards!' he murmured in response.

Emmy turned to the others, mouthing the words again. *Onwards and upwards;* and then, laughing, she raised her eyes to the ceiling.

'Enough, now, Emmy,' said Fortran through clenched teeth. 'We'll see you later.'

The two young men hurried him towards the exit, past tables bearing plates of half-eaten food. When had he last seen anyone fail to eat every scrap? But then they were in a place where plastic was made to look like flowers and chemical substances like real meat. None of it made sense.

'Ignore Emmy,' said Altair. It was only later that it occurred to him that she was probably just the sort of person the Commander wanted him to talk to.

Chapter Nineteen

The Food Store, on the same level, was like a huge version of the place Leo had shown him in the concrete village, although this was sparkling clean and bright with lights, and the sound of electricity hummed steadily from the white cabinets full of frozen foodstuffs. People milled around the shelves, carrying baskets made of wire to collect their chosen items. As they walked around, a number of them stopped Fortran and Altair, although it was clear that Jonas was the real object of their interest. Several of them greeted him with the upraised hand gesture, and he reciprocated with the same. The fact that Fortran and Altair seemed to disapprove only encouraged him.

'Onwards and Upwards,' he said to one young couple, adding a fairly anodyne question about their lives in the Citadel.

'Oh,' the young woman blushed. 'You know. It's OK, I guess.' Her partner pulled a face and glanced at the ceiling. Fortran took Jonas' elbow and steered him away.

'This place is modelled on the old supermarkets,' he said, perhaps more loudly than necessary. 'It helps keep the past alive for people.'

'Is that a good thing - keeping the past alive?'

'Of course.' The sharpness of his tone suggested that there was nothing more to say on the subject.

The moving box - Altair called it an 'elevation chamber' - that they took up to the Medical Floor, was more sumptuous than the one they had used to reach the Food Level, although Jonas still experienced the same sickening lurch as it set off. It was lined with fabric of a kind he had never seen before, and its back wall was entirely covered by a mirror of startling intensity, its silvering complete and unscratched. There he stood, gazing out, alongside his companions, and for the first time glimpsed himself through their eyes: dirty, unkempt, but rudely healthy against their willowy fairness.

He drew in his breath sharply at the gleaming whiteness and fully stocked cabinets of the Medical Centre. There were the same glass-fronted cupboards he had seen in the Hexadome, stocked with packets and bottles and jars containing, no doubt, drugs and medicines far more sophisticated than the simple potions he was able to make.

'My grandmother would have given anything to be able to work with all this,' he said, the wistfulness in his voice arousing the interest of his companions.

'Tell us,' said Altair, and Jonas felt encouraged to tell them a little about her and about his own attempts to use her knowledge of healing plants to help people.

'She sounds wonderful,' said Fortran, his tone devoid of the irony Jonas might have expected.

This emboldened him to ask if he might look more closely at the contents of the cupboards. After a moment's hesitation, Fortran nodded, and Jonas stepped forward and was about to pull the handle of the nearest one when a uniformed assistant stepped forward to prevent him.

'That is not allowed.'

'No, it's all right,' said Fortran, lowering his voice. 'The Commander has authorised him to look at anything he wants to.' He turned to Jonas. 'This is Aiken, one of our most hard-working pharmaceutical assistants.'

Jonas turned to Aiken, feeling a little ridiculous as he raised a pointing finger in greeting. 'Jonas. Pleased to meet you. Onwards and Upwards!'

Aiken looked quizzically at Fortran and Altair, and then, hesitatingly, half raised his own hand. Jonas felt his smile freeze. What had just happened?

Finally, Aiken stepped aside, and Jonas proceeded to examine the contents of the cupboard. As he lifted the first packet of analgesics he was surprised at how light it felt; picking up other items to examine, he realised that most of them were almost empty. He turned to Aiken.

'You'll need to restock soon,' he remarked, remembering how insistent his grandmother had been about keeping her medicines, such as they were, well topped up.

Aiken glanced at Altair, who gave him an almost imperceptible nod.

'I wish I could,' he said in a low voice. 'The original stores are running low.'

'I thought you would be able to manufacture more in here?'

'We could, if we had the ingredients.'

Fortran spoke then. 'Let's show our visitor the hospital.' There was some urgency in his tone, and he ushered Jonas quickly along the passageway.

In the Hospital Area Jonas was again awestruck as he gazed at the surgical equipment stacked behind the glass fronts of tall cupboards. The operating theatre, white and gleaming, took his breath away. He was introduced to a middle-aged woman in a white coat, Dr. Garrett.

'I'm pleased to meet you,' Jonas said, raising his hand to point at the ceiling. 'My grandmother was a doctor.'

Dr. Garrett returned his greeting without hesitation, then asked. 'Are there still doctors out there?'

'Not in the sense you have them,' said Jonas, ruefully. 'I try to use natural remedies where I can, and I have assisted a woman in labour whose baby was stuck in the birth canal.

Dr. Garrett looked surprised. 'Did either of them survive?'

'Thankfully, both did.'

She looked impressed. 'We too have problems,' she said carefully. 'The first generation made sure they included skilled surgeons in the initial intake, but it's been harder to train people since, and now the seniors have passed away, we have to train as best we can using what knowledge we have and some old books and recordings.'

'Best not to get ill if you live in the Citadel,' added Altair. Fortran looked at him sharply.

'Especially if you suffer from a rare condition,' added Dr. Garrett. 'There are so few of us doctors, and we cannot gain wide experience among a reduced population.'

Jonas gave a short laugh. 'It's the same with us. I've reached the point where I need to pass on my knowledge, such as it is, and to exchange ideas with other healers. The world out there needs so many more people who understand the nature of sickness and how to make the medicines.'

There was the sound of a door opening in an adjoining room.

Fortran raised his voice. 'But if you kept the knowledge to yourself, you would be important, would you not?' He spoke as though this were self-evident. His tone had become unfriendly again.

'And rich,' added Altair.

Jonas stared at them with incomprehension; it was as if they were speaking a foreign language.

The Gymnasium level puzzled him even more, as he stared at the strange machines and the straining and sweating men and women using them.

'I don't understand why...'

'Well...' It was clearly a struggle for Fortran to explain something he had never himself questioned. 'It's so everyone can keep fit and healthy.'

Seeing that Jonas was still puzzled, Fortran tried to explain further. 'Much of the work here is boring and repetitive, and a great deal of it involves long hours sitting in front of a computer screen.

'Hm.' It seemed a strange world where artificial activity was needed because everyday life lacked it; where work involved sitting in one place all day, and the equipment made to remedy the situation had the look of instruments of torture.

The running track made more sense, though. He could imagine Big Brendan working off his anger and frustration by pounding round it; not that he'd ever seen Big Brendan running anywhere. His own life included many times when he'd had to run, such as when they went after the wild goats or deer, or when he heard the sound of wild hogs a little too close for comfort. Sometimes, though, he ran for the sheer joy of running, when the sun shone and the new grass was green and tender. Then he remembered the frantic pace of the approaching fire, when he had run for his life, finally outrunning it by plunging into the river; he remembered especially the sense of exhilaration afterwards. This circular track in a barren space looked a poor substitute for such experiences.

A pair of guards passed them, saluting and looking curiously at Jonas as they did so. He did not greet them with *Onwards and Upwards.*

'Shall we go on?' said Altair, tersely.

As they headed back to the elevation chamber, Jonas asked more about the computer screens. He had understood from the Commander that there was no longer a connection with what his grandmother used to call the worldwide web.

'True,' said Altair. 'But we still have computers for all the planning that goes into keeping the Citadel going. You know: how many tons of protein need to be produced in the labs for the next so many months, how many pairs of shoes, of what size, which elevation chambers are due for servicing? They monitor the CO_2 levels, the purity of the water, control the heating and ventilation functions; they deliver education at all grades.'

As if to illustrate his point, Altair opened a door and they looked briefly into a room where dozens of young people were seated in front of computer screens, their faces bathed in the flickering light of the machines before them. To Jonas' eyes they looked miserable. No-one looked up at the intrusion.

'And the surveillance systems,' added Fortran, continuing the previous conversation. 'The computers are linked to the cameras both in here and outside. Up there.' He waved a hand in the direction of the surface. 'Central Control can see at a glance what is happening in the Citadel at any given moment.'

Jonas was unable to conceal a shudder of distaste. 'That must be awful!'

Both young men shook their heads. 'Not at all,' said Altair. 'It ensures everyone is kept safe.'

'Yes,' added Fortran. 'Safe, cared for, and of course it stops anyone from transgressing the rules and expectations of the Citadel. That's essential for the smooth running of our society.'

'The Citadel couldn't operate without rules and careful surveillance. That was the problem before, out there.' Altair's tone suggested there was nothing more to be said.

When Jonas asked, 'And so *does* everyone obey the rules and accept the expectations?' they answered simultaneously.

'Of course.'

'What happens if anyone transgresses?'

'They don't.'

Were they unaware that Keegan had spent time in the - what had Shanti called it? - the Correction Unit? They must have been completely unaware of the advance party of rebels sheltering the crowd of PA and Seeker people in the small Hexadome. Or were they in denial? Then he thought back to Big Brendan and his erstwhile followers. Living in denial was common enough, in here or up there on the surface. He wrenched his thoughts back from what might be happening on the surface, and began to wonder how he was to gather the kind of information the Commander wanted while he was with these two young men who appeared completely satisfied with their lives, while the conversations he'd had with others so far had been very guarded; in fact Altair and Fortran had not really facilitated the kind of conversations he needed to have in order to fulfil his brief, and he wondered what the Commander would say - or do - if he failed in the task. On the other hand, the medical personnel he'd met – neither of them youthful rebels – had shown, without saying as much, a very clear need to leave the Citadel in order to acquire experience and the raw materials for medicines. Yet he felt instinctively that it would be risky to report that to the Commander.

His brain reeling from what he had seen so far, Jonas struggled to suppress his anxiety about what was happening above ground. He so desperately needed to get away, return to Shanti and the others; there were important decisions to be made, and he couldn't expect the PA and the Seekers to wait indefinitely. He must complete the Commander's task as soon as possible to gain his freedom. At the same time, in some other compartment of his brain, it occurred to him that whatever he learned while in this terrible place might be of use to him, and his friends, once he was free.

'The young woman we met, earlier,' he began, hesitantly, as Altair and Fortran ushered him along yet another corridor. Their air of disapproval as she had spoken to him seemed to imply that criticism of the SAR was distasteful to them; and they had seemed in a hurry to end the conversation.

'Emmy?' said Fortran. 'Oh, take no notice of her.'

'Yet my understanding of what the Commander was asking of me was that the sort of people I should be talking to were - '

Altair interrupted him, 'It really is time we were moving on. Come on, let's go!'

Attempting to stand his ground, Jonas tried again. 'I have been asked to explore the nature of the rebellion that the Commander believes is growing amongst the young people of the Citadel. Those are the people I must talk to.'

Anxious looks passed between Fortran and Altair, as they had earlier in the eating place.

'Later,' said Altair, and began leading the way towards the elevation chamber. Jonas had to jog to catch up with him.

'And, for the record,' Altair threw over his shoulder, 'Emmy is not a rebel.'

As the day wore on, the various floors and sections were beginning to run together in Jonas' mind. Each time they entered one of the elevation chambers the sudden motion had the same brutal effect on his innards as on all the other trips he'd made before. He wondered how long it took to get used to it. He also had a sudden discomfiting thought: what would happen if the power failed? He hadn't noticed any stairs anywhere on his travels.

Down at the deepest level he was shown a brief glimpse of the manufactories, where the practical needs of the Citadelians were met. There was a chill in the air which he had not experienced before in this place.

'Yes,' said Fortran. 'We are so deep here it's impossible to keep the temperature even. The computer intranet doesn't function down here either.'

Jonas was about to ask how the rest of the Citadel was heated, but in the vast room they were now entering his attention was taken by the huge metal receptacles, heaving and bubbling with liquid, and his mind was drawn away from the other question. It was only much later that he registered the particular emphasis of Fortran's last remark.

'Fermentation vats,' said Altair. 'Microbes are fed with hydrogen, oxygen and something else...'

'Nitrogen,' Fortran supplied. 'You always were a bit of a duffer in Chemistry!' He gave his friend a playful cuff on the arm, and for a few seconds Jonas had a vision of them as schoolboys, relaxed, unguarded; then it was gone.

'That liquid you see is rich in protein.' Altair had taken up the explanation again. 'If we go next door, you'll be able to see the next part of the process.'

One of the operatives in the adjoining room showed him the yellow powder, huge silos of it, while others were packing it into tubs and loading them on to trolleys. Jonas looked enviously at the wheels, which moved with the smoothness of swans on a lake.

'It's used to make bread, noodles, pancakes, porridge – whatever is needed.'

Another added, 'Upstairs in Food Processing, they make it into meat substitute products.'

'Thank you,' said Jonas, raising an upward pointing finger in response to the same gesture from some of the workers gathered around him. The people down here seemed less subdued than the ones he'd met on the higher levels. Some even murmured the *'Onwards and Upwards'* response, and he thought he heard one of them murmur 'Things will change.'

As they walked, Fortran told him that the workers on this level were mostly the descendants of the original builders.

'They had to be given space in here to prevent them from giving away the secret to the outside world.' He spoke dispassionately.

Jonas wondered how much his companions knew about the history of their home. He ventured a direct question. 'So when, exactly, was the Citadel built?'

'Long before the worst of the disasters,' said Fortran. 'The government of the day had been planning something of this nature for a very long time. Shall we look at the Fabrics Room?'

So they did know. Why then were they not showing more concern at the implications of that action? Learning about the dissatisfaction of the young people of the Citadel was beginning to seem an impossible task.

'If you have other things - other duties - you need to attend to, I'm sure I could find my own way around for a while,' he ventured.

'That is entirely against our orders,' said Altair. 'Besides…' he gave a nervous laugh, 'I don't think you'd be safe on your own. Trust me.'

He would have to be content with that, he supposed, although as for trusting his companions, well, that was another matter entirely.

As if to put a stop to this conversation, Fortran walked briskly towards the rubber-edged doors of the Fabrics Room; they flipped open at his touch, and Jonas found himself in a room noisy with the clatter of machinery. One or two of the workers raised a hand, and Jonas signalled back.

'In here,' Fortran said, raising his voice and facing Jonas, 'Is where fabrics are made from plastic and cotton waste.' Jonas could barely make out the words above the noise.

'Where does the power come from?' he yelled.

'Photovoltaic cells, mostly. Highly efficient ones, using the most recent perovskite technology.'

Of course! He had seen them, with Shanti. His heart contracted at the thought of her.

'And in here,' said Altair, sweeping on through another set of doors, his voice booming in the quieter space, 'Is where the stuff is broken down for recycling.'

Jonas stared down into the great tanks of plastic porridge.

'Plastic-eating enzymes,' said Altair, following his gaze. 'Plastic alone in this one, and over here, plastic and cotton combined.'

'Makes dirt-repellent fabric,' added Fortran.

Another reminder of Shanti: the soft fabric of her dress, so different from everything he'd known before; different, like her.

They continued at a dizzying pace, through Stores and Leisure Sports and Engineering, up and down in the elevation chambers, along passageways and through doors all made from the same materials. Jonas could only begin to imagine the scale of the operation to construct this place.

Horticulture had been mentioned a number of times. Fortran and Altair seemed quite keen to show it to Jonas, and for his part it was the place he was most interested to see, although he found it hard to imagine how anything could be grown within the Citadel. Then he remembered the fresh vegetables he'd been given at lunchtime and his heart lifted a little.

They were finally on their way up to the highest level, where Horticulture was situated. The first section they entered was Hydroponics. He saw a high ceiling, painted light blue and dotted with stylised representations of white clouds; powerful lights beamed down on rows and rows of troughs. Plants in various stages of growth reminded him a little of what he had seen in the Hexadome, except that here their roots were visible in the channels of water flowing slowly towards some unseen destination, to be chemically recycled, he supposed. Beyond the troughs were circular ponds, stocked with fish. Pity for them swelled in him as he watched the creatures swimming round and round in the murky water. He hoped the others would take his silence for admiration.

'This is where fresh fish comes from,' said Fortran, a little unnecessarily. 'Obviously, it is for special occasions only.'

'But,' Altair added, 'The fish also provide fertiliser for the fruit and vegetables we grow.'

Jonas continued to watch the sad creatures swimming futilely round their small ponds and said nothing.

'In addition to human waste, of course,' said Fortran.

In the next room they showed him the results of the fertiliser programme; he was impressed by the healthy-looking salads and beans growing in long rows, and found that, again, it reminded him of the Hexadome, although this place was far more rigidly organised. Around the walls, trees grew in huge pots, their branches trimmed and stretched to form a spread-eagled network along the walls. Up close he was awestruck by the unflawed nature of the fruit: plums and pears and apricots, all quite even in size. He remembered how his grandmother had gone over the fruit they collected from around the fields and woods, carefully cutting out the rotted or diseased parts. For the first time in his life, he looked at apples that were perfectly rounded, their skin shiny and unbroken. Then a question occurred to him.

'How are they pollinated? You have no insects in here, do you?'

Fortran called over one of the assistants. 'Pascal! Can you tell Jonas about pollination?'

Pascal was happy to explain, pointing to a collection of small brushes lying on a table. In his turn, he asked,

'And what about in the Outlands? There are no bees?'

'They've begun to return,' Jonas said, with a smile, 'And a few other insects besides.' He tried to imagine the tedium of collecting pollen from every single blossom to pollinate all the others.

Suddenly, Fortran asked, 'Are you tired?' and then, without waiting for an answer, 'There's a place you can rest.'

The place they chose to sit was a surprise. It was a small room adjoining the one in which he had admired the fruit and vegetables. The lighting was dim, and he found it a relief after the unrelenting evenness of the light that suffused the corridors and public rooms. Fortran and Altair led the way to a corner where some chairs were placed, facing one another as if having a casual conversation of their own. Jonas sat gratefully and looked up at the ceiling, which was completely festooned with vines, real ones; he almost wept at the sight of the bourgeoning clusters of fruit.

Before he could comment Fortran smiled and said, 'No, they're not made of plastic!'

The chairs they sat on were, however, made of plastic, and not unlike ones Jonas had sometimes seen on the middenheaps, except that these were unbroken and sparkling clean.

'Now it's your turn.'

'Sorry?'

'We've shown you how we live. Now we want to know about your life. Your life out there.'

Chapter Twenty

Back at their makeshift camp the Seekers and the remnant of Big Brendan's PA were growing fidgety. The ground was hard and people were beginning to move about restlessly to stretch their legs. Some of the children had begun a game of tag, and their squeals of laughter lifted the general mood for a while, until a small girl tripped over another child's foot and began to howl. There was an argument as to whose fault it was, and parents ran to separate the children. Now the mood turned to uneasy speculation.

'They've been gone a long time.'

'Do you think something's happened to them?'

'No, it's a big place that Hexadome, isn't it?'

'Yeah, stands to reason it'll take them a while.'

'But what are we supposed to do in the meantime?'

'Mum, I need a wee.'

'Over there, in the trees.'

'Will you come with me?'

'Oh, I wish they'd come back.'

'I hope they're all right.'

Finally, Big Brendan was sighted heading back in their direction, followed by the small group chosen as their representatives. They were immediately surrounded by a crowd shouting questions.

Big Brendan told them to sit down, then deferred to Robin to address the crowd. As he began, someone called out, 'Where are Jonas and Shanti?' and a hubbub of consternation broke out.

'It's all right,' said Robin, as soon as he could make himself heard. 'They're fine; they're just behind us.'

He looked around, making eye contact with as many of the crowd as he could, Seekers and PA alike.

'This is important. Will you please sit down?'

The people duly did, sitting as close to Robin as they could and hushing the small children.

Robin continued to address them.

'We have decisions to make about what we do next. We've seen the Hexadome and it's breath-taking, full of growing things.'

There were exclamations of excitement at this, especially among the Seekers, and questions were thrown out. Robin used his outstretched hands to signal the need for calm.

'You will all get your chance to see it for yourselves – much better than listening to me trying to describe it.'

The crowd quietened down a little.

'But it is no longer in use. The plants are growing wild; some of them are dying. It needs to be cared for.'

'What about the SAR?' one of Big Brendan's followers called.

Big Brendan shook his head, but again deferred to Robin.

'No,' Robin said. 'We saw no people, no sign of government. The Hexadome is clearly no longer in use by them.'

'Is it beautiful?' someone asked.

'Yes.' It was Big Brendan who answered. 'Very beautiful.'

There was silence for a time.

Alison stood then. She had been quietly cradling young Jonas, and now that he was asleep she laid him carefully on the ground and went to stand beside her husband.

'As Robin said before, we have decisions to make. There is no enemy here for us to defeat: wouldn't you agree, Brendan?'

Brendan nodded.

Alison continued, 'The Hexadome is a good place, even though bad things happened there in the past. I'm not sure we can make any decisions until everyone has had a chance to see it.'

There was a murmur of approval.

'I think we need to wait for Shanti and Jonas to help organise that, though.' Alison was craning her head. There was still no sign of them.

Brendan stood up. 'Do you think we should go and look for them?'

'Perhaps we should all go and look for them?' Alison could see that the people were becoming increasingly restless. After walking so far, driven by a powerful sense of purpose, the waiting and not knowing was hard.

Someone else said, 'We can go to the Hexadome and see if they're there. Two birds, one stone.'

Robin held up his arms to still them for a moment. 'OK, but remember, it may not be exactly what you were expecting.'

'Understood,' said Tabitha, hanging on to Sam as she stood. 'But you're right: we do need to see for ourselves.'

Despite their eagerness finally to reach the Hexadome and see it up close, the crowd moved slowly, weary and perhaps reluctant to have their dreams spoiled. It was, after all, the dream that had sustained the Seekers for so long. For the Warriors it was different; they had been kept going by the idea of an enemy to fight. Their futile onslaught on the Old City had been disillusioning, but now the hope of something better than revenge was held out: a place of peace and light and green and growing things, a place that had been so important to the builders of the Old City that they had made it before abandoning their cold, hard buildings of glass and steel.

As they walked, Big Brendan was puzzling hard. He had assumed all along that the Hexadome - The City as he had stubbornly called it - was some kind of fortress, even if others had clearly entertained different ideas about what it was. In the end everyone had been surprised. They had found the Old City a deserted ruin, and the Hexadome too, for all its fading beauty, was also deserted. So where were they, the politicians he'd hated all his life? Shanti had said The City was not there. Then where? No-one else seemed to have even asked the question. He said as much to Robin and Alison.

'No. That's why we really need Shanti here.' Robin peered ahead anxiously, but the space before the Hexadome that they were now crossing was empty.

Alison said, 'We won't be able to get inside without her.'

'Are you worried about her?'

'A bit. Aren't you?'

The shout startled them. They barely recognised her as she came running towards them, her hair flying and tears streaming down her face, a Shanti they had never seen before.

'Have you seen Jonas?'

'We were going to ask you the same...'

'I don't know what's happened to him.' For the first time ever, she sounded defeated.

'Shanti...' Robin faced her, taking hold of her arms to still her. He could feel her trembling. 'Try to stay calm and tell us what has happened. When did you last see him?'

She took a few gulping breaths. 'We were heading back, and he said he just wanted to look around.'

'In the Hexadome?'

She hesitated. 'No. Somewhere else.'

'So you came on ahead?'

'Yes. He said he'd follow me in a few minutes. We felt we needed to come back and discuss what we are going to do next...' Her voice faded and she looked round wildly.

'It's OK, Shanti. We'll find him. We haven't come all this way with him to lose him now.' Despite his words, Robin's expression was grim.

Alison spoke up again. 'Would it be a good idea to let the others into the Hexadome while we try and find out what's happened?'

Shanti shook herself. 'Yes, good idea. But we'll need to limit how many are in there at a time.' She turned to Big Brendan. 'Could you be in charge of that, Brendan?'

'Oh no. I'm coming with you.' Brendan's fists were clenched in front of him, and he seemed to grow in size, flexing his muscles. 'If those bastards have harmed him...'

In the end it was Tabitha's son Sam who undertook crowd control, while Brendan rounded up a few of his henchmen and Joe Farmer agreed to show the groups round inside the Hexadome. Shanti opened the big entrance door for them and returned to the others.

Oblivious of the anxieties in what had now become an unofficial leadership group, the first group of Seekers and Warriors filed slowly forward, while the others waited as patiently as they could.

Shanti rejoined the little group waiting outside, looking apprehensively at Brendan. She murmured a warning to the big man.

'All I ask is, please don't go looking for trouble.'

'No,' he grunted. 'Understood.' He jutted his jaw. 'So, what do you want us to do?'

By the time they had searched extensively round the Hexadome and the field of solar panels, it was beginning to get dark, and reluctantly Shanti agreed that they should postpone further searching until the next day.

'He'll probably be back by then anyway,' said Alison.

The change in Fortran and Altair's manner was puzzling. They seemed both more relaxed, seated in the room with the grapevines, away from the main lights, and yet at the same time more on edge. Having been tasked with explaining their lives to him, they hadn't been very forthcoming; nor had they offered Jonas much opportunity to ask the ordinary people of the Citadel any really searching questions. Responding to their request for information about his life, in what they called the Outlands, would require some effort.

'I don't know what you've been told about the world as it was when your predecessors left it. Whatever you've heard, it is still like that, probably worse than you imagine.'

And yet that was only part of the truth: how to tell them about the way people who had lost their families grouped together to form new families, as he had with Robin and Alison; about the raw beauty of nature, even in that wasted land; how they grubbed about on middenheaps to find old things to reuse, and made new ones only when there was nothing suitable? He described the attempts at farming the land to grow food with limited resources; the joy of catching a shining fish in clean, unpolluted streams, the way the song of the birds lifted

263

their spirits, and how the sight of the trees growing green again filled his heart.

They were listening intently, he could sense it, hanging on his words. His description of the squirrels and the deer and the other creatures his companions had never seen seemed to draw from them a longing that was at odds with their loyalty to the SAR.

Fortran asked, 'Who makes decisions?'

This was a question he had never needed to consider before: he would need to think for a minute before answering. His companions waited patiently.

'Well... we do; we make decisions. If we're on our own, we make our own decisions, and if we have a family, or live in a village, we try to make decisions together. It's the only way to survive when life is tough. And there is no longer any government, benign or otherwise, to make decisions for the people.'

Fortran winced at his final comment. 'So life is tough?

'Of course, what would you expect? We have no electricity to speak of, no secure buildings, no hospitals, no means of transport - although I have heard some people are trying to train horses to carry them.'

'What? Really?'

'I've not seen it myself, but of course that's what people did hundreds of years ago, before the age of motor vehicles. The animals pulled carts, too...' His mind went to his own cart, and the hard labour it had been to push it. 'And not everyone is contented, of course. Some people are still angry...'

There was another pause; it seemed Fortran was trying to decide whether he should say something further.

Finally, he began.

'Look, Jonas, please don't be offended; I hear what you are saying about the hardships, and I can understand that people are angry, but you know, some of us find life tough in here too. Especially since the rumours started.'

Rumours! He must be careful to give nothing away. Shanti had told him the network was spreading, but that might not be what Fortran meant, and if it was, then there were people he must protect, like Keegan and Vector. How could he forget the openness of their welcome at the small Hexadome, or the kindness with which they had treated the bedraggled Seekers? Strange to think that there were rumours here too, when it was rumours out there that had spread and grown and raised people's hopes and finally brought so many of them here, brought him to this place.

His tone was guarded as he asked, 'Rumours?'

'That there are people on the outside seeking the Hexadome; that they believe it can be brought back to life; that things could be different...' He hesitated. 'For *all* of us.' Fortran dropped his voice. 'That it might be possible to live on the outside.'

What was he saying? Was this sympathy, or a trap? Instead of responding directly, Jonas asked another question.

'You said "some of us find life in here tough." Does that include you? Because your lives seem pretty easy to me.'

'If you consider complete lack of freedom easy.'
This was Altair, and there was a bitterness in his tone that hadn't been there earlier in the day.

'Complete regimentation, severe punishment for thinking for yourself - '

'Whoa, whoa, Altair.' Fortran placed a restraining hand on his friend's arm.

Cautiously, Jonas asked another question.

'What does the Commander say about these rumours?'

His companions shook their heads. Altair gave a nervous laugh, but neither spoke.

'I don't understand. What does he say?'

They remained silent. There was still the trace of a nervous grin on Altair's face.

'Why is that funny?'

Still nothing.

'Look...' he spoke more sharply than he meant to. 'I had no intention of entering this place; it was entirely accidental. I don't want to be here, but I seem to be a prisoner. I have been asked by the Commander for my insights into why the young people are rebelling against the regime, and I am hoping very much that when I have done that I will be allowed to leave and rejoin my own people.'

Fortran and Altair once again exchanged glances. Jonas was getting tired of it. He was also trying very hard to suppress his anxiety about Shanti and their friends.

'What is this? What are you not telling me?'

Fortran nodded to Altair, who leaned forward and spoke in a low voice.

'OK. Here's the thing. We are out of camera range here -- '

Fortran completed the sentence. 'But we can't stay too long or they'll get suspicious.'

It took him a moment. Of course: the black dots on the ceilings! But this ceiling was obscured by vines.

'You're being spied on! You said there were cameras...'

'The Regime call it 'nurtured'. But look...' Altair began to speak quickly. 'When the time comes, we can get you out. Wait, hear what I have to say, please!' He took a deep breath. 'We understand that you want to get out.

There is a growing movement of people in here who also want to get out. It's vital the Commander has no idea we're involved in that - '

'Which is why,' Fortran interrupted, 'We have had to pretend to be completely orthodox members of the SAR.'

The look he gave Jonas was deeply serious. 'We are trusting you with our lives, Jonas.'

'OK. Go on,'

'But there are plenty of people who are completely opposed to any sort of change, especially if it came from outside. Their grandparents made this place to keep the SAR safe, and they would die to defend it.'

He should have felt greater surprise than he did, but somehow the feeling of his whole world once more shifting on its axis was by now simply familiar. Ever since leaving the Woodlands, nothing had been as it appeared; and so he was unsurprised at his own quick acceptance of this change in his companions.

He returned to what they had said about the danger they were in if the SAR knew their real feelings.

'You say they are capable of killing? And they have weapons, the regime?'

'Oh yes. There's a surveillance system on the surface, with weapons ready to target any incursion.'

'I was lucky to escape then!'

'The Commander must have given orders to capture the first Outlander to approach – precisely for the purpose he is putting you to.'

'And...' Altair shuddered, 'They wouldn't hesitate to use them on anyone who tried to leave, us included.'

'So how do you propose to get me out, when the time comes?'

Altair grinned openly now. 'How do you feel about dark tunnels? You're not claustrophobic, are you?'

It took a moment or two to compose himself. Were they talking about the same tunnels Shanti had told him about? Tunnels like the one beyond the small Hexadome? During the short silence, Fortran said, urgently,

'Look, we've trusted you not to betray us. You must know the consequences for us would be...' He left the rest unsaid, but his expression was enough for Jonas.

'Then you have to trust me too. And first of all I need to know more about life in here, because I still have to report back to the Commander. Unless, of course, you're planning to get me out before then?'

'No, we can't do that. There is still a lot to do before the full extent of the plans for the Evacuation can be realised.'

'The Evacuation?'

'Yes. Up to now it's been a vague plan. Those signs you have been exchanging with people; all that *Onwards and Upwards* stuff. It's how the rebels communicate, how they recognise each other.'

'So Emmy...'

'Yes, she's part of it. And now you are officially part of it too.'

'Which is why...' Altair leaned forward, earnestly, 'We must deflect any suspicion from ourselves; otherwise, they'll separate us from you.'

Jonas nodded. 'OK. Yes, I understand.'

'Then the chain of communication would be broken...'

'And... I didn't imagine it, did I? You were keeping me away from people?'

Fortran nodded. 'We don't think the SAR know about the network, but it was safer not to risk people being obvious about it.'

They remained silent as an attendant came in to perform some task on the vines. When he had left, Jonas asked them to tell him something about the social structures of the Citadel.

Altair pulled a face. 'It's based on family. This whole place is one big family – supposedly! The ruling elite are literally family, have been since the beginning. The First Commander set this place up with our grandfather, the present Commander, and the whole of the ruling council is related by blood. There are no elections, like there were in the old world. The First Commander brought in his family and closest friends and allies - '

Jonas interrupted. 'In other words the ones with enough money and power to build this place.' It was the sort of thing Grandmother used to say about the government of her own day.

'They had the foresight to see what was going to happen on the surface. They put walls around the Old City, but the building of this place was begun a long time before the disasters, so that, when the time came...'

'And they knew there wasn't anything they could do for the people...' Fortran added, 'Because by then it was too late.

'So they abandoned the Old City and sealed this place.'

'And then they had to institute a regime that would subdue the inmates, keep them in line...'

As they continued to speak, it became clear to him: this was a place where hard-hearted and hard-headed pragmatism ruled, the inhabitants treated as objects to be managed, and at the same time encouraged to spy on one another. He learned that, as children were born in what might at first have been seen as a temporary refuge, they were separated from parents for most of the time, educated to a narrative of a ruined world, that they were the only people worth keeping alive, that there was nothing out there for them...

A thought struck him.

'There must be a limit to how many people this place can hold. What happens if too many children are born?'

The look that passed between Altair and Fortran was enough to quell any inclination to pursue this question.

He sighed.

'So what am I going to tell the Commander about his young people?'

'Tell him you need more time to talk to us, to take in all you've seen.'

Altair was looking anxious. 'We'd better move now.'

As they stood to begin moving back into the main part of Horticulture, Emmy appeared. She looked disappointed to see they were leaving and dragged another chair over to their corner.

'We can't stay much longer, Emmy.' Altair sat down again but looked ready for flight. 'We've already been here a while.'

'OK, quickly then: I've been around and about, spreading the word. We meet tomorrow down in Manufacturing.' She turned to Jonas. 'There are so many people wanting to meet you.'

Fortran looked panicked. 'That's a sure way of getting us caught.'

'Oh, it's all right, it won't look like a mass meeting; I've told people to drift down there in ones and twos over the course of the morning.' She turned back to Jonas. 'They can't track us down there.'

He nodded his understanding. Of course: Fortran had said that the intranet didn't function at that depth.

'So...' she looked meaningfully at Fortran and Altair. 'When is the great Evacuation? Have you set a date?'

'Maybe,' said Altair, through clenched teeth. 'But we're not ready to make it public yet.'

'OK. I'll just have to wait,' she said, and raised her hand to Jonas, pointing upwards as before.

He reciprocated. 'Onwards and Upwards.'

Emmy repeated the words, adding. 'Freedom. Change will come.'

Fortran and Altair both said, 'Shh!'

Chapter Twenty-one

Jonas was following Altair and Fortran along yet another corridor, distinguished only by the colour coding for the different levels – this one had a purple stripe along the walls. Two men were coming towards them, and he had only enough time to comment on the fact that everyone seemed to be dressed identically before he registered with a shock that one of them was Keegan.

'There you are. The Commander was wondering where you were.' His tone was clipped, slightly irritated. He turned to Jonas, looking him up and down. 'So this is the Outlander?'

There was no flicker of recognition as he escorted Jonas back to the Commander's office.

'Have you got all the information you need?'

Jonas kept his gaze on the corridor ahead. 'No, not really. Altair and Fortran have told me why this is a good place to remain, but I have no idea why anyone would want to leave.'

'Then perhaps you need to speak to those who do.'

He was still feeling stunned after Keegan had escorted him back to the Commander's room, with no opportunity to say goodbye to Fortran and Altair.

The Commander was sitting where Jonas had last seen him. He wondered if he ever left his office.

'So, tell me: what have you seen?'

Briefly, he enumerated the various sections, mentioning the Hospital, with its failing supply of drugs and the difficulties of training new medics. He presented this as his own observation, anxious not to incriminate the people he'd met.

'Yes.' The Commander spoke as if with great reluctance. 'It is true that we are beginning to run into serious problems in that regard. Our supplies are inevitably depleted and we can't source the ingredients needed to make new medicines. We lack the knowledge of how to make new medical instruments... we have problems, yes.'

Jonas couldn't prevent a wry smile.

'You are just like us! Worse off, in some ways; at least we can use the resources that are out there, even if they are inferior. We can go on developing new ways of treating sickness. What will you do when you run out completely?'

The Commander frowned. 'You must understand that this is a problem not widely known. Even Altair and Fortran cannot know the extent of the problem. In any case, our scientists are working on it. That cannot be the cause of the unrest amongst our young people though, surely?'

'No, not on its own; and if, as you say, most of them have no idea there is a problem.'

'So what else have you seen?'

Jonas replied that he had seen the running track, the manufactories, the restaurants, the hydroponics and so on.'

'And?'

'They don't tell me much about your people's state of mind. But if you've never seen the beauty of the natural world...'

The Commander's response was one of genuine surprise. 'Beauty? Even now?'

'Yes, even now.'

The Commander was no longer fully upright in his chair. He seemed somehow to have sunk into it. When he spoke again, it was a little hesitantly.

'The originators of the Citadel expected this to be a short-term solution to a problem – once it was solved we could all go out and continue as before. That is something you may not be aware of.'

Jonas looked at him pityingly. Didn't he know that it would never be as before?

Suddenly the Supreme Commander looked weary and defeated.

When Jonas woke next morning in the small, prison-like room he had been allocated, he was initially unable to make sense of his surroundings. It had been dark when he went to sleep, but now it was growing gradually lighter. There seemed to be light, not from the unit on the ceiling, but from a window that revealed the sun rising over a ruined landscape. Puzzled, he got up and crossed to the window. There was no means of opening it, but as he pressed his face to the glass he could see a little further to the side. A forest of blackened, shrivelled trees met his gaze: he couldn't recall seeing anything any trees close to the perimeter of the Citadel, charred or otherwise.

Someone tapped sharply on his door, and he jumped back from the window, guiltily. There was another knock, and a voice said, 'Jonas? Can we come in?'

So he hadn't been locked in then? He hastily opened the door, and his companions from the previous day entered, carrying a tray of food and drink.

'We will have breakfast with you,' said Altair, placing the tray on the small table.

To begin with, they ate in silence, apart from a few polite questions about what sort of night he had passed.

Then Altair said, 'The Commander has told us we must introduce you to some of the suspected rebels

274

today,' his eyes raised towards the black dot on the ceiling.

'Ungrateful scum!' Altair's lip curled as he spoke.

'Brace yourself!' said Fortran as they left the room.

Night was falling and the people were still gathered in the open air near the Hexadome, weary and completely undecided as to what they should do next. They had marvelled at the unexpected nature of the domes, even the erstwhile PA members, and then decided they should find somewhere to spend the night. The suggestion of returning to the ruined city was not popular, especially when the word rats was mentioned, and there wasn't room for all of them in the Hexadome. In the end some volunteered to sleep out under the stars – after all, they had been doing that, off and on for months as they travelled; others bedded down under the hexagonal panels of the great dome itself.

The search for Jonas had proved fruitless, as Shanti had suspected it would. If they were unable to find him above ground, then that strongly suggested that he was below, and not by his own choice. As the people quietened down Shanti and some of the others held an urgent meeting.

'If Jonas isn't back by morning, we'll have to make decisions without him.' Shanti bit her lip; it had cost her a lot to acknowledge that he might not be back.

Robin looked doubtful. 'We can't make decisions for everyone here.'

'True, but we should help them look at what the options are.'

Alison joined in. 'What about the Hexadome? Joe Farmer looks ready to begin restoring it any minute, if not sooner!'

'What if they all want to? There isn't room, is there?'

'No, not for them to live inside it, obviously. But if those who want to work it had some sort of shift system, and
meanwhile built places to live…'

'But I thought you said it had to be a sealed system, Shanti?'

Shanti thought for a moment. 'Yes, it had to be, if it was going to be completely self-sufficient, but it was made in a time when they believed the air would become unbreathable out here. We know that's no longer the case. And in any case, the airlock still works.'

'I hate to mention this,' said Robin, but we have a more immediate concern: people are starting to get hungry.'

Shanti took a deep breath. 'OK. I can do something about that.' She smiled at their puzzled looks. 'We provided food before, didn't we? Right from under the Regime's noses.'

Robin began to speak, 'It's a long way back to the small dome; you can't expect…' but Alison cut him short.

'No, I don't think Shanti means that, do you?'

Shanti drew a deep breath. 'I need to tell you something.'

If they were only mildly surprised by Shanti's account of the Citadel, it was because so much had happened in the past weeks that they were past being surprised by anything new.

'Ah, yes,' said Brendan. 'I'd been wondering where the SAR were hiding.'

'I showed Jonas where it is. I think that's where he must be; otherwise he'd have come back before now.'

'And you're thinking of going in there for food supplies, and while you're in there you just might rescue Jonas.' Robin shook his head.

Alison asked, 'Will Jonas need rescuing?' and Shanti's expression was answer enough.

'Then it's too dangerous for you to go back there, Shanti.'

'Shh, Robin. I'm not going to go in the front door. But the tunnel to the small dome is only the main one: there are others that join it.'

'And is there one near here?'

'Oh yes.'

Brendan spoke up again. 'You'll need help transporting the supplies. Count me in.'

'I'd sooner you stayed here and kept an eye on things. Will you do that?'

To no-one's surprise, Brendan refused.

'You need someone strong. To look out for you.'

Alison and Robin looked at each other and Alison spoke for both of them. 'Yes. We'll help.'

Shanti shook her head. 'I'm sorry, but you can't take a baby in there. It's really too risky.'

After a brief discussion, Robin and Alison reluctantly decided that she would have to stay with young Jonas, as she was still giving him some feeds. It was further agreed that they would need someone else with them, and they decided to ask Leo.

They slept and were up before the dawn.

'So you see,' Fortran was saying, somewhat pompously, as they headed along another interminable corridor, 'Sleep is regulated by the changing light coming through the windows. Most people think they are in a tall tower, looking down on the surrounding land. They can see it is utterly barren and destroyed, so no-one wants to venture out.'

'Yes. People are such simpletons!' Altair now seemed to be enjoying the role he was playing, although privately Jonas thought he was overdoing it a bit.

They took him to yet another area he hadn't seen. His eyes opened wide with astonishment: a gently lapping pool, for swimming, he was told, fed by a waterfall and surrounded by rocks that might have been real, until you touched them. There were even imitation bird calls. They lingered for some time, Altair and Fortran glancing periodically at the time-tellers they carried.

Finally, Fortran said, in an exaggeratedly casual tone, 'Do you think it's time we moved on? There's still a lot
Jonas hasn't seen.'

'Why not?' said Altair, with a grin.

They had reached the entrance to the elevation chamber, where they were met by Keegan. He gave a curt nod to Fortran and Altair and then addressed Jonas.

'We'll take you back to the lowest level this morning, where the manufactories are situated,' he said, looking slightly to the left of him. 'There are some things you haven't yet seen.' His tone of voice had the same clipped quality as the previous day.

This was disorientating. Of course, he had known that Keegan spent his time moving between the small dome and the Citadel, and it would be essential, when inside, to maintain an orthodox persona as an important member of the SAR – or was it the other way round? With a shiver of fear, he found himself wondering which was the real Keegan, and which the pretence.

As they passed through the various rooms in Manufacturing, with their different processes and robotic machines, he recognised the familiar damp chill in the air from his previous visit, and the mind-numbing sounds of the machinery. In the last room of all - one he had not been shown before - a large group of people was already gathered. He was greeted by the now-familiar raised index finger, wondering that they dared to make it in the presence of Keegan. But surely that was a good thing, showing he could be trusted?

Abruptly, Fortran began to speak, raising his voice to make himself heard. 'You have been summoned here today to give evidence of your grievances to our visitor. You should also know that any attempt to create any kind of uprising or protest about the way the Citadel is regulated will be seen as a criminal attempt to undermine the whole fabric of the Citadel and its governance.'

What was going on? This didn't feel like a protest meeting. Why the formality all of a sudden? He wondered again if Fortran and Altair were unaware of Keegan's part in the movement.

Just then Emmy sauntered in, followed by two or three more at intervals. She came to stand next to Jonas, as though they were old friends.

He was watching Altair, who now also raised his voice to add, 'You are advised to be completely honest in your responses to his questions; your activities are already known, and so you have nothing further to lose. Do you hear me?'

All this time, Keegan had stood stiffly by, his face revealing nothing. After being asked to believe so many impossible things in the past weeks and months, to say nothing of the past few days, Jonas still felt unsure of what was real here. And if the whole rebellion movement had been a ruse to trap the rebels, he would have to believe that too. He was also acutely aware of his own knowledge of the planned evacuation, the tunnels, the stealing of equipment, and began to feel seriously afraid. What might happen to him, far below the earth and beyond the reach of his friends; beyond the reach of Shanti? But Shanti: she was the one true thing in the shifting sands of his life at present, wasn't she? And she trusted Keegan.

He watched, numbly, as Keegan jumped up on to a piece of machinery to make himself visible to the entire meeting. The background murmur ceased.

'I'm sorry we've had to be so formal about things today, but it is important that you understand the risk you are all taking by being here.' He paused to look around the crowd. No-one stirred. 'Good. As Fortran has said, we have an important visitor among us today.' He turned with a smile to Jonas.

'It's OK, Jonas,' he said, seeing his bemused expression. 'They can't actually spy on us this far down. We've met here before, although not usually with quite so many rebels. This is where all the planning happens.'

He hopped down from his place on the machine and clapped an arm across Jonas' shoulder. In a quieter voice, he said, 'I'm really sorry about all this. You did so well not to give me away.' He turned to the others, raising his voice again. 'You are all safe here. Jonas is entirely on our side.'

In the discussion that followed, Jonas learned more about the discovery of the old computers that had come to light during Keegan's period of correction. It seemed quite a number of those present had been privy to that discovery, and those who hadn't had soon learned the truth. They described what they'd seen in the old films, and told how their suspicions about the world outside had grown as they watched.

'They thought I was a perfect example of how well the Correction Programme worked,' Keegan said, grinning.

Emmy explained to Jonas the shock and disgust they had felt on being faced with the falsehood their lives had been based on. 'You see, we went from really believing that this - ' she waved her arms around to encompass the whole of the Citadel - 'That this was all there was, to, well, realising that it couldn't be. As we grew older, and wondered where the water came from, where the waste went to, why our windows showed a world outside that we couldn't access, well, the questions just grew.'

'Then the rumours began,' said someone else. 'We were told that there was a world out there, that there were even people, living out there despite the poisoned air and ruined land.'

'And,' Emmy added, 'No-one would explain what had happened to the Hexadome. We were intrigued by it, and the rumours spread that it was a kind of better place...'

'A place without cameras and lies,' someone else said.

Keegan took over the story. 'That's when some of us decided we needed to find out for ourselves. You know about the tunnels, about Shanti's part in this...'

A man seated over by the wall, who had remained silent until now, stood up eagerly. 'Can we ask Jonas some questions?'

For the next hour Jonas did his best to satisfy their curiosity about the world beyond the Citadel. He was honest in describing the challenges and hardships.

'So where would you rather be?' someone asked. 'In here or out there?'

He answered without hesitation: he preferred the world outside. Why? Because out there were people he cared about. His family? No, they had died, but there were others...

He answered their questions about how people out there lived, how they felt about them, the privileged ones in the Citadel; how they too had heard rumours of a better place, how people's hopes had centred on the Hexadome. He described the journey, the finding of the Old City, finally the exploration of the Hexadome...

By the end he was exhausted.

The crowd dispersed, a few at a time so as not to create suspicion. As they left each raised a hand to Jonas and whispered *Freedom,* or *Onwards and Upwards!*

'Thank you,' some of them said to him. 'We are happy to follow you.'

This was alarming. He turned to Keegan. 'I'm not the leader of your rebellion!'

'That's how they see you. You led your people here, didn't you?'

But he hadn't, had he? Not really; not at all. They had all just, well... travelled. Yet, thinking about it later, he remembered how he had felt somehow called to make the journey, to travel alongside the people who had become his friends, his family... He had hoped he might do some good, without having any sense of what that good might be, and now, because of him, because of his presence among them, these people of the Citadel were ready to risk their lives to regain a freedom that they might even regret.

Jonas and Keegan and the other two returned to the highest level, an uncomfortably long journey for Jonas' stomach. In Horticulture, Keegan revealed a dark alcove just off the vine room that he hadn't noticed before. Once there, he could see that it opened out into a tunnel.

'You've been in the other end of this,' Keegan said.

'The small dome!'

Keegan nodded. 'What I don't think we explained to you at the time is that there are shorter tunnels branching off it. One of them comes out quite near the Hexadome itself.' He looked at Jonas. 'That is the tunnel we will all use to leave here; and that needs to be soon.'

He described how the tunnel that linked the Hexadome to the Citadel had been blocked up a while ago, in his parents' day. It was the first time Jonas had heard Keegan speak of his parents, and he recalled Shanti's sadness when speaking of them. He saw it mirrored now in her brother.

'It's been hard for you,' he said. 'You and Shanti are very brave.' Keegan gave him a grateful smile, then stopped to speak to some of the Horticulure staff, the only people Jonas had seen in the Citadel with dirty clothing. He commented on their unusually dishevelled state.

Keegan smiled. 'Yes, working in Horticulture is a perfect cover for people who've been in the tunnels. They need a certain amount of maintenance work.'

They sat for a time under the vines, and Keegan said, quietly, 'Shanti's all right. She's been collecting supplies for the others. They're all still out there. I'll get a message to her, let her know you're OK. She's been really worried about you.'

Two uniformed guards looked in. When they saw Keegan they saluted and moved on. Keegan raised his voice. 'On your feet, Outlander scum!'

Jonas let out the breath he'd been holding.

'You know, you really had me going, Keegan. I was beginning to think you were some sort of double agent.'

'I'm sorry, but I couldn't risk…'

'I understand. It was the same with Fortran and Altair – I really thought they were totally orthodox…'

'Oh yes. We all know how to play our parts in here.'

After a pause he indicated with a gesture that it definitely was time to get moving. 'This way! Move it!'

None of the day's conversations really helped him decide what he should tell the Commander. If he said there was no rebel movement, nothing to worry about, he didn't think he would be believed. On the other hand, if he said there was, he'd be asked for names, details. He decided to tell him that some of the young people were restless, that rumours about the outside world had been circulating – who knew how these things started? Yes, he had spoken to young people on his way round the Citadel. They were intelligent, well educated – and therefore just wanted to know more. Perhaps telling them the real history would help?

The Commander was not particularly receptive to this account.

'You clearly need to delve deeper. I am entirely convinced of the existence of an underground movement.'

Jonas choked back a laugh at this unintended pun.

'They will probably try to enlist your help. Pretend you are on their side, find out as much as you can.'

Jonas assumed his most serious expression. 'What makes you so sure there's an actual movement?'

The Commander sighed deeply. 'This is not to be repeated, Jonas…'

Jonas nodded his understanding.

'I believe my granddaughter is part of it. No-one will tell you this, but she has not been seen for some time. I even wonder if she has found a way out…' A shudder ran through him, as though to rid himself of such a thought. 'Although that of course is impossible…'

Chapter Twenty-Two

Back near the Hexadome, where, despite the Commander's words, Shanti had already done the impossible, it would no doubt have surprised him considerably to know that his missing granddaughter was at that moment attempting to find her way back into the Citadel, having led a group of Outlanders to the Hexadome. She and Robin, Leo and Brendan were not heading in the direction of the flat circle with the winking eyes that Shanti had pointed out to Jonas some twenty-four hours previously, although they passed it. It made Robin shudder, and Brendan's fists clenched involuntarily. They moved on until they came to a place where the flat land rose gently towards an area encircled by a border of rocky outcrops. It had the appearance of what might once have been a lake; and perhaps it had been. If the land itself could speak it would have told stories of constant change and upheaval, even greater than those which had taken place within living memory.

'Over here,' Shanti whispered to Robin and Leo. 'See that gap between the rocks?'

They peered in the direction she indicated.

Robin whispered, 'Is that it, the entrance to the tunnel?' adding, 'Why are we whispering?'

Shanti shook her head, and they all laughed. 'We will have to be quiet once we get inside, though,' she said. 'Voices echo in there.' Before the others could catch up with her, she had already slipped between two rocks, almost disappearing from sight.

'OK.' Her voice came as an amplified whisper. 'Here goes. Just follow me, and remember…' She turned and placed a finger on her lips, a touchingly old-fashioned gesture, to Robin's mind; but he understood its meaning.

It was dark in the tunnel, and they walked with arms stretched wide, fingertips just brushing the sides. The earth beneath their feet was uneven, and Leo stumbled a number of times. As their eyes grew accustomed to the gloom, they became aware of faint lights along the walls. Shanti said they were phosphorescent strips, and the others wondered what that meant.

They came at last to a place where the tunnel broadened out a little. Shanti sat down on the ground, and Robin and Leo joined her. Brendan, for all his brave words, was clearly uncomfortable in the confined space, and took some persuading to sit.

'What now?' Leo spoke quietly.

'We wait.'

'What are we waiting for?'

'For Keegan. He's gone back in; he knows what we need.'

'Gone in?'

'He comes and goes all the time. I'll tell you more later.'

It wasn't long before they sensed the presence of others coming towards them in the tunnel. Keegan was accompanied by two other young men, laden with boxes and packs. They handed them over quickly, without speaking, and returned in the direction of the Citadel.

The journey back to the world outside was completed in silence, and as Shanti and the others emerged thankfully into the fresh air, she told them quickly to meet the others outside the Hexadome before she turned round and disappeared back down the tunnel.

To Brendan's expression of alarm, Robin simply said, 'She knows what she's doing - and why she's doing it.'

If Jonas had pinned his hopes on being released once he had spoken to the Commander about the discontent of the young people, he was sorely disabused next morning. The knock on his door revealed two strangers.

'Good morning,' he said, cautiously.

'Good morning,' said the older of the two. 'Pixel.' He didn't offer a hand to shake. 'This is Titan.'

'Are Altair and Fortran not coming today?'

'That will not be possible.' Pixel gestured for Jonas to follow them into the corridor. 'They are not available.'

The rest of the tour, around the Education level and the Housekeeping Stores, was conducted with very little conversation and a frosty air. As they continued, Jonas recognised some of the young rebels he had been introduced to the previous day, and they made brief eye contact with him, discreetly raising a hand. Jonas gave a nod of recognition and sometimes a little wave in return. Others, whom he did not recognise, also seemed to be wanting to hold his attention, and he realised that they were signalling that they too were part of the network. The movement was clearly spreading, and fast.

Later, in the Commander's office, he was requested to sit, in a rather peremptory manner.

'Did you have a good day?'

'Yes, thank you. I saw a lot more of the Citadel,' Jonas replied cautiously. 'I didn't have the opportunity to speak to many people though.'

The Commander gave a twisted little smile.

'Today there was no need. Pixel and Titan took note of all those who gave you the secret sign. You have helped us a great deal. We can now round up and segregate all those who are disloyal.'

Jonas was too shocked to say anything.

The Commander stood. 'You can return to your room, for now.'

A guard was summoned and escorted him towards the elevation chamber without speaking. As the door slid closed behind them, the man raised a hand, palm outward.

'It will be all right,' he whispered.

Jonas hoped he had understood correctly.

'I missed seeing Fortran and Altair today,' he ventured. Do you think I could say hello to them?'

His companion shook his head. 'They are in the segregation area.' The chamber was still plummeting downwards. 'I could ask Captain Keegan to speak with you, though.'

Some hours later, as Jonas sat in his room listlessly toying with the plate of pale and unappetising food issued curtly by a guard, his door opened softly, and Keegan's face appeared.

'The Commander has asked me to check on you.' His tone was official, even a little hostile. For one, dizzying moment, Jonas wondered, even now, after everything that had happened, if it had all been a pretence.

'What is wrong with your food? Let me see.' He came into the room closing the door behind him. 'I'll just wash my hands first...'

He went to the little wash basin, running the tap until the room was steamy. Jonas watched, fascinated, as he rubbed the soap until his hands disappeared beneath the froth.

'Ah, I think I've steamed up the...' He stood quickly on the bed. 'I'll just give it a wipe.'

Jonas wondered what would happen next.

'Good,' Keegan said, as his wipe smeared soap across the black dot. 'That's better.'

As soon as he was back on the floor, he said, 'What's going on?'

The other Keegan was back. Jonas breathed a sigh of relief.

'It seems I've inadvertently betrayed everyone in the network. The Commander has sent Fortran and Altair to the segregation area; the others too, for all I know.'

'It's all right. Something like this was bound to happen sooner or later. We'll bring our plans forward a bit, get everyone out tonight, by the usual route. You too, but for now, just lie down and pretend to sleep. Don't do anything until you hear the knock on your door.'

Hours crept by as Jonas waited for the signal. Tempted to go searching for the others, he was in the end too fearful of arousing suspicion if seen wandering about alone. At last, when his nerves were stretched to breaking point, he heard a soft tap, and began to open the door cautiously, but before his hand could reach the handle, the door was pushed open forcefully, almost knocking him over; and then he stopped breathing for a moment.

Shanti fell into the room, slamming the door behind her, and stood without speaking, drinking in the sight of him, before crossing to where he stood. They held each other for precious minutes in a silent embrace, until Shanti pulled back in order to look at him once more.

'You gave me such a fright when you disappeared! I wondered if I'd ever see you again!' Her voice was a little unsteady. 'I'm proud of you, Jonas, what you've done... making it possible for all these people to leave.'

Jonas shrugged. 'I only ended up here by accident. I did nothing.'

'That's not what Keegan says.'

'All I did was tell them about the Outlands and listen to their stories…'

'And they were inspired by you; seeing you was what they needed to give them the courage to join the rebellion.'

'So what are you doing in here?'

'Come for you, of course. We've been back and forth with supplies for the Seekers. Now we're leaving. Didn't you get my message?'

'Keegan said you were well. But why come here? It's dangerous for you: the Commander knows you're part of it.'

Shanti frowned and smiled at the same time. 'And yet for some reason I was always his favourite grandchild. He's going to be very disappointed in me.'

Footsteps could be heard in the corridor.

'Is it time to go?'

'Yes. Come on.' She reached for the doorhandle, her other hand seeking out Jonas' hand. Jonas took it and his heart lifted with hope: to be together, free, out in the world again, knowing they had done something worthwhile for people both inside and out… Shanti had made her choice, chosen to be with him, in his world…

The door was flung open, sending Shanti stumbling off balance. As the guards entered, their bulk blocked the light from the corridor.

It all happened so quickly. Jonas caught hold of Shanti to stop her falling. As he did so she reached up, flung her arms round his neck and whispered, 'I will distract them. Run: the others are waiting. Turn right. The elevation chamber is at the end of this corridor. Up to Horticulture – to where the tunnel is. I'll follow.' She gripped him even more tightly. 'Promise you'll do as I say?'

They heard the harsh tones of the first guard before they saw him.

'Stop right there!'

The next moment a second guard was striding towards them.

'OK, that's enough!' He raised his hand; there was some sort of weapon in it.

'Promise me,' she whispered, urgently. 'I love you Jonas.'

He gave a barely perceptible nod, and at that moment she gave him a push. 'It's all your fault. You traitor… I should never have listened to you.'

She began to wail, flinging her arms around and making as if to overturn the little table. Both guards stepped forward in an attempt to calm her, and as they did so she shot out a foot so that one of them fell heavily, the other tripping over his companion's body.

By then Jonas was already at the end of the corridor, hoping he could remember how to operate the elevation chamber. To his relief Keegan was there before him. As the door opened he bundled Jonas inside and reached for the control panel.

'But Shanti…' Jonas couldn't believe he was planning to leave his own sister behind.

'It's all right, Jonas; calm down. She knows what she's doing; she knows where the tunnel is.'

For a moment, Jonas grappled ineffectually, trying to stop Keegan from touching the controls, but it was too late. Sobbing, he slipped to the floor, his hands over his face.

'We have to go now. You can't put all these people in danger. We've got to go…'

The elevation chamber lurched upwards, but this time Jonas was entirely unaware of any sensation in his stomach. It was his heart that was hurting now.

The people milling about near the rocks were feeling better now that they'd eaten. Brendan had moved the entire company to the space near the tunnel entrance, and he and Robin and Leo had organised the transport and distribution of the food with impressive speed. Now they were watching and waiting.

And then it happened: one by one the pale young people staggered up into the light, stepping cautiously out from the rocks that disguised the entrance to the tunnel. Some had bags, others carried coats or jackets, but most had nothing but what they wore. Blinking, they looked around them, squinting to make sense of the landscape and the huge open expanse of the sky.

Keegan, Robin and Leo stood a little apart. Jonas hung back, staring back into the dimly lit tunnel. At last, Keegan called to him.

'OK: this is the plan: Brendan and some of the others are going to lever the rocks up at the top there – do you see? That should start a landslide that'll block the tunnel. The authorities were close behind us.'

Jonas reacted as if punched in the stomach. 'No! Shanti is still inside.'

'If we don't do it now they'll come out firing. You know how ruthless they are.'

Jonas began to run. Keegan caught him, but Jonas again broke free.

'Calm down, Jonas. She knew the plan. It was her idea to rescue you, to cause a diversion, get out if she could, but if not...'

There was a rumbling sound. Jonas' cry of dismay was heard by everyone as he hurled himself towards the rocks, but it was already too late. Roaring and crashing, they fell in a cloud of dust and grit that had the people running backwards and covering their eyes.

As the cloud settled, Keegan took hold of Jonas.

'She loves you, Jonas.' He gestured towards the rockfall. 'That's how much she loves you.'

Granny Tabitha was the first of the Outlanders to approach one of the pale young people. She spoke warmly.

'Welcome, my dears. Come and sit down. We've kept some food and water for you.' A young woman followed her to where Sam, Tommy and Ginger had laid out a rug. The remains of their meal were in one of the plastic boxes Jonas had rescued from a middenheap many months ago.

'Thank you.' The young woman smiled shyly. 'I'm so very pleased to meet you.' She sat as the others made room for her, while Tommy and Ginger helped Tabitha to seat herself.

'I'm Emmess,' she said. 'My friends call me Emmy.'

'Then we'll call you Emmy,' said Tabitha.

Fortran and Altair were standing awkwardly. They kept glancing over to where Jonas sat, his knees hunched, well away from the others. Keegan had explained what had happened with Shanti, and they were still trying to decide whether or not an approach from them would be welcome when Alison and Robin came forward. They were each holding one of young Jonas' hands, and the child was carefully placing one chubby foot after the other and laughing with the sheer joy of doing it.

Altair knelt to be level with him. 'Hello, young man,' he said, and grinned broadly as the child blew a raspberry and then cooed with delight at his own efforts. Before long the little group were sitting and talking as they began trying to make sense of each other's worlds.

Behind them, Joe Farmer and Veronica were in earnest discussion with Pascal from Horticulture, who was explaining his work in Hydroponics. The little clusters were soon replicated across the whole scene, like so many families meeting up.

'Look, you mustn't give up hope.' Keegan was kneeling beside Jonas, one hand on his shoulder; Jonas gave no sign that he had heard. Keegan persevered. 'Look, you know what she's like; she's strong, she's resourceful. If she can get out, she will.'

This time Jonas raised his head. 'If? Through a tunnel blocked by a rockfall?'

'There are other ways out.'

'And if she doesn't get out?'

'Then you have to remember that she wanted you out here, helping these people. You have to get on and do it; don't let her down.'

'That's not what I meant.' Jonas' face was bleak again.

'Keegan sighed. 'No, I know it wasn't. The truth is, I don't know what will happen to her...but you have to remember that it was her choice.'

Alison called across to Keegan and he reluctantly got to his feet. 'I'll be back,' he said patting Jonas' shoulder. Jonas once more slumped down in a heap of misery, entirely oblivious to Keegan's efforts at encouragement.

'We're very close to the Citadel here,' Alison said. 'Should we move people on before they get too settled?'

Keegan considered. 'We're out of range of the cameras, which means we're out of range of their weapons.'

'So Brendan was right? They do have weapons?'

'So long as they remain inside they will only use the defensive lasers, in case someone gets too close.' He smiled reassuringly. 'Nobody is going to come out after us. I think we should let people be for tonight, and then tomorrow we need to make some decisions.'

The great winged birds circling impassively overhead might have observed the final intermingling of the two groups of people, the pale ones and the others; they might have noted how they formed little groupings and sat together on the ground, talking until late into the night; how they stretched out there on the bare earth, covering themselves with lengths of cloth until they were still.

Further off, but not very much further, they might have heard the rustle of many more of the creatures approaching through the trees that lined the road, converging from all points of the compass. Compass points were unknown to them, but while the birds knew nothing of north and south, east or west, they knew their direction as innately as Alison and Robin's baby knew that these were his parents and that he was loved. So they watched, and they saw things the human creatures couldn't see.

Next morning Alison and Robin, Keegan, Altair and Fortran, gathered instinctively, together with Emmy, Brendan, Joe Farmer and Veronica. Reluctantly Jonas joined them. His whole demeanour reminded Alison painfully of how he had sunk down into himself after Skylark died.

'We can't just hang around here,' Robin said. 'Keegan, what was your plan for when you began to explore the Outlands?'

'Well, of course, the first thing we hoped for was to make contact with people like yourselves.'

'And to find a way of living out here. A new way of living.'

'You do know it's not easy?'

'Now he tells us!'

There was gentle laughter before they returned to the serious business of decision-making.

'But, you do know, don't you, that you will find it hard.'

Emmy, her energy undimmed, said brightly, 'We were prepared for that.'

'So...'

Robin found himself stepping into what he thought of as rightfully Jonas' role.

'The first question is: do we stay here or move away?

There were various views: it was dangerous to remain so close to the Citadel; the land here was unpromising if they hoped to farm it in order to feed all the people. But what about the Hexadome? Surely they weren't going to abandon it now?

'How many are we?' Alison asked. 'Has anyone counted?'

Keegan reckoned that about sixty or seventy young Citadelians had come out with him.

'And with the numbers here, that's probably still well under three hundred.'

Robin said, 'And if we split, you know, some staying at the Hexadome and the rest travelling to find a good place to settle, well that reduces the numbers again. The problem with the other settlements has always been numbers. While everyone is focused on the basics of living from day to day, there's no way we can develop separate skills.'

He turned to Keegan. 'It's good to have you along, but we still need more people. If we are going to farm seriously, we need some who can devote all their time to it, to release others to build and make things…'

Veronica, who had been quiet throughout, now spoke tentatively. 'There must be others, though. I mean, the rumours about the Hexadome were flying around when we set off. We can't be the only people to have made it here, surely?'

The meeting ended without any firm conclusions. Decisions about the long term were deferred as it became clear that something had to be done in the shorter term.

Brendan disappeared and was later seen digging latrines.

Human beings are infinitely resourceful. How could our race have survived for millions of years without that ability? When they are equal in their need they have a gift for creating community. When they are not, what they create is division, which is where our story has its roots.

And so, seemingly without planning, the people began to organise: some entered the Hexadome - for Fortran and Altair it was the first time since early childhood - to begin harvesting what was there and planning for the future. Forward thinking is another of the talents that human beings have. Others searched for firewood, while yet others took a census of the people there, assessing needs and offering what support they could.

'Digging latrines? Big Brendan is digging latrines?'

Robin spluttered, spilling precious drops of drinking water and startling young Jonas as he took in this news. 'Whatever next?'

The sense of purpose was energising, and after so many days of sitting around and waiting, the experience of physical tiredness at the end of the day was welcome. For the newcomers too, the tensions of planning for escape were swept away in the new experience of working alongside others.

The only person untouched by all this activity was Jonas, who began half-heartedly making game traps, only to abandon them unfinished. It wasn't until Alison spoke to him sharply, reminding him that the people needed meat, and that if he couldn't make the traps himself he could at least show others how to do it, that he opened his eyes wide as if seeing her for the first time.

'You sounded just like Shanti then.'

'Of course I did. You're not the only one still carrying her around in your heart.'

He had wept at that, and it gave him some relief; besides, Alison was right: the skill of trap-making and setting was one he could pass on to others. He gathered a small group and began explaining, showing them how to set up the forked branch, stretching the cord to make a loop just in front of the bait. Joe Farmer provided a few carrots, harvested in the Hexadome.

It was clear to Jonas, though, that they would have to go a little further afield to set them; there was too little vegetation here to provide cover for small mammals. As the rest of the community saw them setting out, various people joined them, and as numbers grew Jonas was forced to speak to them to warn them against scaring away the very creatures they were trying to catch.

During a rest period, Tabitha, seated on a rug and propped snugly against someone's bundle, said, 'I thought, when we set out, that when we reached the Hexadome, that would be the end of the journey, but it seems it was only the beginning.'

Those with her nodded in agreement. They understood what she meant: it still felt unfinished. Besides, after walking for so long, it was strange to be in one place, even though most people had found useful activity to occupy their time. A number of them decided to undertake a serious walk of exploration.

Others remained where they were. Tabitha was becoming increasingly frail and, clearly in pain, was now no longer able to walk far. It was likely to be too long a trip for Alison with young Jonas, and, besides, the little network of mothers with young children was already gathered around her, deep in discussions about starting a school.

'That's one thing we have to do,' she was saying. 'We really must educate our children. They have to grow up with a belief in a better world.'

'And the knowledge of how to make it better,' someone else said.

As the others gathered, ready to set off, Sam hesitated. He was desperate for some activity, but worried about his mother. In the end Harry and Ginger persuaded him to go, and promised to stay and take care of Tabitha.

A group of around fifty people, including many of those from the Citadel, walked around the Hexadome, still marvelling at its size, its perfection, each hexagonal pane fitting exactly with its neighbours and emitting its mysterious green glow.

'The people who built this must have learned it from the bees,' someone said, starting a conversation about pollination that lasted for some time.

As they walked, they reached the place where the field of solar panels lay. At first they were so dazzled by the sheet of light that they turned away or raised their arms to shield their faces.

'I've heard about this all my life,' said Fortran. 'The source of our power down there.'

'The source of your power?' Brendan had been standing behind him.

'Electricity,' Jonas explained, with an effort. 'Electric power. Their machines, their light, their elevation chambers that connect all the different levels.' There had been something about the way Brendan had seized on Fortran's words that made him uneasy.

Jonas shuddered as they continued on to the circle of posts and blinking lights. It was only the fear of the same thing happening to any of the others that enabled him to recount his own experience, as he stressed the danger of entering the circle. He emphasised the fact that the tunnel they had used to escape was now blocked. It cost him an effort to say that, and Robin was right there with him as he did so.

'Come on, Jonas. I think we're finished here. Time to go back.'

Altair had just arrived at the edge of the little group.

'You said you'd seen the Old City. Would it be possible to go and see for ourselves?'

Not everyone wanted to return to that dark and forbidding place; it was largely the newcomers who were curious. Sam was anxious to get back to his mother, and a number of others were undecided. Finally, Veronica and Joe agreed to take them, so they set off, and the column of people split in two as they left. The rest returned to where the others were encamped, not far from the Hexadome.

There was a little huddle on the ground where they had left Old Tabitha. As Jonas and the others approached, Harry and Ginger stood awkwardly.

'Sam, I'm so sorry...' Harry faced Old Tabitha's son. Sam's face was white.

'You said you'd take care of her. You said she'd be all right.'

Out of habit, Jonas stepped forward and felt her pulse. He craned round to where Sam was standing.

'She's not gone yet.'

The others made room, and Sam knelt beside his mother. Her eyes were closed and she made no sign that she knew him.

'I'm sorry, Ma. You were right about so many things. I wish I hadn't argued with you the way I did'.

He took her hand, pressing the papery skin to his cheek.

'I've learned things, so many things, coming on this journey with you. We have to make our own future, don't we? A better one...'

Old Tabitha opened her eyes and looked directly into his. He leaned closer to catch her words.

'Keep travelling, Sam. Always keep travelling... even if you stay in one place.'

The piece of land where they buried her was hard to dig, and Jonas was glad of Brendan's help. He was glad, too, that the big man made no comment on the tears that Jonas let fall. How many was he weeping for this time? He no longer counted them. Perhaps he was weeping for all the things human beings had lost, for their carelessness in losing it, for the terrible harms they inflicted on each other.

Perhaps that was why he was so distraught the next day when he got wind of Brendan's plan. He and a large group had been up early, gathering branches and leaves and blankets and anything they could find, and were already on their way to the field of solar panels when

Jonas caught up with them. He sprinted to place himself ahead of them, then turned, arms outstretched to stop them.

'What in the name of all that's good and right do you think you're doing?' he bellowed.

Startled, they stopped. Someone stepped forward. Jonas didn't know his name, although he recognised him as a former supporter of the PA.

'Easy, Jonas,' the man said, like someone approaching a wild animal. 'Thanks to you we know all about the Citadel now. We know about where their power comes from. We can stop it, easily.'

As Jonas continued to stare at the crowd, another voice called, 'We're going to stop the sun getting to the panels; then their electricity won't work.'

The big man moved towards him. 'Their power will be gone. Ended!'

Jonas found that he was clenching and unclenching his fists.

'They no longer have any power, Brendan. No power that means anything. That's all in the past.' He looked around at the crowd, those at the front straining to hear what the two of them were saying to each other.

'But if you cut off their electricity, they won't be able to live underground: no air pumps, no water, no waste disposal... Don't you see? If you do this, you'll be killing them.'

There was a buzz as those at the front turned to relay this to those behind them. A few were heard to murmur, 'So what? They deserve it!' but mostly they were shushed by others.

'No.' Brendan raised his voice to make himself heard. 'We won't kill them. That's not what this is about. But if we cut off their electricity, they'll have to come up from out of there, won't they?'

'Then they'll be like the rest of us,' someone shouted from near the back, and there was a general murmur of agreement.

'No, Brendan, you don't understand. They won't be able to get out.'

Brendan looked disbelieving. He turned to Keegan, who had followed Jonas once he'd learned of the plan.

'That's right, isn't it? There are still tunnels? Still a way out? You said…'

'Well, yes, there are other tunnels, but…'

At his first words the crowd had surged forward, waving their branches, relieved that they would not, after all, be thwarted from their purpose.

'No, wait. Wait!' Jonas looked at Keegan in desperation. 'Help me.'

The two of them once more raced ahead of the crowd and then turned to face them.

'Brendan, you don't understand. If we cut off the power supply they won't be able to access the tunnels. They need the electricity to reach the top level, where the tunnels begin. Don't you see? They have things they call elevation chambers, little rooms that move upwards…'

The big man's mouth gaped.

Jonas turned back to Keegan. 'How many people in there?' he asked.

Keegan shrugged. 'Two or three thousand? I'm not sure.'

'Do you want to kill all those people, Brendan?'

It was thanks to Keegan's quick thinking that they found a way of diverting the crowd's energy and anger. Of course, they had to warn the crowd once again about the danger of stepping into the circle, but they were happy to set to and smash the cameras that had been set into the surrounding posts. Jonas took no part in this. He stood back, reflecting that he must have been the first person to come within range during all those years since the Citadel was sealed. Their great prize! They must have been regretting the outcome now.

The mob were already halfway round the circle as Keegan said, close to Jonas' ear to make himself heard above the triumphant shouting and crashing, 'Their knowledge of the Outlands was already limited, but now it will be lost completely. The only thing is...'

Jonas stared at him. What now?

'Yes, the only thing is, the cameras are part of the defensive system.'

'So they have weapons up here?'

'Yes. Some sort of laser-powered beam that...' He left the sentence unfinished. 'You were lucky because they wanted you alive, and - '

Keegan's gasp was echoed by everyone around the circle. It all happened so fast that no-one was able afterwards to describe exactly what they saw; to Jonas it looked like an uncanny reversal of his own experience.

Catapulted from a chasm that opened in the earth, Shanti fell full-length before getting to her feet and looking round. Her eyes searched frantically for Jonas. She took in the crowd, the branches being used to smash the flashing eyes of the perimeter cameras. She turned and turned. Almost three quarters of the cameras were blank. The crowd had halted, stone-still, its collective mouth agape. Finally, she located Jonas, who was staring in total disbelief, and they stood, taking in the sight of each other for long moments. Finally, Shanti began moving towards the edge of the circle where Jonas was standing with arms outstretched. She moved carefully on the pitted earth, agonisingly slowly, and her back was to the remaining cameras that watched her progress. She didn't see the beam of red light that shot from behind her, although she must have heard the screams of the crowd.

For a bulky man, Big Brendan moved remarkably fast. He was alongside Shanti before anyone knew what was happening. He knocked her to the ground – for a moment Jonas thought he was venting his rage, but then he saw, when it was too late to do anything, the beam of light as it struck the big man. It passed clean through his body, and he lay, still and silent, his battles ended.

Shanti crawled away, out of the circle and into Jonas' arms, and behind them in the circle there was nothing but silence.

Chapter Twenty-Three

The swallows had departed; they had business elsewhere. The sorry band that huddled below them, like pilgrims of old, had set out with a goal and a destination. They had nurtured a sense of purpose; they had reached their journey's end, but they had not yet found the thing they were seeking. Perhaps they had been looking in the wrong place, for the wrong thing. But every pilgrimage has a purpose beyond the miles you walk or the shrine you visit. Big Brendan had been on a pilgrimage of his own to find a way of leaving behind his anger, although he didn't know it at the time. Joe Farmer, too, found something he didn't know he was looking for. The Seekers had wanted to know how they could live in harmony with each other and with creation, but they had thought that such a venture involved a place, a physical location. The pilgrimage is not over when the journey ends; there is a further journey, the one that takes you home, but by a different route, and not necessarily back to where you started.

There came a great rustling from within the woods, treetops swaying, clouds of woodland birds rising into the air. A sound like human voices grew and grew, until suddenly, there they were: hundreds of people, just like themselves, travel-stained and weary. They continued until they came face to face with Jonas and Shanti, who had stepped forward to meet them.

One of their number came forward, an older man with careless grey hair tumbling down his shoulders and eyes bright with expectation.

'Greetings, Friends. It's good to see so many of you. The more there are of us, the more we can restore the land to life. We have been searching for the Hexadome. Do you know where it is?'

It seemed the news had continued to spread like wildfire after all. People, though, sometimes take a little longer to get there. For Jonas, there had been so much loss, so many dead, and now, before him was a chance for life, renewal, hope. Now there were enough people to farm and to hunt, to build and to teach and to grow. And he had a role to play in all that.

Did they stay there, close to the City? Did they scatter out, bringing the land slowly, painfully, back to life? Did some of their number make the long journey back to the Woodlands? Time alone will tell.

If they had cared to look up, they might have seen the ever-present kites. From their place high above the troubles of the terrestrial world, they could see what the people could not: here and there settlements of the human kind, little groups of dwellings, earthbound homes for earthbound creatures. Here and there too were the beginnings of a new agriculture: fields ploughed with roughly crafted implements, ready for the seed to be sown, the grain to be harvested, the bread to be baked and the feast to be eaten.

It was not the first time the soaring kites had seen it; the creatures of the land below always began like this; the methods changed, the fields grew in size, but in the end it always fell into decay, until it began once more: the endless cycle of human endeavour thwarted by human greed.

ABOUT THE AUTHOR

Carolyn Sanderson has dipped her toes into the world of academia, and worked in a number of fields including counselling, training and working for the Church of England. She has also had a number of years of being at the sharp end in front of a classroom full of adolescents!

She has written articles, reviews and a number of hymns, and lives in Milton Keynes, a surprisingly green city. When not writing, she loves tending her garden.

Also by this author:

Times and Seasons (in the Weidenfeld &Nicolson series
Hometown Tales)

Women don't kill animals (in The Word for Freedom,
Short Stories of Women's Suffrage, Retreat West Books)

The World Was All Before Them
© *Carolyn Sanderson* 2023

No Abiding City

Printed in Great Britain
by Amazon